The Road to Devotion

CAMERON KENT

PRESS 53
Winston-Salem, North Carolina

PRESS 53
PO Box 30314
Winston-Salem, NC 27130

First Edition

Cover image by Benita VanWinkle
www.busybstudio.com

Library of Congress Control Number: 2009913147

Printed on acid-free paper

ISBN 978-0-9825760-2-1 (paperback)
ISBN 978-0-9825760-3-8 (hardcover)

The Road to Devotion

Dedicated to

Julie Wilson, my beloved English teacher at Mount Vernon High School in Alexandria, Virginia, who saw the potential in all of us, and who taught me volumes about literature and life.

And to my childhood minister at the Old Presbyterian Meeting House, Dr. William R. Sengel, who had the courage to march in Selma before everyone else realized it was the right thing to do.

1

Sarah Talton was ashamed she couldn't cry. Everyone around her wept unabashedly while her own cheeks remained dry, except for the beads of perspiration rolling down from the dying heat of the August afternoon.

Divine as they may be, the words the minister recited from the Bible carried no significance as they sailed by Sarah's ears. As the simple pine box holding her father's lifeless body was lowered into the same burial ground where her mother had rested for twenty years, Sarah's mind wandered. The sharp dagger of clarity briefly punctured her private thoughts as she theorized that her inability to shed tears was part of her father's legacy. Her inheritance would be his iron will, and although his death had been sudden, the passing of that particular character trait was not unexpected.

Their journey through their thirty-four years together had been on a road paved with respect and discipline, yet pocked with anger and resentment. Had he been flinty in his approach to Sarah because she had the same look and mannerisms of his wife? The identical hazel eyes and auburn hair? Had the ache of missing his partner translated into a relationship with his daughter that teetered between love and reproach? Or had he been hard on her because he had always assumed one of his progeny would be a male? Despite his best efforts to make her so, Sarah was clearly not. She had not been the boy who would eagerly join his father for hunting and fishing. Yes, she would still tag along with him into the forests around their farm, but it was always at his insistence. She had not been the adolescent lad a father could help to navigate the complexities of puberty and groom into a proper gentleman. Nor had she been the young man with whom he could share a cigar and a brandy as he revealed the secrets of trying to make something grow and prosper from unforgiving southern soil. To him, she was merely a girl, with all the inherent shortcomings thereof. Weakness, frailty, and tears were all traits Miles Talton detested.

The one word he used most to describe his eldest daughter was *capable*. He only wanted Sarah to be able to run a farm, and nothing more. He cared not that she was intelligent or well read, or that she had any introduction into the world of music or art. In his mind, any time devoted to outward appearance was time wasted. His life had always been about making a living by tilling soil, so he made his life hers, even if it meant making her miserable in the process. Sarah could distinctly remember dreadful farming lessons where her father would keep her out in the wilting sun for hours, castigating her as if she were a young mule, but then ending each day with a kiss on the back of her head. He would often revile young Sarah for her inability to pitch hay like a man, but then she would overhear him in town bragging to the other men about the tensile strength of his eldest daughter. Even a rare embrace in his rough-hewn arms felt like a test of how much pressure she could withstand. And then there was the episode with the horse. Even though it had been twenty-eight years ago, the echoes of the violent, verbal whipping he unleashed on her that day in the winter of 1832 still took up residence in the darkest chambers of her mind. Just the smell of anything equine sparked the awful memories of that day, and triggered a rush of adrenal fear. What frightened her most that day, man or beast? She still didn't know.

Her father's penchant for uncensored criticism that knew no boundaries, often juxtaposed next to modest expressions of affection, made no sense to her, and thus their entire relationship made no sense. She was not what he had hoped for in a child, and consequently he was not what she had craved in a father. And thus, no tears flowed as the red North Carolina clay flew from the shovel onto his casket. The same dirt he had turned over for decades with the dull blade of a plow would now encase him for eternity. Even then, nothing resembling grief awoke in Sarah Talton's soul. It was time to emote, but after absorbing three decades of her father's misplaced anger, she had simply forgotten how.

Sarah's eyes scanned the sparse gathering and saw one other person who was not wiping away tears. Braxton Smithwick was dressed in attire that seemed better suited for a wedding than a funeral, and he was the only gentleman in attendance who had not removed his hat. As the reverend read Psalms, meant to soothe grieving souls, Sarah noticed that Braxton remained inattentive, keeping to himself on the far edge of the proceedings. He surveyed the fields and forests of the Talton farm with narrowed eyes, as if estimating her land's potential yield and market value. She had known Braxton for as long as she could remember, and detested him the entire time. Nothing he did at this moment changed her mind.

As the service concluded, Sarah forced a thin smile and silently nodded her appreciation to the minister and the mourners, then gradually moved away from the burial plot. She slipped her arm around the shoulder of her sister Rebecca, who was crumbling with emotion. Steadying her younger sibling's wobbly legs and sagging spirits, she turned and walked away. Braxton moved swiftly to her side and attempted to take her by the crook of her arm, as if he were escorting the mother of the bride at a wedding. Without a word, without even so much as a glance, Sarah jerked her elbow away and held it fixed across her midsection as her pace quickened.

The path from the Talton family burial ground back to the main house cut directly through the dusty rows of their fields. Leaves that should be as green as frogs' backs were instead maple brown and curling at the edges. Sarah looked up as she walked, gazing beyond the clouds that had failed to produce any measurable rain in weeks, and into the heavens. If God were testing her, she felt like she was failing.

2

Sarah settled into her usual spot in the sanctuary of the wooden-frame church on the hill. For generations, the Talton family had occupied a pew in some house of worship on the Sabbath, and there was never any thought given to breaking that tradition. The rituals performed on Sunday mornings did little to fill her. The sermons, even when she could force herself to listen to them, were bereft of any practical application to her daily life. Her faith remained the cornerstone of her existence, her strength during difficulties, and the guiding hand for all her important decisions, but communal worship failed to energize her spirit. She felt closest to God when she was alone, reading her worn Bible by dim candlelight, or when she observed the Creator's awesome power in nature. A sunset, a snowfall, a summer thunderstorm and the rainbow that followed... these were the images that proved to her there was a meaningful God in her life. And yet, Sarah dutifully attended church services every Sunday, because she found spiritual comfort in an innate feeling that God had a special purpose for her. She didn't know what it was, but she had convinced herself that a hard pew in a tiny country church was as good as any place to find enlightenment.

She liked most of the other people in the tiny congregation, and she'd appreciated the outpouring of sympathy they'd shown her in recent weeks following the death of her father. Even though each covered dish from the women of the church had been accompanied by veiled advice from their husbands, at the end of each lonely day it had been comforting to know that someone cared about her in her supposed hour of grief.

Rebecca sat next to her with the pew Bible opened to the approximate middle. When Sarah leaned over to get a closer look at what passage her young sister might be reading, she discovered Rebecca was secretly harboring a copy of *Great Expectations*. Dickens or Deuteronomy? thought Sarah. A difficult choice. She decided to allow Rebecca to continue the ruse, for it would surely enhance her life more than what she was about to hear.

The reverend ascended to the pulpit, pushed his spectacles higher onto the bridge of his nose, and cleared his throat. It was time for his sermon to begin, which meant it was time for Sarah's mind to wander back to the list of everything she had to get done before day's end. Her Bible told her that Sunday was supposed to be a day of rest. Her farm dictated otherwise.

A candle with less than a quarter-inch of life left in it flickered over the ream of papers Sarah had spread across the scarred wooden table in the drawing room of the farmhouse. Her father had been dead two months, and the strain of running the farm by herself was growing greater by the day. A week ago she had been forced to sell another four acres of land and two more slaves. That left her with just twelve field hands, barely enough to keep the operation solvent.

As she did at least five times a day, Sarah scanned the handwritten list of everything that needed to be done, day by day, season by season. The list seemed endless, insurmountable most days, yet there was no choice. It was a microcosm of the wisdom of Ecclesiastes; there is a time to plant and a time to pluck up what has been planted, or it will be a time to die. With so much on the list, there was little time for anything else.

Sarah's mind was numb with the intricacies of planting schedules and crop rotation spelled out in her father's almanac. She allowed herself a few moments to venture into the lands she'd only read about in books. Tropical islands with pearl-white sands, deserts with devil winds, walled cities of Old Europe with castles and teashops. For a woman who had never ventured more than fifty miles from her place of birth, she took great delight in these vacations of the mind, projecting herself into a future where a thousand far-flung places would all be under her footsteps. To love, to travel, and to travel with someone she loved... these were the simple dreams she harbored. It helped her to fend off the depressing notion that she had already lived for more than three decades and had never seen an ocean.

"Are we going to make it?" Rebecca stood in the doorway, biting the corner of her bottom lip and tugging on the strands of hair that fell across her shoulders. Rebecca was twenty years old, but didn't possess nearly the worldly knowledge of her older sister. Despite their father's objections, Sarah had insisted that Rebecca spend more time with her head in a lesson book than her hands in topsoil, and Rebecca's devotion to education had insulated her from many of the harsh realities of daily farm life.

Sarah forced a reassuring smile as she stood up from the table. "We'll be fine. There's nothing for you to worry about. I promise." Sarah walked across the room and gave her sister a comforting embrace.

"Is there anything I can do?" Rebecca asked.

"If you could make it rain, that would certainly help." Sarah broke into a broad smile and tousled Rebecca's hair.

"I'm serious. What can I do?"

"The best thing you can do, Rebecca, is to go back to school, study hard, and find a way to get off this farm. The world is a lot bigger than these fifty acres, and you need to explore as much of it as you can. Somewhere out there is a better life for you, just waiting to be discovered."

Rebecca nodded in agreement as she forced a smile and headed to the staircase. "Coming up?"

"I'll be there in a moment."

Snapping back to the harsh fiscal reality laid out on the table in front of her, Sarah scooped up the papers into a disorganized pile. She intended to stuff them into a drawer where they would be unseen and thus less weighty on her shoulders, but she looked up and saw the portrait of her father over the fireplace mantle. He stared down at her with disapproving eyes, so she retreated to the tabletop and took several minutes to neatly organize the jumble of papers before carefully placing them in the drawer.

Too weary to even read, Sarah extinguished the candle and trundled up to bed. She would force herself to let go of the financial troubles swirling in her mind and try to get some rest, for she knew the next morning would be difficult.

With the sun barely up, Sarah paced in front of the dozen slaves mustered in the yard outside the Talton farmhouse. They stood shoulder to shoulder, an arm's length apart. Not quite at attention, but more like children lining up to get picked for a schoolyard game. They were well fed, and clothed better than most slaves, but there was no joy in their collective souls, especially on a morning like this. They knew that when they were called in from the fields it meant only one thing: somebody was leaving.

Sarah could never bring herself to take her slaves to the public auctions in the bustling town of Winston. What was the difference, selling them to a specific buyer versus the highest bidder? Sarah knew there probably wasn't any, but for some reason, selling her slaves this way made her feel better. Besides, by avoiding the public transactions, she didn't have to endure the critical looks and whispers of the men in town if they thought she'd been shortchanged in her bargaining.

Standing alongside Sarah was a wealthy gentleman farmer from Germanton. She didn't know his name, nor did she really care to. Looking more like a politician than a plantation owner in his white linen suit and straw hat, he inspected the laborers like a cattle rancher surveys livestock before deciding which ones should be taken to the slaughterhouse.

"I'll take that one, that one, and those two," he said matter of factly, pointing to two young men and two young women.

A look of horror careened through the dozen black faces as they realized a family was about to be torn apart. A muscular slave in his twenties, who had been tabbed for sale, turned his wide eyes to Sarah.

"Beggin' yo pahdun, Miss Talton, but I gots a wife and two lil' younguns heah. Ain't der no way I kin stay wit you?"

Sarah listened to his plea and looked over at the gentleman farmer. He lifted his chin and forcefully reiterated his order.

"That one, that one, and those two."

Sarah took a deep breath as she pondered the man's offer and tried to balance the business side of running a farm against the social implications. While it didn't set well with her to separate family members, she had to constantly remind herself that she was operating a farm and not a charity. If she didn't sell off part of her assets, the entire operation might go under and then there would be nothing left for anyone, black or white. She had already sold several parcels of land, and thus she required fewer hands to work the fields. It made good business sense to auction some of her slaves and invest the proceeds back into the land. She was determined to not only survive as a farmwoman, but to succeed, even if it meant a few distasteful decisions along the way. She could almost hear her father voicing his approval over her deduction.

"I'm sorry," Sarah said to the muscular slave.

"But—"

"Get your things."

She nodded to the gentleman in the linen suit as she turned her back on the slaves. The deal was struck. As the women in the group of slaves openly wept, the buyer counted out the money into Sarah's outstretched hand.

She clutched the bills tightly, like someone holding a snake just behind its head. As Sarah quickly marched back into the farmhouse, she tried to convince herself that she felt no better or no worse than if she had just taken a calf from its mother.

3

*T*he dogs smelled blood. They craved it with insane lust. It was the way they were bred, and neither the jagged thorns of the wild roses, nor their burning lungs seared by the crisp October air, would deter their relentless pursuit. They knew no other way. The mad fervor of the chase was more than instinct, more than generations of insemination with raw, spitting anger. There was a primal pleasure they derived from the hunt, and only a swift, choking yank on their master's leash would save them from self-destruction.

With only torches and the fragmented light of a thumbnail moon, the frenzied hounds and their handlers forged headstrong through thickets of mountain laurel and scrub oak as the scent grew stronger. It was the blood of a runaway slave for which the hounds ached, and their lungs heaved louder with each gallop of their mudstained paws.

As the dogs gained ground they could hear tree branches snapping against skin like whipsaws, and see the frosted blasts of breath from the runaway in terrified flight. The animals locked on to the wind of their prey. The pace of the hunt quickened.

"Thisaway! Over h'yah!" yelled one of the handlers, jerking and whipping the leashes of the dogs, imploring them to charge through the maze of dark forest. "Don't let him git to the river!" he called out to the other patrollers.

Up ahead, the slave could hear the gentle roar of the Yadkin River. Through the intermittent moonlight, the fog rose silently from the surface, like anguished spirits ascending in search of a better place. Water had delivered Moses as a child, and saved him as a man. Perhaps it would provide rescue once again.

Standing in the way of the river of freedom was a threshed cornfield, its brittle brown stalks twisted on the ground like fallen soldiers in endless columns. A two-legged human was no match for a dog in an open field, but there was no other choice. The curdling yelps from the posse of bloodthirsty hounds drew ever closer, and a change in course was the only option.

Waiting for the sliver of a moon to duck behind the clouds, the slave pulled down the sides of a tattered felt hat and dashed madly across the ruddy red clay of the cornfield. Pitch darkness paved the way for the first two hundred yards of the desperate race to freedom. The swiftly flowing waters of the Yadkin were almost within reach, nearly close enough to take a liberating plunge into muddy waters that would mask the scent and deliver the runaway from the evil that lurked behind, but divine providence suddenly evaporated in the chilled night air. The guiding forces of nature parted the clouds, and the slave's position was given away by the traitorous glimmer of moonlight.

"There he is!" yelled the burly bounty hunter through a ragged beard that still carried the leftover crumbs of an ash cake. "Go, now! Hunt it up! Hunt it up!" he cried, releasing the dogs into a full-bore sprint.

With the same fear as the fox who can feel the thunder of hoofbeats, the slave took flight. If only the legs were willing to take the rest of the body the final few yards to the river, there might be hope. It was not to be. The slave's ankle twisted nastily in the hole of a groundhog. With stabbing pain, the weary legs stumbled, then crumpled to the ground in defeat. Within seconds, the hounds arrived, circling and screeching around their human quarry. The two patrollers ran up behind the dogs, kicking them out of the way. A bullwhip in the hand of the bearded one cracked through the night, drawing blood from the exhausted legs of the runaway. He unleashed more brutal whiplashes to a black midsection starving for breath. In barbarous triumph, the patroller lifted a four-foot limb of hardened hickory and dealt out a series of thudding blows, until his captive submitted to the painkiller of unconsciousness.

"Good work, boys, good work," said the burly bounty hunter as the torchlight danced off their assortment of whiskey-brown teeth. "Kinda make you hungry, don't it?" he joked, drawing a cackle of laughter from his scrawny partner. "Go on now, fetch the wagon. This one ain't goin' nowhere."

"Where we takin' him?" asked the partner as he collected the leashes on the dogs.

"Miss Talton's place, I reckon. Lord know she could sho' use some help. Go on now, it's a gittin' late."

4

Hickory smoke rose from the twin chimneys of Bellerive, a white-columned plantation home several miles from the center of Winston. The gravel lane that ran between two long rows of Dutch elms was lined with an assortment of surreys and Hansom cabs, with brushed horses waiting patiently for their owners.

Inside the high ceilings of Bellerive, a concerted effort of viola, cello, and harpsichord provided the festive undertone for the social gathering. It was the autumn of 1860, and the music and wine numbed the rumblings of war for the dozens of gentlemen and ladies in attendance.

The host of the evening was Braxton Smithwick, just thirty-five years old, but already a captain of capitalism. He was a dirt farmer like his father and grandfather before him, and although not highly educated, he possessed a keen business sense his ancestors had lacked. His combined talents of agriculture and shrewd bargaining had allowed him to amass wealth of impressive amounts at a relatively young age. With his polished boots and fine wool suits he brought in from Charleston, Braxton saw a true southern gentleman

15

in his frequent visits to the mirror to inspect and admire his razor-cut sideburns and Vandyke beard. It mattered little to him that most others did not share the same reflection.

The guest of honor that evening was Monsieur Edouard LeGare, whose aristocratic visage, angled sideburns, and deep Parisian voice attracted the romantic attention of nearly all the women in the room. The deep pockets of the French textile manufacturer drew the lustful greed of the men. LeGare had been touring North Carolina to expand his import business in France, lining up contracts for cotton and tobacco that would be shipped overseas. Despite his inability to speak English with any confidence, LeGare still managed to greet the invitees without saying a word. The humble bob of his head, warm smile, and firm handshake conveyed enough meaning to penetrate the language barrier.

Braxton brushed past several guests who were of little economic importance to him and summoned the room's attention with a *clink-clink* of his pipe stem against an Irish crystal goblet.

He held his hand aloft, quieting the crowd. "As your host this evening, and on behalf of all the landowners here in Winston, I bid a warm welcome to Monsieur Edouard LeGare." Braxton soaked in the smattering of applause. He raised his goblet as he addressed LeGare directly. "I trust that your time here has taught you to consider us friends as well as business associates, and that you will spread the word back home in France that North Carolina tobacco has no peer, and that southern cotton is king!"

The guests cheered as they raised their glasses in agreement.

"To Monsieur LeGare, *mon bon ami!*" bellowed Braxton as he beckoned the Frenchman to join him at the front of the crowded room.

The sea of chintz hoopskirts parted as Monsieur LeGare bashfully obliged and joined Braxton at center stage. LeGare wet his lips several times before delivering his comments.

"*Merci, merci.* I... uh... say thank you... *et, et...*" LeGare bowed his handsome head and shrugged his broad shoulders. "*Je ne sais pas... merci... merci, mes amis.*" The monolingual southern crowd sensed his genuine gratitude.

"Well said, well said!" proclaimed Braxton to the guests.

LeGare retreated into the crowd amidst their polite applause, looking for a distant corner where he could minimize his mingling.

Feeling triumphant in the role of gracious host and business leader, Braxton made his way across the room with one particular guest in mind. On the outskirts of the throng, he would spot Sarah, whose rugged attractiveness made her stand out in a room filled with China doll faces and *crème fraîche* complexions. It was the first time Braxton had seen Sarah since she'd refused to take his arm at her father's funeral. Despite her rebuffs of his numerous advances over the years, Braxton still craved Sarah. She simply wasn't like any of the other women of his acquaintance, and the distance she kept from him was as beguiling as it was challenging.

Slender and strong from years of pitching hay and tending gardens, Sarah exuded a physical toughness that belied the emotional insecurities that simmered just below her well-tanned skin. If her flowing auburn hair had enjoyed more frequent encounters with a brush, Sarah might be stunningly beautiful. She chose not to be.

Standing alone by preference, Sarah's eyes were locked on Monsieur LeGare, as they had been all night. In fact, the Frenchman was the only reason she had squeezed into her prison of a dress and traveled the few miles to the party.

"Encouraging, isn't it?" Braxton's sudden intrusion yanked Sarah back from her faraway thoughts.

"Our cotton and tobacco selling in Europe for three times what we get for it here! That is if those damnable northern agitators don't dissuade the Europeans from trading with us."

"Umm hmm," Sarah murmured.

"That's why my new-found friendship with Mr. LeGare is so crucial to my financial future, or dare I say, *our* future."

"Yes, yes, Monsieur LeGare," responded Sarah as the hint of a smile creased her face. "The future."

Braxton followed Sarah's gaze across the room to where the bachelor Frenchman was standing.

"Why, Sarah, it's not like you to invest so much attention in a gentleman."

"I suppose you're correct, Mr. Smithwick." She looked straight at him with a faux feminine demeanor. "I suppose that's because I frankly can't recall the last time I talked to a real gentleman."

Braxton moved directly into the line of sight between Sarah and LeGare.

"Trust me, he's not for you. He's too... inconvenient. Now I, on the other hand—"

Braxton's attempt to sell himself was suddenly interrupted by the arrival of Rebecca.

"Mr. Smithwick, I'm sure there are other guests that desire your presence," said Rebecca. "My sister shouldn't be so greedy with your attention."

Braxton smiled wryly and glanced downward, struggling to remain gracious.

"Do they not teach you anything about manners or respect at that college of yours, Miss Talton?"

"Oh, I think I know quite a bit about respect and when to apply it, sir. Wouldn't you say, Sarah?"

Sarah bit her lower lip to keep from laughing. She laid a matronly hand on Rebecca's shoulder and gently pulled her aside, out of range of Braxton's growing incensement over the interloper.

"Please excuse my young sister's impudence. Sometimes young foals feel the need to stretch their new legs without regard to the other horses in the barn. Thank you for your hospitality tonight, Mr. Smithwick. Have a pleasant evening." Sarah abruptly guided Rebecca away.

"Braxton!" he called to her as she strode casually away. "You can call me Braxton!" Momentarily dismayed, he glared at LeGare, but as he fumed, he caught a glimpse of himself in the mirror on the drawing room wall. Buoyed by the sight, Braxton drew in a mood-altering breath and resumed his purposeful mingling.

Across the room, Rebecca and Sarah stood alone, as they preferred. Rebecca bubbled over with girlish enthusiasm. "Have you talked to him yet?" she asked her older sister.

"Talked to who?"

"First of all, it's to *whom*, and secondly, you're dreadful at lying, Sarah."

"I don't know what you mean."

"Yes you do! Monsieur LeGare! Why won't you ever go talk to him?"

"And how do you propose I do that? He hardly speaks a word of English, and I speak even less of French."

"Which is preferable to someone like Braxton Smithwick who talks all day and never really says anything. Honestly, why do you even permit him to come within arm's length?"

"I'm just being polite. He's a powerful man in this town, and I can't afford to get on his list of enemies."

Sarah gazed again at LeGare. "Look at him... if I didn't know he was a businessman, I would swear he was royalty."

"You need to go over and talk to him," said Rebecca, gently prodding her sister in the direction of the princely Frenchman. "You don't get this opportunity very often, and who knows how much longer you'll have it."

Sarah's short breath and loud exhale indicated that she agreed with Rebecca's assessment. Bracing herself for what she knew would be an awkward encounter, Sarah slowly drifted closer to the regal aura of LeGare. She wondered if he treasured their initial encounter decades before as much as she did.

They were the halcyon days of Sarah's youth, those rare moments in time when a young girl begins to understand all the wonderful experiences the world has to offer and that the notions of accomplishment are endless, that brief span of time where possibilities still outweigh responsibilities. For some, that blissful period can last an entire summer, perhaps even a year or two. For Sarah, it was only that one day in the spring of 1840 when she was fourteen years old.

It was a Sunday, a day of rest, and all she knew was that a wealthy Frenchman was paying a visit to the Talton farm to talk to her father about business. The foreigner was accompanied by his teenaged son, and it was Sarah's duty to keep the boy entertained while the men conducted their financial affairs. Naturally more comfortable in the company of boys than girls, Sarah eagerly accepted her assignment. She envisioned an afternoon of skipping rocks across the farm pond and hunting for salamanders in the gray rocks of the creekbed, but when she first laid eyes on the sturdy young Edouard LeGare, her life changed. Womanly feelings she'd never experienced overtook her as she stood speechless in front of the most handsome man she'd ever seen. She pulled the dangling strands of her bird's nest of hair back behind her ears as if that would magically transform her from an unkempt tomboy into a comely young woman.

"*Je m'apelle Edouard,*" he said, introducing himself.

Sarah's knees buckled slightly as she melted inside. It was the first time she had ever heard French spoken aloud. His words washed over her like a warm embrace. She had no idea what he said, but just the rich timbre of his voice stirred her to the core. After several seconds of staring blankly at his face, the fount of such blessed poetry, she realized a response was in order.

"Yes, me too," she replied.

Edouard smiled and nodded in understanding. "Meetu? Meetu! *Bonjour*, Meetu."

"Bone jewor," she parroted.

Despite the inpenetrable language barrier between them, the two young teens bounded off for a day of adventure. Having been raised in the narrow confines of a Parisian townhouse, the seemingly infinite pastures of the Talton farm were liberating. With Sarah as his guide, Edouard explored the hidden joys of a working farm. The tour included everything from spying on a fox den at the edge of the meadow to the simple pleasure of blowing the snow-white seeds off a dandelion bloom. Not an understandable word was spoken, but hand gestures and untamed laughter provided all the communication the pair would need.

As daylight neared its end, Sarah and Edouard were playing on a rope swing that hung from a sprawling poplar next to the farm pond. Taking flight from a six-foot-high tree stump, they took turns swinging out over the water, screeching with laughter, until the pendulum slowed enough to allow them to let go of the rope and land gently on the softened banks of the pond. With an impish grin, Sarah held up a finger to Edouard as if to say *watch this!* With rope in hand, she scrambled to the top of the launching stump. Leaping as far as possible to her left, Sarah swung in a wide arc out over the meadow grass. As she reached the zenith of her looping flight and started to swing back towards the stump, the rope grazed the outstretched limb of the tree and became momentarily snagged on a smooth knot protruding from the branch. Gleefully, Sarah continued to swing back towards the stump, but she was bracing herself for the violent change in course she knew was about to come. The top of the rope slipped off the tree knot and abruptly plunged her into a five-foot freefall, jolting every disc in her spine. Squealing with laughter, Sarah hung on as the rope straightened taut again and twirled her to a dizzying stop. She hopped off and carried the rope to her French playmate.

"Your turn."

Eager to attempt the new wrinkle in rope swinging, Edouard wrapped his young hands around the braided fibers and scrambled to the top of the stump. He leaned back, took a deep breath for courage, then launched himself on the same parabolic path that Sarah had traveled. The top of the rope approached the overhanging limb, but as it neared the protruding tree knot, Edouard's commitment to adventure suddenly flagged. The knowledge that he was about to be jerked sharply off course was too much for his rational mind, and rather than allow himself to experience the same exhilaration he had witnessed from Sarah, he simply let go.

It was not until young Edouard looked down to prepare for his landing that he realized he was not over dry land. With no other option, he plunged feet first into the pond and briefly disappeared from view.

Sarah's hands covered her nose and mouth in a combination of amusement and horror. Without a second thought, she charged in to rescue him. Edouard breached the surface and shook the muddy water off his head, just as Sarah reached him. Unable to contain her laughter, Sarah pulled him upright and looked into his eyes to make sure his pupils were of normal size.

"Are you all right?" she asked, biting her lower lip to choke back guffaws.

Edouard broke into an embarrassed grin. With her hands still holding his upper arms, he looked directly into her eyes. Without a spoken word all day, the chemistry between the two teenagers was still palpable. Time stood still as they stood in chest high water on the brink of a kiss. They shut their eyes and pursed their lips as their heads instinctively moved closer to each other, their hearts pounding hard enough to create fresh ripples in the pond.

"*Edouard!*" came the throaty voice from up at the main house. "*Allez! Maintenant!*"

Like the rope swing suddenly slipping off the knot of the poplar tree, his father's beckoning had violently shattered the peace. Edouard pulled away from Sarah's grasp, clearly wanting to linger, but mindful of his father's strict orders. The moment was gone. He quickly waded to shore, leaving Sarah standing alone.

The pond water dripped off Edouard's mudstained garments as he sat in the grassy meadow and pulled on his boots. His gaze never left Sarah's, even as he backed away and headed to the farmhouse.

"*Au revoir*, Meetu!" A gentle wave goodbye, and her most perfect day was over.

Though engaged in a semblance of conversation with two gentlemen, LeGare noticed Sarah's subtle entry into his domain. His cobalt-blue eyes now tracked her like an eager birdwatcher as she inched closer. When she dared to marry her eyes to his, LeGare flashed a gentle smile, strengthening his gravitational pull.

With a polite exchange of pleasantries, LeGare excused himself from the conversation and subtly motioned for Sarah to follow him through an open door leading to a veranda. Sarah understood, and they quietly made their way outside.

"*Bonsoir*, Mademoiselle Meetu."

That voice. It was captivating. Soothing and disarming, yet

paralyzing. Sarah stood rigidly in place. Finally alone, but nothing to say. Now what? Unable to speak, much less converse, she simply smiled and looked away as if the correct words might be magically written on the sprawling lawns of the Smithwick plantation; she looked back and smiled again.

From the very first time that she had learned of LeGare's return to Winston, she had longed for such a moment. She had wondered about it, daydreamed about it, even acted it out during private moments. She had danced through dreams where she could inexplicably speak fluent French, even with the hint of a Parisian accent, and had taken timeless strolls by the Seine with Monsieur LeGare. Arm in arm, they had carried on robust discussions about art and architecture and philosophy and a host of other subjects she knew nothing about, and shared glasses of Bordeaux and deep kisses in a cosmopolitan cafe in Montmartre. And even when she awoke, and realized her perfect afternoon with Monsieur LeGare had only been in the uninhibited imagination of her slumber, she smiled to herself, believing it was still time well spent.

Of course Sarah had never been to France, never been to Europe, never even been out of the state of North Carolina. But her passion for reading had taken her everywhere she'd ever desired to travel. Books were her one and only indulgence in her hardscrabble life as a farm woman. No fancy hats from the milliner, no delicate jewelry, no exquisite teas in the pantry. What little profit she scraped out of her meager land was squirreled away and spent on books to provide escape from the drudgery of farm life. Upon meeting Monsieur LeGare, she'd spent considerable more time curled up with Hugo and Voltaire, making her feel more a part of his universe. She'd even searched the entire town for a book that might make her the least bit conversant in French, but her quest had been futile.

During their brief encounters in town in recent weeks, chance meetings at the bakery and the bookshop, she sensed that LeGare could feel the same chemistry between them. A quick glance, an uncensored smile, a restless fidgeting whenever their paths intersected, all giving her joy and hope that her feelings weren't unilateral.

And now here she was, as she had so often imagined in the last two months, alone with him. Finally and mercifully alone, but with nothing to say. The nervous silence only added to the chill of the autumnal air. A remark on the weather was all Sarah could muster. "It is cold tonight, yes?" she offered, speaking slower and louder than normal.

"*Pardon?*" said LeGare.

"It is cold tonight," she repeated, with even greater enunciation. "Cold," she said again, this time crossing her arms to her shoulders in a mock shiver.

"*Ah, oui! Il fait froid!*" exclaimed LeGare with sudden comprehension. He whisked off his jacket and draped it over Sarah's shoulders. She drank in the aroma of his cologne buried in the fabric, momentarily forgetting that he was standing right in front of her. LeGare studied the woman in front of him as if she were a master's work of art hanging in the Louvre.

"*Vous êtes très jolie*, Mademoiselle Talton," LeGare whispered. "*Très, très, jolie.*"

"Thank you," she replied, looking away with a tinge of embarrassment.

LeGare moved closer. He gently took Sarah's hand and stroked his thumb across the back of her fingers. She was suddenly self-conscious that her skin was dry and coarse from thirty-four years of farm life. With the tip of his index finger, LeGare slowly lifted Sarah's chin so that her eyes met his. She had only dared to dream about a moment like this but never fully imagined it would ever come true.

"There you are!" Braxton Smithwick and another guest erupted through the door and onto the veranda. Sarah and LeGare quickly separated, the moment between them shattered.

"I've got a man here you need to meet, LeGare! Grows the finest sorghum in Winston! You know sorghum? Use it for silage or syrup! Amazing little plant! Come on inside, we'll tell you all about it!"

LeGare was brusquely whisked away. He turned back and offered Sarah an apologetic glance, then vanished into the main room.

Bitterly disappointed, Sarah attempted to savor what was left of her stolen moment with the Frenchman. She removed LeGare's jacket and again held it to her nose to escape in his scent. She exhaled a frostbitten breath in quiet resignation, and with the jacket draped over her arm, returned to the drawing room.

Sarah quickly located her sister and pulled her toward the hallway of the plantation house. "Come on!" she whispered with a gleam in her eye. Rebecca knew exactly where they were headed; the Bellerive library. In Sarah's mind, Braxton's only redeeming quality was his impressive collection of literature, all leatherbound with gold lettering, and it brought her joy just to be surrounded by the assembled contents of their marbled paper. By the crackle of their fresh spines, it was clear to Sarah that Braxton had never actually read any of the books he owned, but the mere fact that he cared to collect them provided at least an ounce of counterweight to her otherwise total disdain of the man. She had known Braxton since they were children, when their parents would meet for picnics after church. From the time he'd first admired the way she could skip rocks across the river, she'd always known that Braxton was smitten with her. Their paths had collided hundreds of times since then, either by chance or by his orchestration. To him, it was destiny. To her, a curse. He always made certain she was on his guest list at his frequent social gatherings at Bellerive, and inexplicably, she accepted most of his invitations. Perhaps it was because his parties provided her only opportunity to escape her insular life on the farm. Or perhaps it was the lure of his glorious library, and the thrill of seeing a new novel she coveted on his bookshelves, just begging to be consumed. Perhaps he knew that as well.

As the two sisters entered the French doors leading to Braxton's library, eager to explore and devour the new titles, Sarah's heart sank. Inside the sanctuary of letters were three men, talking as men do, with little verity but much certainty in their opinions.

"What the Northerners fail to comprehend," clamored the first man, a rotund sort with ruddy cheeks, "is that without slavery, there is no order, and without order, there is no civilization!" The other two nodded in agreement. "Without a system of class and subordination, nobody can order anyone else to do anything, and consequently, nothing would ever get done! Is that really what they want?" The men shook their heads.

Sarah pulled again at Rebecca's arm and began to retreat gracefully, having no desire to engage the blustery triumvirate in conversation. The sisters were nearly gone and on their way when the second man chimed in.

"Of course, the same is true of women. It is our duty as men to protect them, and therefore it is their obligation to obey!"

"Here, here!" agreed his cohorts, raising their brandy snifters. "Happy are those who understand and accept their limitations!"

Rebecca abruptly stopped and cocked her head to one side. She broke free of Sarah's grasp and turned back into the library.

"Excuse me, sir?" she said.

"Why, Miss Talton, and Miss Talton," he replied with an affected gentility. "Good evening to you. We didn't see you come in."

"Clearly."

"Is there something on your mind?" inquired the angular man on the end who had just put forth his thoughts on gender.

"I couldn't help but overhear your remarks on the limitations of women," said Rebecca. "What precisely did you mean by that?"

The three men first looked at each other with mild surprise, which quickly gave way to amusement.

Struggling to extricate himself from his chair, the portly man stood up to act as spokesman for the group. "It is the natural order of the universe. God created some of us to be stronger than others, physically as well as mentally. The weak must be subjects to the strong. In the case of men and women, the wife must be subject to the husband, or else the family disintegrates."

Rebecca moved closer a half step. "With all due respect, sir, I do believe that my sister here could chop more firewood and put up more hay in a day than you could in a week. What does that tell you about who's stronger?" Sarah turned her head and looked away, not at all pleased to be involved in this debate, much less being the new focus of it.

"This is true," he replied calmly. "And your sister also runs the lowest yielding farm in the county. What does that tell *you?* "

Sarah jerked her sister's arm as she leaned toward the exit. "I believe it's time to go."

The eldest of the three men stepped forward. "Gentlemen, this is a social gathering! We're not supposed to be debating the natural order of the universe, are we?" The other two men reluctantly nodded in agreement, as he turned to Rebecca. "Now then, would you mind getting me some more brandy? My glass seems to have emptied with all this vigorous conversation." He held out his snifter.

Rebecca narrowed her eyes and bit the inside of her bottom lip. She gracefully extended her hand and wrapped her slender fingers around the stem of the snifter. Even after the man released his grasp, Rebecca continued to hold the glass at arm's-length in front of her, locking her eyes onto his. She then let the brandy snifter slip through her fingers and crash to the floor, shattering both the glass and any semblance of civility that may have remained in the room. She brusquely turned her back, and marched away.

Sarah's hand instinctively covered her gaping mouth. Her eyes widened in an odd combination of horror and pride. She forced a demure smile as she backed out of the room with a half-curtsy to the three shocked men in front of her. "My apologies for my sister. Good evening, gentlemen."

"Come on, we're leaving," said Rebecca to Sarah as they gathered up their coats. " 'Get me some more brandy!' " she quoted. "I'll get you some brandy, and I'll put poison in it!"

The two women headed quickly for the front door. Sarah took one final glance at the throng in the drawing room, spotting LeGare's head rising above the rest. He was again playing the role of listening post to the ramblings of yet another gentleman farmer trying to get into his good graces.

5

Come unto me, all ye that labor and are heavy laden, and I will give you rest.

Matthew 11:28

*T*he aging horse-drawn surrey rumbled down a country lane as a haze of moonlight peered through thin clouds to show the way back home.

At the reins was Cyrus, a slave as black as a raven, with a barrel chest and hands like anvils. Cyrus relished the rare opportunities to drive Miss Talton. Governing a horse with the wind whipping in his face made him feel free. He had a fondness and admiration for his owner, and sincerely appreciated the trust she placed in him to drive her safely to appointments and to wait patiently in the surrey for her return. Vigorous with the whip, Cyrus had the old bay moving at a steady clip. Sarah and Rebecca huddled in the seat behind their driver, buried beneath the warmth of several quilts. Rebecca pulled the edge of the quilt closer to her chin and shook her head.

"That was perhaps the worst party I've ever attended. A room full of pig-headed dullards, every one of them!"

Sarah smiled. "Well, not *every* one of them."

"I stand corrected. But Braxton Smithwick is *such* a rube, he counts double."

"He may be somewhat unrefined, but the man doesn't operate the largest tobacco plantation in Forsyth County by being a rube."

"Oh, please! His political views are insufferable! Did you know he's supporting John C. Breckinridge in next month's election?"

"I would too if I had a vote."

"Oh, Sarah, how *can* you? The Southern Democrats represent everything for which the North holds us in contempt!"

"My, my... the things they teach you in college these days. And who *would* you have us vote for?"

"Abraham Lincoln," said Rebecca.

"Lincoln? *Lincoln?* Do you want to just give away everything we've worked for? The South would never be the same!"

"Precisely my point."

"I'm glad our father isn't around to listen to such blasphemy from his own daughter. Honestly, Rebecca... Lincoln?"

"You're unusually feisty tonight. I do believe Monsieur LeGare has had an effect on your constitution."

Sarah offered a sheepish grin. "My constitution is just fine, thank you."

"You know, he's the kind of man who will keep you up at night," giggled Rebecca.

Sarah blushed, unwilling to admit that he already had.

The surrey rolled onto the grounds of the Talton farm and Cyrus deftly cooled the horse's heels to a gentle stop. Something suddenly caught his eye.

"Who dat, Miss Talton?"

"What do you mean, Cyrus?" Sarah climbed out of the back of the surrey. It wasn't until her head had cleared the canopy that she saw the buckboard wagon in front of her well-worn barn, with the two slave patrollers and their dogs on board. She shot a puzzled glance at Rebecca, and held up her hand to tell her young sister to stay put. Sarah climbed down from the surrey and walked toward the buckboard with Cyrus a few paces behind. The two gnarled men from the woods scrambled down to greet her, removing their hats in a show of respect.

"Evening, Miss Talton," said their burly leader.

"Can I help you?"

"We caught us another nigra tryin' to run. Thought ya might could use 'nother hand on the farm."

For the first time, Sarah noticed the runaway slave strapped to the back of the buckboard, moaning quietly under a covering of stiff canvas. "I see." Sarah moved closer to the runaway, still exercising caution. "And what makes you think I need another hand?"

The bearded patroller nervously shuffled his feet and glanced at his partner, unsure how honest he should be. He hung his head before speaking. "Well, it's just the talk in town, that's all. Ya know how folks is... some of 'em figured ya might need a little, ya know, assistance."

"Well they're quite misinformed. I'm doing just fine."

"Yes, ma'am. I would not disagree with that, not one bit." The man looked to his partner for support and the scrawny man readily bobbed his head in agreement. "That said, then I suppose it wouldn't be a burden on ya to pay us our reward money and we'll be a gittin' on our way."

With the cocksureness of an arm wrestler who was about to pin his opponent's wrist to the table, the burly man lifted his head and stared squarely at Sarah. She locked onto his gaze for a moment, then broke it off, taking a few more steps toward the moaning slave. She knew she couldn't afford to pay the bounty hunter's reward, even if she could use another hand in the fields. But to admit that was to admit defeat, not only to the two men standing in front of her right now, but to the hundreds of men in town who had been standing in her way much of her life.

"It's not the money," lied Sarah as she circled the prostrate body on the buckboard. "Lord knows I've got the money for a silly little reward. It's just that I don't want to upset the balance here. My farm is a very efficient operation, and you may feel free to share that information with anyone in town who may believe otherwise. It's like a man who owns a dog, and is suddenly offered another dog. It's not that it costs that much more to keep another animal, but it upsets the balance of the situation. How will the two dogs get along? Where will the new dog sleep? What if they don't like the same food? Then I'm stuck making two different suppers for two dogs. It's about maintaining the status quo. Balance. Do you understand?"

The patrollers shook their addled heads. "Uhhh... no, not really, ma'am."

"The point is..." Sarah now stood directly over the face of the captured slave. "The point is... while I appreciate the considerable efforts of you two gentleman, I just don't require another slave at this point in time, especially since I'm required by law to return him to his rightful owner. Perhaps you should take your bounty up the road a few miles to Mr. Smithwick, because I'm sure he could—"

A shaft of pale autumn moonlight illuminated the slave's face for the first time. Sarah slowly removed the tattered felt hat. "Oh my good Lord in heaven," she gasped.

"What da matta, Miss Talton?" said Cyrus as he edged closer. "He dead?"

"No," she replied, trembling slightly. "He's a *woman* !"

Equally as surprised as Sarah, the two patrollers gathered around the murmuring body on the buckboard. Rebecca joined them, now standing by Sarah's side.

"And she's hurt!" said Rebecca, reaching out to touch the crusty patches of blood that had trickled down the runaway's muslin smock like tiny rivers. Rebecca turned angrily to the hunters. "Why do you have to do that? Isn't it enough to just capture them? Do you *have* to beat them senseless?"

"We just doin' what the law allows, Missy. Nothin' mo."

"And certainly nothing less!"

Sarah gently lifted the runaway's semi-conscious head into her hands. The mysterious woman's skin was a rich brown, the color of a well-ripened chestnut. Even with the bloody scratches from wild blackberry bushes and cornfield dirt smeared by tears, there was something beautiful, something elegant, something rare about her face. It didn't seem to be the kind of face that should be pressed face down against the unforgiving oak panels of a buckboard wagon. Sarah eased the slave's head underneath the felt hat to provide a modicum of comfort.

"Cyrus!"

"Yessum?"

"Wake up the others. Get this woman into some dry clothes, and have them attend to these wounds."

Acting swiftly on Sarah's orders, Cyrus lifted the limp figure of the slave woman into his powerful arms and immediately departed for a row of rough-hewn cabins.

Sarah turned to the two woodsmen. "What do I owe you?"

"Six dollars," responded the leader. "Three apiece."

The look on Sarah's face indicated she was aghast at the amount, but she fought to hide her disgust.

"Very well. I shall return momentarily."

Sarah lifted up her hoop skirt and walked briskly across the yard to the front door of the modest white farmhouse. Rebecca scurried behind her as they entered the front hallway and turned into a small parlor.

"What are you doing, Sarah? We can't afford this!"

"I don't *know* what I'm doing. It just seems to be the appropriate thing to do and I can't explain it right now."

Sarah strode directly to a bookcase next to a blackened fireplace and removed a leatherbound copy of Washington Irving's *Sketchbook*. She flipped open the pages, removed several pressed bills from inside, and quickly returned the book to its proper spot.

"But you need that money to buy seed!" Rebecca followed Sarah's determined path back to the front door.

"Don't worry. I'll take her in, see to it that she heals up, then return her to her rightful owner. Surely she hasn't gotten far, no more than a day's travel from here, I would think. We'll take her back and get reimbursed in plenty of time for planting season. And you'll still have money for school, I promise. It only means that I'll do without a book or two for the winter, and I have a number I wouldn't mind reading again, so it's not a burden."

The two sisters made their way back into the cold night air and rejoined the two patrollers. Sarah stuck out the money as far as her arm's length would allow. "Six dollars. Now go."

The burly one nodded his head in silent appreciation as he

accepted the payment and immediately divided the spoils with his partner. "Well then, if there's nothin' else—"

"There's nothing else, I assure you," snapped Sarah.

The burly bounty hunter leaned closer to Sarah, his feral beard nearly touching her face. He spoke in a gravelly whisper. "Just a word of advice, ma'am. I'd be keepin' an eye on your stock of red pepper."

"And why's that?"

"The runaways rub it on their feet, thinkin' the scent throws off the dogs. What the nigras don't know is that them dogs is trained now to get wind of red pepper, and once they do, the huntin' part's over. After that, it's just chasin', and ain't no nigra gonna outrun them dogs. All I'm sayin' is, you find you be missin' some red pepper, there's a good chance you gonna be missin' a nigra." He winked at Sarah. "But not for long."

Sarah backed away a considerable distance as she nodded in understanding. "Goodnight, *gentlemen*."

The men pocketed their money, hopped onto their buckboard, and wheeled away.

Cyrus kicked open the wooden door of a slave cabin, the limp body of the runaway draped across his arms. The structure was crudely made of dovetailed weathered logs, chinked with red mud that fought a constant battle with the whistling Carolina winds. The last vestiges of a dying fire glowed in the river rock fireplace, casting an apricot-orange light across the small room. He barked out orders.

"Sibby, Missus say git dis woman inta some dry clothes." Cyrus laid the injured slave on a corn shuck mattress in the corner. Sibby, the matriarch of the field hands, still groggy from only an hour of sleep, crawled out from under the quilts on her simple, straw-covered bed. She found her balance on work-weary legs and rubbed her eyes to bring the room into focus.

Cyrus stood over the runaway and shook his head in disgust. "Some nigras ain't got da sense God give 'em." His duties fulfilled, he quickly left the cabin, slamming the door behind him.

Sibby Quarterman stood barely five feet tall in a permanent stoop. She believed she was in her late sixties, but she didn't really know. Her eyes were merely slits from years of squinting in the bright sun of the tobacco fields, with a crescent shaped bag of skin underneath each eye like the dark side of a waxing moon. It was difficult for her to clearly see the stranger in the room, but with the instincts of a grandmother, Sibby knelt down and examined the body curled up on the floor.

"Dis chile hurtin' somethin' awful," said Sibby. "Luzanne, put a pot on to boil."

Luzanne, her sturdy and slender daughter, readily obeyed. She grabbed the cast iron pot next to the fireplace, filled it with water, and set it on top of the coals. She added another slab of split oak to the fire to bring it back to life.

Sibby reached out with her arthritic fingers, gnarled by years of plunging her hands into North Carolina clay, and rubbed them softly against the stranger's muddy face.

"Who dat, Momma?" whispered Luzanne, leaning over her mother's shoulder.

"Don't know. She look like she bin runnin' a long time. Skinny lil' thang."

In her upstairs bedroom, Sarah delicately rubbed her hand over the fibers of Monsieur LeGare's jacket. She draped it over the chair on her nightstand, twice making certain it was hanging just right. As she started to undress for bed, she looked out her window and saw the fresh, gray smoke rising from the chimney of Sibby's cabin. She wondered what new problems she may have introduced into her life by temporarily taking in the runaway. Admittedly, she had done it only on impulse, but in hindsight, it now seemed like the good Christian thing to do. She convinced herself that days from now, she would return the slave to her owner, accept reimbursement for the six dollars she'd paid the patrol, and everyone would be happy. Satisfied now that her concerns were without merit, Sarah pulled down the nightshade and gave the shoulders of LeGare's jacket a final fond stroke.

Kneeling on the dirt floor of the slave cabin, Sibby took a ladle fashioned from a gourd and dipped it into the warm water simmering on the fire. She held it the runaway's lips, prodding her to take a sip.

"Here ya go, chile."

For the first time, the injured woman opened her eyes, easing back into consciousness. With Sibby's help, she tilted her head forward and sipped weakly. The flickering light from the rejuvenated fire danced across the anonymous woman's face, revealing a natural beauty in her eyes and the delicate structure of her cheekbones. She fell back into a painful slumber.

6

In the house of the righteous is much treasure:
but in the revenues of the wicked is trouble.

Proverbs 15:6

*T*he newest arrival to the Talton farm groaned as she rolled over on the sack of corn shucks. As she opened her coffee-brown eyes to the morning sun filtering into the cabin, the images of Sibby and Luzanne standing over her were blurred. Her first cognizant sensation was that her bare feet were sticking out from the tattered cotton blanket covering her legs. She lurched to attention.

"My shoes!" she screamed in terror. "Where're my shoes?"

"Easy, chile, easy," said Sibby as she gestured toward the fireplace. "Dey right der, dryin' out."

The runaway scrambled to her feet, wincing from sudden pain as she applied weight to her twisted ankle. She limped to the hearth and retrieved her sodden shoes, clutching the muddy leather like a child holds her favorite doll. She hobbled over to the only chair in the room and sat down, struggling to put on her shoes over her swollen ankle.

"Where am I?" she asked without looking up.

Sibby bent down to help her with her shoes. "You on Miss Talton's farm."

"Where dat?"

"Nor Carolina. Winston, Nor Carolina. Where ya from, chile?" The runaway didn't answer. She struggled to lace up the top of her boots, weak with hunger and fever.

The door to the cabin suddenly opened, bathing the room in blinding sunlight. Through the brilliant portal emerged Sarah, with Cyrus a step behind. Nobody spoke as Sarah walked over and took a long look at the runaway, circling the chair to view the slave from every angle.

"Who are you?" she inquired in a gentle voice. The runaway offered no reply. "It's all right, you can tell me. I'm not going to hurt you."

The runaway glanced over at Sibby and Luzanne. Sibby nodded her endorsement, but still no response came from the newcomer.

"Very well," said Sarah. "In due time." Sarah noticed beads of moisture forming along the runaway's hairline. Without giving notice, she reached out to touch the slave woman's forehead, the way a mother takes quick stock of a child's temperature. The runaway instinctively snapped back her head, certain she was going to be slapped. Sarah pulled back her hands and held them benignly in the air, making it clear she meant no harm. The slave slowly sat up straight. Sarah cautiously moved her hand closer, like a stranger attempting to pet a skittish dog. She placed her hand on the runaway's perspiring brown skin.

"This woman is extremely ill. She needs more than folk medicine. Cyrus, see that she's taken into the house. Get her some horehound and plenty of spice tea."

"Yessum."

"Ya might wants to brew up sum branch elder twigs an' dogwood berries for dem chills, too," offered Sibby.

Sarah nodded. "Good idea, Sibby. Cyrus? Can you take care of all that?"

"Yessum, Miss Talton. Fo sho." Cyrus motioned for the runaway to follow him. She stood slowly, again wincing from the pain of her throbbing ankle. Gingerly, she attempted several steps, forcing herself not to cry out in anguish. Sarah motioned to Cyrus to help the limping woman. He extended his powerful arms, the envy of any blacksmith, and helped the runaway out the door. He had always had an uncanny acumen for interpreting the unspoken nods and gestures of his mistress, and took great pride in carrying out her wishes, especially in front of the other slaves. He wanted to make certain they fully understood who was Miss Talton's favorite, and that the position he enjoyed in the farm's pecking order was not to be challenged. At the same time, Sarah understood how vital her bond with Cyrus was to her survival. With no master in the household, and the inability to pay a white overseer to handle the slaves, she leaned heavily on Cyrus to keep her servants in line. Aided considerably by his imposing frame, rippled with muscles carved out by hard work, no one had ever dared to challenge his supremacy. And though not quite reaching the rank of slave driver, Cyrus was nonetheless the voice of authority inside the slave quarters, and the distributor of justice and punishment behind them. Heaven help the slave who didn't fully understand that.

As the midday sun washed through a translucent window, the runaway awoke from a fitful sleep. She found herself in a small trundle bed in what had once been the maid's quarters of the Talton farm in more prosperous times. She fondly stroked her hand across the cotton sheets and colorful quilt, having never slept in a real bed before. Rubbing her weary eyes with the heels of her open hands, she rose to her feet, struggling through the weakness of fever and the discomfort of her ravaged ankle. Limping to the door, she opened it just a crack and saw that it led to the kitchen. She ventured cautiously to the fireplace, continually glancing around to make certain she was alone. The runaway knelt down next to the hearth, lined with sooty bricks the color of fallen leaves from a red oak. The bricks were coarse and chipped from years of hot cast iron skillets filled with steaming cornbread and bacon being dropped on them. Taking one final glance behind her, the slave woman placed her hands palm down on the abrasive surface of the hearth and vigorously rubbed them in circles until she drew blood.

Outside in the yard, Sarah fumbled through a small iron ring holding a dozen passkeys. Even though she used them nearly every day, the vast array of skeletons always looked the same, and each entry into a storehouse or outbuilding was always an embarrassing exercise in trial and error. It also angered her somewhat that she was forced to keep the farm's provisions under lock and key, but years of theft by her slaves had proven it to be a necessary evil. The Talton family had always done their best to feed their slaves a decent meal, better than most from what she'd heard about other plantations, but even that didn't seem to slow the plundering of rations. If the smokehouse were inadvertently left unlocked or unattended, by morning a sizable portion of the pork and turkey would be gone.

Sarah finally found the correct implement to liberate the door to the storehouse and drew a generous amount of sugar from the hogshead. It used to bother Sarah that she couldn't afford the fancy loaves of sugar they sold in town, but it had been so long since she'd tasted it, she could no longer tell the difference. With Rebecca home from school for a few months, she took great enjoyment in cooking for the two of them, especially cakes and cookies, and sugar from a hogshead was just fine for that.

As she closed the door to the storehouse behind her, her mind flashed back to her days as a teenager when baby Rebecca would dive into gingerbread fresh from the oven. The smile and faraway look of reminiscence that spread across her face suddenly evaporated. Galloping up the lane was Braxton Smithwick, his wild shock of unrestrained hair flying around his head like summer sawgrass in a hurricane. To show off his riding abilities, Braxton raced his mount into the open space in front of the farmhouse, recklessly scattering chickens. He jerked the animal to a sudden stop and dismounted in one fluid motion, the leather of his polished boots thudding onto the dirt directly in front of Sarah. She backed away with instinctive timidity as Braxton's horse twitched in place, waggling his wild mane and exhaling the frosty fire of chilled autumn air. Braxton yanked on the reins to quiet his horse and tied the straps to the hitching post.

"And to what do I owe the pleasure of this surprise?" asked Sarah with a tone of disinterest as she turned her back to Braxton and made her way to the front door of her farmhouse.

"I just talked to John Parker."

Braxton's deadly serious tone momentarily stopped Sarah in her tracks. She turned back and stared at him with deep concern and embarrassment. She exhaled audibly and with a nod of her head, motioned him toward the door.

Sarah poured Braxton a cup of piping hot coffee into an earthenware mug and then one for herself as she joined him at the small wooden table in the kitchen.

"John Parker says you're three months behind paying your bills." Sarah spooned a measure of sugar into her coffee, watching it swirl around in the mug. She bit her lower lip and looked up at Braxton with as much pride and defiance as she could muster.

"Since when did my financial affairs become the topic of conversation at the feed mill?"

"It's not just there, Sarah. Rumors are everywhere that you can't meet your obligations."

"Things are a little difficult right now. The fall harvest wasn't what I'd hoped for. But I'll take care of it."

"How? Ever since your father died, I've watched this farm slowly wither into the ground, and I don't see that changing."

Sarah offered no defense as she resumed stirring her coffee. Braxton put his wrists on the edge of the table and leaned forward. "Sarah, listen to me... I can help you!"

"But I don't require any help, Mr. Smithwick."

"I can pay off your debts, and we can make this farm profitable again."

"I notice you use the word *we* when referring to *my* farm."

"You have some of the best farmland in the entire county, but you can't tend it alone."

"And why not?"

"It's just not possible. Look, it's not your fault that you're a woman. All I'm saying is—"

Sarah abruptly stood up and shoved her chair under the table with indignation. "Good day, Mr. Smithwick."

"Sarah, you're gonna lose this farm! Your crops aren't growing, you aren't working your slaves hard enough, and on top of it, you're wasting money sending that uppity sister of yours off to school! I'm offering you a business partnership... and who knows, maybe more."

"Mr. Smithwick—"

"Braxton! Call me Braxton!"

"Mr. Smithwick, we've known each other as long as I can remember, and I just don't look at you that way. I'm sorry. I just don't."

"You mean like the way you look at that Frenchman?" he responded, cocking his head and raising an eyebrow.

"I'm asking you to leave now."

Braxton snorted in frustration, then downed the remainder of his hot coffee. He wiped his mouth with his sleeve.

"By the way, he's leaving for Charleston in two weeks, so maybe then you can get your mind back to running this farm. In the meantime, consider my offer. It's the best one you'll get. Most likely the only one." Braxton cocked his eyebrow and snapped his head down and back as if to say *"you best believe it."* He brushed past Rebecca in the hallway without speaking as he marched to the front door with heavy footfalls.

With a frown of concern and confusion, Rebecca found Sarah in the kitchen, fumbling with two potatoes on the table.

"What was that all about?" asked Rebecca.

"Nothing."

"Who's leaving for Charleston?"

"Monsieur LeGare," she whispered.

"Who?"

Sarah angrily tossed the potatoes aside. "Monsieur LeGare! And I fear that if I don't somehow communicate with him before then, I might never again have the chance."

"Reverend Williams knows some French. Perhaps you could get him to translate a letter."

Sarah struggled to resurrect a smile, battling the lines of worry etched into her skin. "Dear sister, I will not be sharing my most intimate thoughts with Reverend Williams."

Rebecca sighed. "Perhaps it was not meant to be."

"My head agrees with you, but my heart says differently."

"Too bad your heart doesn't speak French."

A genuine smile blossomed across Sarah's face. "Oh, but it does."

Unseen behind the adjacent walls of the maid's quarters was the runaway with her ear pressed up to the solid oaken door.

7

*Foolishness is bound in the heart of a child;
but the rod of correction shall drive it far from him.*

Proverbs 22:15

*O*nly the most stubborn of autumn leaves still clung to the branches of the giant elms lining the carriageway of the Talton farm as the buckboard wagon of the slave patrol thundered onto the grounds. Strapped to the back of the wagon was Will Quarterman, a young man, muscular and lean. The patrollers dragged him off the wagon and let him land on the ground like a sack of flour, the chains of his wrist-shackles and leg-irons clanking around him like a ship weighing anchor. Will struggled to his feet, defiant anger seething out of his fatigued body. The patroller raised his hickory stick and clipped Will behind the knees, sending him crashing to the ground again. He raised his staff again.

Sarah charged out of the front door of the farmhouse.

"Enough!" she screamed at the patroller, jarring him enough to make him lower his arm. "You're paid to bring them back, not break their bones!"

"If folks is gonna act like animals, then you gotta treat 'em like animals."

"Then perhaps I should be paying you in raw meat." Sarah motioned her head toward Will. "Unchain him."

The patrollers pulled Will to his knees and removed the chains that bound his lower legs. Bands of raw, pink skin encircled his ankles where the chains had scraped away his outer flesh. As the men gathered up the chains, Sarah tossed several bills onto the ground in front of them to pay the reward.

"Good day."

Wilting under the heat of Sarah's glare, the patrollers snatched up their payment and climbed back onto their wagon. The driver released his frustrations through his horsewhip and rumbled away in a cyclone of dust.

When the patrol had vanished, Sarah circled Will like an angry prosecutor interrogating a hostile witness. He remained on his knees and stared straight ahead. Searching for words, she pounded her closed fists against her upper thighs.

"Why? Why do you do this to me? Do I not treat you fairly? Are you not given food, shelter, and clothing? You only make it harder on everyone when you do this! It costs me money... money I need to be spending on more important things... so unless you want to see the Talton farm sold to someone who may not treat you as well as I do, then this is going to stop. Is that clear?"

Will's only response was to spit away the lingering dust from the buckboard's exit.

Sarah turned to call for Cyrus, who was already behind her in anticipation of her needs.

"See that he's properly punished."

"Yessum."

"And for the others, no meat for three days. I can't have this happen again."

"Yessum."

Sarah lifted her chin and breezed quickly past Will, the edges of her skirt brushing past his taciturn face as she returned to the main house.

Cyrus clamped his sturdy black hand around Will's bicep and yanked him to his feet. With resignation as to what was about to happen, Will allowed Cyrus to drag him along like an unruly child being escorted to the woodshed by an angry parent. As they passed in front of the main house, Will caught a glimpse of something in the window. It was the runaway, observing events through the milky glass. Their eyes connected for only the briefest of moments before she ducked from view.

Inside the maid's quarters, the runaway moved from the window to the door and peered out cautiously, making certain of no interruptions. She sat on a footstool at the base of the bed, tugged off her threadbare right shoe, and with great care slowly pried off the worn leather heel. The center of the heel had been hollowed out and inside the secret cavity was a tattered letter, folded and folded again.

Trembling with anticipation, she gingerly unfolded the note and silently read the words on the thin parchment.

> *My Darling Jacquerie... I have written you a hundred letters, and a hundred times have wondered if any of them have made it into your hands. They all carry the same message... I am a Free man now, living in Canada and working for an honorable merchant and gentleman. My journey here was difficult but my Freedom has been worth the suffering. My only sorrow now is my separation from you. I will be with you every step of the way as you follow the drinking gourd to Freedom. I know in my heart that one day you will both join me, and I pray every night for your safe passage.*
>
> *I will wait Forever.*
>
> *Your faithful husband,*
>
> *John Bodin*

With tears welling up in her eyes, Jacquerie Bodin clutched to her aching chest the precious letter she'd read a thousand times, covering her mouth to keep from releasing an audible cry. She kissed the precious note, then carefully folded it along the same worn seams and tucked it back into the safety of the hollow heel of her shoe. She lined up the cobbler's nails on the heel with the holes on the bottom of her sole and like a carpenter driving a finishing nail, carefully pounded the heel onto the hardwood floor to secure it back into place.

It was the early spring of 1858 when John Bodin first appeared on the cotton plantation of Peter Duval, his face still gleaming from the sweet oil his seller had rubbed on him to make him more attractive at auction. The Duval family owned one of the largest operations of its kind in the entire state of Louisiana, covering more than a thousand acres outside the town of Crowley. It required hundreds of slaves to maintain the frenetic output of raw cotton, with at least a dozen house slaves working in the massive plantation home at any given time.

John had been purchased at auction for a princely sum.

With leg and chest muscles that rippled like the shoulders of a Brahma bull, he was worth it. Most days he could perform the work of three men. There were horses at the Duval farm who couldn't pull as much weight as mighty John Bodin.

While his new owners anticipated a tremendous output of work in the fields, they hadn't foreseen the disruptive social impact that John would have on the population. Men and women, mostly women, couldn't help but stop what they were doing and simply watch John in action. From daybreak to dusk, he worked the fields like an untracked locomotive and he never seemed to tire. The reaction to his prodigious feats of labor ranged from admiration to amazement, and from lust to jealousy. The other men soon grew tired of hearing the nightly stories brought in from the fields about how much work John had accomplished that day. As his reputation quickly grew, so did the resentment of some of his male counterparts.

Of all his admirers, none did it with more ardor than a rail-thin young woman named Jacquerie. Each morning she made a particular effort to pass by him as he headed into the fields and she reported for work inside the main house. Whenever possible, she would slip away from her assigned duties of watching the Duval children and sneak off to an upstairs window, hoping to catch a distant glimpse of John. If he were close enough to the main house, he was easy to spot. A head taller and a foot broader than most of the men around him, his sweaty charcoal skin stood out in stark contrast to the snowy white carpet of the cotton fields.

John had been on the Duval plantation for nearly half a year before he would take any notice of Jacquerie. One steamy August night, as the exhausted tribe of laborers trudged back from the fields, Jacquerie made her way from the big house to the crumbling rows of slave quarters. Hidden inside her blouse were two large molasses cookies she'd stolen from the kitchen. Making certain her path intersected with John's, she quickly whipped out the forbidden treats and surreptitiously jammed them into his massive hands as he passed by. She knew she had to be quick about it, because to get caught stealing food from the plantation house would mean serious punishment for both of them. Taken aback by the unexpected act of kindness, John spun around to express his thanks, but Jacquerie was gone before he could open his mouth. He shoved the cookies into his pocket and headed on.

Every sundown that followed brought the same brief encounter. A biscuit, a hunk of jerky, a crisp apple... anything she could swipe would find its way into John's mudstained hands and eventually into his stomach. A word was never uttered between them, but the attraction grew stronger by the day.

As was his custom, he would hide the items that Jacquerie brought him under a loose plank in the floor next to his bed. After he'd had a chance to wash up and eat the meager meal that was provided to him, he would slip back to his bed and retrieve the hidden gifts. On this particular night he had nearly an entire turkey leg and a piece of horehound candy waiting for him. His mouth watered as he knelt down and gingerly lifted up the plank to reveal the spoils.

"Whatcha got der, boy?" came the gravelly Cajun voice behind him. John slammed down the floorboard, but it was too late. He turned around in abject terror to see the Duval family's overseer lording over him. John said nothing as he remained on all fours, unsure of his next move.

"Where'd you git it, boy?"

John still said nothing. Without warning, a hard leather boot slammed into his midsection. It hurt, but not terribly so, as John's stomach muscles were close to an even match with the overseer's swift kick.

John already knew he wasn't going to reveal his source and he fully understood that some horrible punishment surely awaited him, but he had other decisions to make. He knew he could overpower the man who stood over him. In fact, he knew he could kill him with his bare hands. He also knew there would be more angry white men to follow, and he could never kill them all. On the other hand, even if he surrendered quietly, the punishment would still come.

As the overseer again swung his leg forward for another brutal kick, John raised up and grabbed him by the ankle. With one swift motion, he yanked his white attacker to the floor and pounced on him. With his knees pinning the overseer's arms against the floor, John wrapped his iron hands around the man's white throat and pressed his powerful thumbs against his windpipe. As he did so, he turned around and looked at the two slaves he rightly suspected of turning him in. It was a silent yet clear message... *if I can do this to him, imagine what I can do to you*. Still staring down the two men, John relaxed his grip on the overseer and allowed him to choke his way back to consciousness. John stood up, then reached down and grabbed the overseer by his wrist, helping him to his feet. With great ceremony he bent down and pulled the stolen food from its hiding place. He tossed the turkey leg to one of the traitorous men, then popped the piece of hard horehound into his mouth. With great dignity, he slowly walked out the front door, not knowing his fate, but clearly unafraid to face it.

John's legend grew exponentially overnight when others heard what he'd done. Their awe and respect would reach new heights in the coming days as they watched the pain and suffering he would be forced to endure at the whipping post.

Jacquerie was sick with worry, for the Duval plantation was notorious for harsh discipline, particularly for thieves and runaways. It wasn't just the usual floggings that drew red blood from black flesh, but torturous punishment, barbaric in its ingenuity, savage in its execution. She had seen white men pour tar on a slave's head and ignite it with a torch, causing incredible pain before dousing it with a bucket of water. On other occasions, she'd seen slaves stuffed into a wooden barrel that had dozens of nails driven through the sides so their sharp points protruded inside. The barrel was then rolled down a steep hill with the man inside, inflicting hundreds of puncture wounds that were often fatal.

John had one thing working in his favor. The Duvals were not inclined to kill a slave as valuable as he was, no matter what the perceived crime. On the other hand, it would serve them well to make an example of him in front of the others. *If we can do this to him, imagine what we can do to you.*

When one of the cotton presses was dragged into the common yard in front of the slave quarters, they all knew John's fate. The cotton press was in essence a large-scale version of a wine press. Instead of a man turning the large screw by hand as on a wine press, two horses were attached by a rope to the top of the screw. The horses would walk in a circle to slowly lower the screw, which in turn pressed a large block onto the raw cotton underneath it. When the cotton was sufficiently compressed, the horses would reverse course and raise the screw.

On this day, only one horse was connected to the top of the screw handle. Dangling from the other side, hands lashed above his head, was John Bodin. As the horse trod in the circular path, John swung freely from the rope, eight feet above the ground, like a fish at the end of a line. Every so often, as his fancy would strike him, the overseer would whip John as he swung past him. Depending on how high the leather bit into him, John's back, buttocks, and legs were turned into a bloody mess.

After a merciless hour of this corrective measure, the overseer lowered John to the ground. It was as much to give the horse a rest as anything.

John's penance was not over. For the next four days and nights, he was chained to a wooden bench in front of the slave quarters. He provided a constant visual reminder to the others about the importance of obedience.

The misery was almost intolerable, even for a man as strong-willed and powerful as John Bodin. It wasn't so much the terrible thirst that sent him to near hallucination, but rather the infestation of flies and maggots that flocked to his oozing sores. All the other slaves walked by him, unable or unwilling to help. All but one. Risking severe punishment herself, Jacquerie slipped out of her cabin in the middle of the night and crept quietly to John's side. She gave him cornmeal balls to eat and cool water to drink as she washed his sores with the liquor of Oak of Jerusalem which she'd picked and boiled earlier that evening. She rubbed his shredded back with a slab of stolen meat fat. For four nights she did this, risking her own life each time. Not a single word was spoken as she nursed him. Their eyes said all that needed to be said.

In the days and weeks that followed John's release from his own private purgatory, he would find Jacquerie at every opportunity. The love that had blossomed between them was strong and pure, a shining island in what was otherwise a sea of damnation. She loved everything about him. The touch of his mighty hands, the feel of his weathered skin. She just loved the way he looked at her when they shared a meal of Indian corn. They would kiss madly, with quiet desperation, as if it were going to be the last time.

By year's end, they were married, and permitted to share the same quarters. They saw little of each other during the day as he made his way into the cotton fields and she returned to the big house, but at night they were inseparable. Even as they slept, each would reach over in a state of half sleep and touch the other on the hip, just to make certain they were still there.

On nights when the moonlight would allow, Jacquerie taught John to read by scratching letters and words into the Louisiana dirt with a sharp stick. They knew it was dangerous, but John's zeal for learning outweighed their fears of getting caught.

It was as happy a life as they could make for themselves under the circumstances, and the love they shared helped to neutralize some of the indignities they suffered each day at the hands of the people who owned them.

It was nearing the end of winter of 1859 when the lives of John and Jacquerie Bodin would be changed forever.

Owen Duval, the twenty-five-year-old son of Peter Duval, and heir to his fortune, walked the fields of the family plantation as if he already owned it. He'd never put in a single day of hard work in his life, had done nothing to earn the enormous inheritance he would one day receive, yet he carried with him a grand sense of entitlement that most around him found infuriating. He took great pleasure in riding horseback up and down the endless rows of cotton, as if inspecting them with a keen eye, unaware that he was trampling tender plants underfoot. He would often take the whip from the hands of the overseer and help mete out punishment to unruly slaves for the sole reason that he could. Owen also had a penchant for bedding down slave women, for unlike the white women of the town, they were in no position to refuse his unwelcome advances.

It was just after dusk when Jacquerie made her way from the main house back to her cabin. As she passed by the storehouse, Owen stepped out of the lengthening shadows.

"I need to see you for a moment," he said in a hushed tone.

Jacquerie stopped obediently in her tracks. "Yessuh?" she asked politely.

"In here." Owen motioned furtively, beckoning her into the storehouse.

Fear gripped her. She'd heard the stories from the time she was a little girl, and she'd always gone out of her way to avoid a situation exactly like this. "But Massa Duval, I ain't got no business in there."

"Get in here, woman! Now!" The oily locks of Owen Duval's straw-blond hair fell down across his forehead as he stepped forward and grabbed Jacquerie by the arm. He yanked her inside the narrow confines of the storehouse and slammed the door behind them.

Jacquerie backed into a corner, trying to retain her composure. "Is there somethin' I kin do for ya, Massa Duval?"

"Oh yes," he replied, leering at her. "There certainly is." He stepped closer, a salacious grin cracking across his face. "I've been watching you. Been watching you for the longest time."

Owen removed his jacket and hung it on a nail as he moved closer, biting his lower lip.

Jacquerie braced herself against the shelves of the storehouse, trembling with terror. There was nothing she could do to stop Owen's advances. To scream would only result in an immediate punch in the face or worse. To escape his clutches and run away, however unlikely, would only mean a flogging later that night and another assault in the future. She had only one choice: pray it was over quickly.

Owen's hand slithered up her sleeve. He tucked his fingers underneath the collar of her blouse. With a violent tug, he yanked her garment down over her shoulder, tearing the fabric. He closed his eyes as his lips moved across her bare shoulder and onto her neck. Her chest was heaving with dread as he moved his mouth toward her breastbone.

Owen had no time to react as the door to the storehouse suddenly crashed open. With nostrils flaring and muscles twitching, John Bodin charged inside, a cotton hoe clutched in his hands. As Owen spun around, the oak handle of the hoe caught him squarely in the jaw. He raised his hands to his mouth as blood spurted out. With Owen's midsection now exposed, John delivered a bone-snapping blow to his ribs. Owen dropped to his knees, sucking for a breath. The rigid shaft of the hoe cracked across the crown of Owen's head, sending him slumping to the floor in a pitiful heap. Alive, but barely.

John and Jacquerie stood paralyzed. It had all happened so fast.

"You have to go!" yelled Jacquerie. "You have to go now!"

John looked at the crumpled body of young Owen Duval on the floor in front of him. He knew his wife was right.

"You come wit me!"

"I can't!"

"What? Why not?"

"I'm gonna have a baby, John. I was gonna tell ya tonight."

"A baby?"

She nodded as she folded her arms across her stomach. "A baby. Which is why I can't go with ya. I'll just slow ya down. They'll kill us all."

"Then I cain't go! I'll take da whippin'."

"John, look at him!" She gestured to Owen. "They'll *kill* you for this! There's no choice to be made! You *got* to go, and you got to go *right now!*"

John's breaths came harder and faster as he weighed his options. Jacquerie was right. To stay was a certain death sentence. To take her with him jeopardized three lives.

John yanked off Owen's boots and trousers from his listless legs and tied knots in the end of each pant leg. Together they filled the makeshift knapsack with as much food as the bulging cloth would hold. He pulled on Owen's canvas jacket, his biceps bursting through the seams.

In a matter of mere minutes, the course of their life had been changed forever. It was time for John to leave. They kissed with desperation, understanding that this could very well be the last time.

"I'll git word back to ya where I am." He rubbed her soft belly. "Take care of yourself. I *will* see you again. I promise."

John hoisted the knapsack onto his broad shoulders. A final kiss, and then out of the door and into the growing darkness of the new night. He was gone.

The following months would bring difficult journeys for John Bodin, slogging through dismal swamps and dark forests, using only the North Star as his guide. When the stolen supplies from the Duval storehouse ran out, he foraged for wild fruit and gleaned vegetables from farms.

Every step he took put him further away from Jacquerie, but at the same time, brought them closer together.

The door to the maid's room suddenly opened, revealing Sarah standing underneath the transom.

"What's that stamping noise?"

"Scu' me?" said Jacquerie, scrambling to her feet.

"The noise coming from this room just now. What are you doing?"

"Oh, *dat* noise. Cricket, ma'am. But he gone now."

"A cricket. In late October. I see."

The tone of Sarah's voice and the look on her face were clear indications that she didn't really believe the explanation, but she let it pass.

"Well then, now that you're talking again, why don't you tell me your name?"

"My name is... Mary."

"And where are you from, Mary?"

"Sou' Carolina."

"South Carolina. Where in South Carolina. What town?"

"Don't rightly know. Cain't say fer sho."

"Do you know who owns you?"

"Massa Johnson."

"Johnson. I see. Must be a lot of Johnsons spread across South Carolina."

"I reckon der is."

"And you wouldn't be making all this up, would you?"

Jacquerie raised her eyebrows in surprise, as if to say *why would I do a thing like that?* "No, ma'am. Dat der be da God's onnest troof."

"Good." Sarah pulled a printed sheet of paper from behind her back. "Because I found this at the telegraph office."

Sarah took another long look at Jacquerie, then read aloud. " 'Reward. One hundred dollars. Ran away from my plantation near Crowley, Louisiana, on the first day of September, 1860, my house servant, Jacquerie Bodin.' " She peered over the paper at Jacquerie. "I think I'm pronouncing that correctly."

Jacquerie didn't flinch at the mention of her name as Sarah continued.

" 'She is five feet five inches high, weighs between one hundred and one hundred ten pounds, has dark eyes and a thin jaw. I will give one hundred dollars reward to whoever secures her, no matter where taken. Signed, Peter Duval.' "

Sarah handed the sheet to Jacquerie, who held it upside down as she examined the words.

"One hundred dollars," mused Sarah out loud. "She must be a *very* valuable slave."

Jacquerie shrugged and handed the missive back to Sarah. "I wouldn't know nothin' 'bout any a dat. I belongs to Massa Johnson."

"Yes, you did say that. And what did you do for Mr. Johnson?"

"Field hand, ma'am."

Sarah reached over and took Jacquerie's hands into hers, feeling their texture. While rough in spots from where she'd scraped them against the bricks of the fireplace hearth, they just didn't seem quite weathered enough for a field hand.

"Field hand. I see. Well, I can use another good hand to bring in the fall harvest. Now that you seem to be feeling well enough, I'll see to it that Cyrus gets you clothing and quarters. In the meantime, I'll try to track down your Mister Johnson and see about getting you back to him."

"Yessum."

Sarah took one last distrustful look at the slave woman, then exited the room. An ocean of worry washed across Jacquerie's face as she considered what her new mistress might have uncovered about her past. She took several steps across the wooden floor, testing her injured ankle. A *cracking* whip tearing through the autumn air suddenly drew Jacquerie's attention to the window, and though she couldn't see who was administering the pain, she knew it was the unmistakable sound of a slave being flogged. The hideous snap of seasoned cowhide raping human flesh was something she'd heard all of her life, but to which she had never grown accustomed. It dredged up frightening memories inside her head, and triggered perspiration outside of it.

Mercifully the assault ended, and moments later Jacquerie saw Cyrus pushing Will Quarterman toward his cabin, his wrists still in shackles. The back of Will's shirt was shredded like a battle weary flag, bloody from the stinging tentacles of the overseer's whip. As if suddenly struck by the impulse of a sixth sense, that instinctive feeling that someone is watching you, Will suddenly turned and saw Jacquerie standing in the window. Their eyes met once again, but this time she made no effort to disappear from view.

8

When I'm in trouble, Lord, walk with me.
When my head is bowed in sorrow, Lord, I want Jesus to walk with me.
When storms are raging, Lord, walk with me.
When I am sinking, save my soul. Lord, I want Jesus to walk with me.

African American Spiritual

Jacquerie's thin black arms were wrapped around a bundle of clothes and an old quilt as she followed Cyrus from the big house out to the row of slave cabins.

"Ya do like ya bin told, ya don't get into no trouble. We don't allow no troublemakers on da Talton farm, ya unnerstan?"

Jacquerie offered no reply, as if he'd not even spoken. Cyrus pushed open the door, harder than he needed to, and motioned for Jacquerie to go inside.

Will was hunched over on a handmade stool, wincing in pain as Sibby soothed his lash wounds with balm. All motion in the small room stopped as Cyrus barged in. He showed no remorse over the raw flesh he'd whipped into Will's back, and the indignation that poured from the eyes of the people staring back at him had no effect on his frigid conscience.

"Find room fa her," barked Cyrus.

Luzanne moved slowly toward the door, taking Jacquerie's bundle from her arms and pulling her deeper into the cabin in a gesture of obedience and acceptance. Cyrus nodded and slammed the door behind him.

Sibby resumed her therapeutic massage of Will's back as he slowly lifted his head and forced a smile.

"Well lookie heah. Seem like we have us one mo mouth to feed. And a pretty mouth, at dat."

Jacquerie snatched her quilt back from Luzanne and staked out the corn shuck mattress in the corner. "Don't worry... I don't intend to be here very long."

It wasn't so much *what* Jacquerie said but rather *how* she'd said it that brought Sibby, Luzanne, and Will to rapt attention. They froze in place and stared at her, as if they'd sensed the chilling presence of an apparition in the room.

"Where ya learn to talk like dat, chile?" Sibby asked in a hushed tone.

"It's not important."

"Why ya say ya won't be here long? Ya buckin' fo a job in da house?" asked Will.

"I plan to get further away than that."

Sibby closed her eyes and shook her head vehemently. "Don't be talkin' like dat! It's dangerous!"

"I'm not afraid of anyone," said Jacquerie.

"Ya may not be now, but ya best start gittin' 'fraid. See what dey done to Will? Think 'bout what dey gonna do to you!"

"I can take care of myself."

"Dat what dis fool son of mine thought, now look at him. When y'all people gonna learn to stop causin' trouble? I don't need no mo trouble! No mo. Ugh uh. No."

That would be the final word on the subject for the night. Sibby crawled into her bed and closed her eyes. Luzanne exchanged a quick glance with Will, then turned over to sleep.

A brief moment of silence was broken as Sibby raised her voice in somber song.

> *Dey crucified my Lord,*
> *and He never said a mumbalin' word.*
> *Dey crucified my Lord,*
> *and He never said a mumbalin' word.*

Not a word, not a word, not a word.
The blood came tricklin' down,
and He never said a mumbalin' word.
The blood came tricklin' down,
and He never said a mumbalin' word.
Not a word, not a word, not a word.
He bowed his head and died,
and He never said a mumbalin' word.
He bowed his head and died,
and He never said a mumbalin' word.
Not a word, not a word, not a word.

Sibby exhaled loudly and crossed her arms over her chest. She lay motionless like a prepared body in a casket.

Jacquerie tried in vain to find a comfortable spot on the floor as Will continued to leer at her.

The long shadows of dusk melded into early nightfall, bringing a calming blanket of silence over the Talton farm. It provided Sarah's only peaceful moments, the brief respite wedged in between the work that had been completed that day, and a restless night of sleep worrying about what needed to be accomplished tomorrow.

She stood at her bookshelf in the parlor, tallow candle in hand, and reached for her Bible on the top shelf. Instead, there was an empty slot in the Bible's usual space, with the adjacent book falling over like a lean-to shed. Somewhat puzzled, Sarah rummaged through the other books on the shelf, but the worn black leather of her Bible was not among them.

"Rebecca?" she called into the darkness of the farmhouse. "Rebecca, did you borrow my Bible? Rebecca?" There was no response from her sister, and Sarah was suddenly too tired to pursue the matter. She sat down in the wingchair next to the fireplace, rubbed her weary eyes, and watched the candle flame quietly devour the soft wax below.

9

To every thing there is a season, and a time for every purpose under heaven:
A time to be born, and a time to die; a time to plant,
and a time to pluck up what has been planted;

Ecclesiastes 3:1-2

A thin veil of dust illuminated by the morning sun swirled like a sheer curtain in front of each window inside the Talton farmhouse. Rebecca moved swiftly around the house, clearly searching for something. She nearly collided with Sarah as their paths crossed in front of the staircase.

"Lose something?" Sarah asked.

"I can't find my issue of *The Liberator.* Have you seen it?"

"Yes, I've been using it to wrap fish."

"Sarah! How could you do that?"

"Because that's about all it's good for. How can you read that abolitionist rubbish?"

"Call it what you want, but you know it speaks the truth."

"The truth? William Lloyd Garrison's only purpose is to stir up hatred for the southern way of life, and my own sister is contributing to him!"

"Have you ever actually read it?"

"No, and I don't intend to. I've never stuck my head in a bear's den either, but I'm smart enough to know better."

"Perhaps not a bear's den, but southerners seem to have no problem sticking their heads in the sand like an ostrich."

"This is not a game, Rebecca! It's not some chapter from one of your schoolhouse history books! This is life! *Our* life, and the abolitionists threaten that!"

"Yes, yes, dear sister, and heaven forbid we ever allow change into our midst! Perhaps we should just go back to the days when men dragged us back to their caves. And while we're at it, we should abolish fire, and of course there's the wheel... we should have *never* allowed them to invent that—"

Sarah violently jerked Rebecca by the arm. "Listen to me!" She bristled with a mixture of anger and warning. "Up until now I've let you speak your mind within these walls, but it *has* to stop! If our slaves start to see signs of weakness, we'll have another Nat Turner on our hands, and we simply cannot allow that to happen! Do you understand?"

Rebecca shook free of her grasp and took several steps back.

"What has gotten hold of you, Sarah? Since when were we not free to express our feelings in this house?"

Sarah drew in a calming breath. "I'm sorry. It's not you. It's everything. Slaves running away, northern agitators trying to change our way of life... everything."

"Sarah, you've got to stop worrying so. Everything is going to turn out just fine, you'll see."

"I wish I could believe that. But that's not the reality, Rebecca. There's going to be trouble. There's going to be bloodshed. There's going to be change, and I don't think any of us is really ready for that."

The two sisters embraced, not only in a show of apology and mutual affection, but as if to buttress each other in the face of the impending political and social storm.

Sarah raised her head from Rebecca's shoulder and looked squarely at her father's dour face hanging over the fireplace. Sarah swallowed hard, fighting back tears. "He never told us it would be this hard."

The high October sun offset some of the chill in the air as Jacquerie hunched over in the field, picking squash alongside Sibby. She looked awkward as she slowly loaded her apron, limping slightly on her tender ankle as she made her way down the endless row of yellow. The other slaves moved with a quiet rhythm, bending and picking, bending and picking, their hands and bodies flowing along the ground like an army marching to a silent cadence.

Sibby moved closer to Jacquerie, observing her struggles.

"Where ya learn to pick like dat? Squash goin' be rotten by da time you gits to it!"

The other slaves within earshot laughed.

"We didn't grow squash where I'm from."

"Don't matter, chile, pickin' is still pickin', and ya don't look like ya done too much of it." Without warning, Sibby reached over and grabbed Jacquerie's hands and gave them a quick but thorough inspection. "Dem ain't no field hands, dat's for sho. Look to me like ya been tryin' to rough 'em up some, but dem still ain't no field hands. Why in da world would a house slave wanna be out da fields?"

Jacquerie jerked her hands back and clenched her fists.

"Y'all out here ta work or hold hands?" snapped Cyrus. "Git to it!"

Both women obediently nodded their heads and immediately resumed picking. As Cyrus walked away, Sibby casually but purposefully positioned herself along the row so that she was shoulder to shoulder with Jacquerie. Without saying a word or even sharing a glance, she gave the younger slave a remedial lesson in squash picking. Her skilled hands slid gracefully down to the base of each plant, and in a swift, simultaneous motion, twisted the vine and the squash in opposite directions, like a washerwoman wringing out a wet towel. The momentum of the plucking motion carried the ripe squash directly into her gathering apron, and in an instant her hands were set to grasp the next one. It was like a choreographed ballet as Sibby picked her way down the row, her aging arms moving with effortless efficiency as she left nothing behind. After a dozen demonstrations of her technique, Sibby started to leave a squash behind for Jacquerie to glean. Together they made their way across the field, Sibby outpicking Jacquerie three to one, then two to one, and soon nearly on pace with one another. Only then did Sibby finally look up and offer her pupil a warm smile, and for the first time, received one in return.

"*King of kings, Lord of lords, Jesus Christ, the first and last, no one works like Him,*" Sibby began to sing. "*He built His throne up in the air, No one works like Him. And called His saints from everywhere, no one works like Him.*"

The other women joined in, their bodies starting to sway in unison as they rhythmically moved down the rows. "*He pitched His tents on Canaan ground, no one works like Him. And broke His oppressive kingdoms down, no one works like Him.*"

Sibby focused on Jacquerie with a look that said *why aren't you singing, child?* Jacquerie disengaged from Sibby's eyes and refocused on the vines in front of her as the others continued in song. Like a simmering pot that finally boils over, Jacquerie finally allowed a few notes to trickle out. "*O He is King of kings. He is Lord of lords, Jesus Christ, the first and last, no one works like Him.*" Sibby greeted Jacquerie's inclusion with a smile that nearly shut her eyes. Jacquerie's voice grew stronger, melding with the others. "*I know that my Redeemer lives, no one works like Him. And by His love sweet blessing gives, no one works like Him.*" Their collective voices rose from the field, a soothing gift to the heavens.

A quarter mile away, Sarah stood on the front porch of the house and sipped from a cool glass of spring water. She heard the echoic voices wafting in from the field and took it to be a good sign.

That night in the cabin, Sibby, Luzanne, and Will slept hard in the fading light of the fire, their only reward for another endless day of toiling for their mistress.

In the corner of the room, Jacquerie eased off of her thin bed of corn shucks and crept closer to Will. She shook him out of his slumber.

"Whatcha want, woman?"

"How far did you get?" she whispered.

"What?"

"Last time you ran. How far did you make it?"

Will finally comprehended the question. Clearing his head and making sure the others weren't listening, he leaned closer to Jacquerie.

"Almost ta Virginia dis time."

"You've run before?"

"Oh yeah. Gots all da way ta Ohio da first time. But I ain't runnin' no mo'."

"Why not?"

"It ain't as good out der as ya wants to believe it is." Will moved closer to Jacquerie and grinned. "And now that you here, I gots one mo' reason to stay." Will inched even closer.

"Keep your distance," she warned, backing away.

"Come on now... pretty thang like you, so far from home? Ya must be thinkin' 'bout havin' a man."

"I am, but not you. I'm married."

Will bolted upright. "What you say?"

"My husband is a free man in Canada," whispered Jacquerie with pride, "and I'm goin' to join him."

"You crazy, woman. Y'ain't never gonna make it to no Canada. I ain't even sho' where dat is, but I'z sho' a skinny lil' thang like you ain't never goin' ta git der."

"Maybe not. But I'll die tryin'."

Will sensed from the determined anger swirling in Jacquerie's eyes that this was no idle promise. He quietly nodded his head as if to say "*I believe you*," and nestled back down into his thin blankets. Like a candle that had been snuffed out, Will immediately fell back asleep. Jacquerie slid back across the floor, the expiring glow of the fire penetrating the tears glossing over her eyes. She reached down and massaged her injured ankle, wondering when it might be able to once again give her the gift of flight.

10

Thou shalt not deliver unto his master the servant which is escaped from his master unto thee.

Deuteronomy 23:15

The heavy mist of late November hung over the fields, silently waiting for the morning sun to chase it away.

With frostbitten grass crunching underneath her boots, Jacquerie wrangled an oaken bucket filled with water from the well, changing hands every ten paces to rest her weary arms. Cyrus charged across the field to intercept her.

"Miss Talton be wantin' to see ya," he snapped.

"Me? Why?"

"Don't be askin' no questions, woman! Do as ya tolt, unnerstan?"

Jacquerie glared at Cyrus, caught between her utter contempt for his abuse of power, and her lack of power to do anything about it. She turned her head in a subtle display of disrespect. "Yes *suh*. Where is she?"

"In da barn. Ya best git goin'."

Cyrus could clearly see that Jacquerie was struggling with the heavy bucket of water, but he chose to walk away, letting her fight the battle alone. Fueled by rising anger, she switched hands once again and pressed on with her burden.

Moments later, she arrived at an enormous washtub just outside the main house. With one final burst of energy, she lifted the bucket to her knee and tilted it over, pouring the ice cold spring water into the tub. As the rippling water calmed itself, she saw her reflection slowly come into focus. She gasped at the sight, like a funeral mourner unprepared for an open casket. Her hands rose to her cheekbones, sunken and hollow from weeks of eating little more than berries and rotting kernels of grain and corn as she'd followed the rivers from Louisiana to North Carolina. Will was right. She *was* too skinny to run right now. Jacquerie cupped her hands and dipped them into the crisp water, drawing out a rejuvenating drink. She closed her eyes to savor it, imagining how delicious the waters of the Ohio River might taste.

Inside the barn, a futile battle was being waged between a woman who had precious little talent to strap a feedbag onto a plowhorse, and a twelve hundred pound beast of burden who sorely didn't want to be wearing one. The horse tossed her vanilla colored head back and forth to avoid Sarah's reach, her wispy mane slashing through the air like a willow switch.

"Settle now!" commanded Sarah. The horse readily disobeyed, stamping her hoof hard enough to send Sarah reeling back in fear. Determined to not be outmaneuvered, Sarah grabbed the riding crop hanging on a peg next to the stall and smacked it across the horse's neck.

"I said *settle!*" yelled Sarah, again to no avail. She cautiously advanced again, lashing the recalcitrant horse, then retreating, then moving in for another blow, in and out, like a lightweight boxer delivering jabs. Eventually it became clear to her that the flogging was only serving to make the horse wilder. Her patience spent, Sarah picked up the feed bag and flung it at the unrepentant creature. Only then did she see Jacquerie standing in the shadows at the end of the barn. Smoothing back her own tousled mane, Sarah swallowed hard and drew enough deep breaths to restore an air of false confidence.

"Ya wants to see me?" asked Jacquerie.

"What sort of stupid animal doesn't want to eat?" Sarah forced a grunt of laughter to reinforce the notion that she was in control of the situation. "Some of God's creatures just don't know what's good for them, do they?" She drew another deep breath to steady herself. "Now then, about you."

Sarah started to pace nervously back and forth, gathering her thoughts and her courage for the speech she was about to deliver. The warm riding crop in her hand had Jacquerie's full attention.

"You know, Mary, or whatever your real name is... I consider myself to be a woman of integrity. I don't like to be lied to." Sarah slid her hand into the pocket of her apron and pulled out the reward notice from the telegraph office. "I checked on your Mister Johnson in South Carolina. Odd thing... couldn't find him. Now why do you suppose that is?"

"Don't hab no idea, ma'am. Mebbe he ded," she replied as she hung her head and kicked at the straw on the barn floor.

Sarah shook her head in disgust as she turned to hang the riding crop on the wooden peg in the stall. "I'm sending a telegram to Mr. Duval in Louisiana. I'll make the necessary arrangements to send you back."

Jacquerie's head snapped up in panic. "*No!* " she cried out impulsively. "You can't send me back there! You *can't!* "

Sarah spun around, completely startled by the outburst. Her eyes narrowing, she slowly took two steps closer to Jacquerie, not only trying to comprehend how a slave woman would dare to talk to her mistress that way, but how she could suddenly speak with vastly better diction than ever before.

"Well now, it would appear as though Mister Johnson is not the only thing you've lied about. No wonder Mr. Duval wants you back so badly."

"They'll *kill* me back there!"

"Nonsense! Nobody pays a hundred dollars for the return of a slave only to kill it."

"They will! They've done it before!"

"Well, how they handle their property in Louisiana is their business, not mine." Sarah wiped her hands on her apron. "The law in North Carolina states that escaped slaves are to be returned to their owners, and I intend to uphold the law. I have no choice in the matter. So back to work now."

With deliberate force, Sarah pegged the printed sheet onto a nail in the side of the stall. She turned her back to indicate the conversation was over. Trembling slightly from the unpleasantness of exercising her authority, she looked for something to occupy her hands. She took a folded horse blanket draped over a stall, unfolded it, and proceeded to fold it again exactly as it had been before. With a quick glance over her shoulder, Sarah confirmed what she had sensed; Jacquerie had not budged.

"I told you to go on!"

"I would rather die right here than go back there."

"I'm sorry. There's no choice in the matter." Sarah continued folding the blanket with no real purpose. "Now get going!"

Jacquerie remained frozen in place, fully aware that she was at a crossroads. Her slender frame visibly convulsed as she realized her limited options. If she walked out of the barn as ordered, they would be her first steps on the grim road back to Louisiana, where she would face brutal punishment, maybe worse. Each step would also take her further away from Canada. "I can help you."

Sarah slowly raised her head, seething. "Woman, are you *trying* to get punished?"

"Please, listen to me!"

Sarah tossed aside the blanket with exasperated anger and marched directly to the barn door. "Cyrus!" she yelled. "Cyrus, quickly! I need you!"

"Je parle français," blurted Jacquerie.

Sarah abruptly stopped and whirled around, not at all certain she'd heard correctly.

"What did you say?"

"Je parle français. I speak French."

"And what does *that* have to do with anything?"

"You're in love with a man you can't talk to. If you keep me here, I can translate for you."

Sarah's face was instantly flushed from both the shock of this startling proposal and the embarrassment of a slave having any knowledge of her romantic affairs. She was the one now frozen in time as she tried to process the sudden lightning storm of information.

Cyrus appeared at the doorway of the barn. "Miss Talton? Ya need me?"

Sarah barely moved, her eyes locked onto Jacquerie's as she pondered the possibilities now in front of her.

"No. Never mind." She waved him off without looking.

"Yessum." Cyrus respectfully backed out of the barn, but his eyes darted back and forth between Jacquerie and the paper hanging on the nail until he was gone.

Sarah pointed to bale of hay. "Sit," she commanded. Jacquerie obeyed. "So... where did you learn French?"

"Most everybody speaks French in Louisiana. Just keep your ears open and pretty soon you know it too."

"I see. Say 'good evening' in French."

"Bon soir," Jacquerie said with the hint of a Cajun accent.

" 'Bon soir.' Yes, yes. All right, say 'good morning, the weather is nice today.' "

"Bonjour... il fait beau aujourd'hui."

Sarah wrung her hands with newfound excitement, momentarily forgetting the social divisions of mistress and slave and black and white.

" 'I love you'... how do you say 'I love you'?"

"Je t'aime. Je t'aime, Monsieur LeGare... Je t'aime."

Sarah closed her eyes and clenched her fists in rapture, imagining how those words might sound rolling off her own tongue.

"And you can teach me to speak French?"

"I can teach you, yes. Oui."

Sarah nervously tapped her index finger against her lips, narrowing her gaze as she mulled over her surprisingly new situation.

"Perhaps..." she started, her thoughts fermenting. She walked over to the printed sheet hanging on the nail. She grasped it with both hands and slowly pulled it downward. The nail tore through the top of the paper, leaving a stain of rusty iron ore on the jagged edges of the parchment. She folded it four times without looking and tucked it back into the pocket of her apron. "Perhaps we can delay your departure to Louisiana, just for a time, until your health improves. I can't very well send you off with that sprained ankle, now can I? That would be most unfair to Mister Duval. In fact, I want you to work in the house for a few days. That'll take some of the strain off your legs. There, it's settled. Go get your things."

"Yes, ma'am." Jacquerie got up from the bale and limped out of the barn, holding back tears of joyous relief.

Sarah turned to the horse, cocked her head, and nodded in the manner of a dignified greeting.

"Bonjour. Il fait beau aujourd'hui." She smiled. "Bonjour, Monsieur LeGare! Il fait beau aujourd'hui!"

11

The kingdom of heaven is like to a grain of mustard seed,
which a man took and sowed in his field;
Which indeed is the least of all seeds, but when it is grown,
it is the greatest among herbs.

Matthew 13: 31-32

*T*he butcher block in the Talton kitchen glistened from the iridescent skin of a dozen rainbow trout fresh from the stream. They were laid out in a column, wide eyed and palpable, having surrendered to their transition from freedom to frying pan.

Sarah lorded over the catch with a dullish knife, struggling mightily with the slippery blade as she fileted the trout.

Jacquerie was a few feet away, scrubbing the kitchen floor on her knees while secretly stealing glances of Sarah at the butcher block.

"Ow!" yelped her mistress as the edge of the filet knife sliced into the tip of her index finger. Jacquerie cocked her head as she continued to scrub.

"You needin' some help, Miss Talton?"

"No!" she snapped, directing her anger at the inflicting knife. "I can do this!"

Sarah attempted another incision on the uncooperative trout, but the bloody knife slipped out of her hand and rattled across the freshly scrubbed kitchen floor. Jacquerie stopped in mid-scrub, unsure whether or not to retrieve it. Wiping the blood onto her apron, Sarah motioned with her head that it was all right to pick it up. Jacquerie slowly grasped the handle of the filet knife, stood up, and joined Sarah at the butcher block. With Sarah's nodding approval, she deftly carved into the fish.

"Ya starts up here at da geel—" she narrated as she cut a vertical line just behind the opalescent head of the trout. As Sarah looked up and wrinkled her forehead with confusion, Jacquerie immediately realized she didn't have to fake her accent anymore.

"You start up here at the gill... then you slice along the backbone all the way down to the tail... then down to the belly, then back the other way to the head again. Then you flip it over and do the same to the other side. Like that. You try."

She handed the knife to Sarah, who still had difficulty getting the blade to cut cleanly. Jacquerie wrapped both her hands around Sarah's and guided them along, cutting the fish together.

"That's right... that's right... you're gettin' it... good."

Sarah couldn't help but take particular note of Jacquerie's gentle and skillful hands as they continued to slice through the pink and yellow meat.

"Why did you pretend to be a field hand?" asked Sarah. Jacquerie offered no response. "So you could run away easier?" Still no reply. "Why are you running, anyway? What's out there? Honestly, what's better than this?"

Jacquerie again offered no direct answer as she continued to prepare the fish. She finally summoned the audacity to change the subject.

"Can I ask you a question?"

"I suppose," said Sarah.

"Beggin' your pardon, ma'am, but why is the woman of the house cleanin' fish?"

Sarah took a moment to respond, not because it was an insulting inquiry, but because it had never really crossed her mind before. "Well, I imagine it's because there isn't a *man* of the house anymore. My father died three months ago, and I've had to sell some people just to keep going. The house slaves were the first to go. I keep trying to do more with less, and I don't know how much longer—" Sarah stopped cutting, visibly trembling. She leaned her full weight on the butcher block, fighting to choke back raw emotion. "I'm tired of everybody telling me I can't do this! Because I *can*! And I will!"

Jacquerie stroked Sarah's hand in an effort to soothe her. "I'm sorry, I didn't mean to upset you."

Sarah locked her jaw and shook her head. "It's all right. I just get this way sometimes. Up 'til now, it's always been in private." At that instant, Sarah suddenly realized the line between slave and mistress had been crossed, and she snapped out of her wallowing in self pity. She snatched a newspaper off the table and quickly started to wrap up the fish. "Here... take these to the others," she ordered. "Go! I'll meet you in the barn in a half an hour."

Jacquerie obediently took the fish and started to leave. She turned back, pausing momentarily to gather her thoughts. "Ma'am, beggin' your pardon, but I noticed those two fields behind the barn aren't being used right now."

Sarah was slightly taken aback, unaccustomed to such discourse with a slave. "That's true. Well, not entirely... the horses are using them for pasture."

"Why?"

"Those fields had tobacco in them last year, but that takes a lot out of the soil, so I'm giving the land a rest... let it replenish the nutrients." Sarah suddenly felt defensive. "Why am I explaining this to you?"

"Well," continued Jacquerie, treading carefully, "again, beggin' your pardon, but two horses don't need twenty-five acres. You might want to consider planting some winter wheat on that patch of land. Winter squash does real well too... acorn, butternut... easy to grow, and they keep real good after you pick 'em. Would bring in a good sum at market. And you need somethin' to sell while you're waitin' for that tobacco to cure. Just a thought. But you'd need to get it in the ground soon... before a hard freeze."

Though it was difficult for Sarah to admit it, the slave's advice made abundant sense. She knew nothing of winter wheat, but from the sounds of things, there didn't appear to be much to learn. She nodded her head in agreement. "Yes, I've been thinking about doing that. I'm glad you reminded me."

"Can I mention one more thing?"

"I suppose."

"You got mustard greens in the four acres down by the creek."

"That's right."

"You irrigate them?"

"Uh... no. Should I?"

"Yes, ma'am. Mustard greens love water. You give them a good, cool drink now and again, and they'll thank you tenfold. You give them some good manurin', and they'll thank you again."

"How am I supposed to irrigate?"

"Just dig a few trenches coming out of the creek... the water will find its way."

"That sounds like a lot of work."

"It is. You have to move a lot of dirt the first time, but then it's done, once and for all. Then, just sit back and watch 'em grow. They'll be good and ready before Easter."

Sarah mulled it over. It all sounded possible. Still, she had her doubts. She scrunched her forehead. "I'm just curious... how does a slave who spent most of her time in the big house know so much about what goes on in the fields?"

"In the big house is where they *talk* about what goes on in the fields. Like I said... just keep your ears open. Amazin' what you can learn."

Sarah nodded in agreement. "You best be going."

Jacquerie obediently lowered her head and left the kitchen.

Sarah saw her own reflection in the oval mirror on the wall. Dirty face, disheveled hair, reddened eyes. "Yes, Sarah," she inquired aloud of the reflection. "What could possibly be better than this?"

Two bales of hay provided the necessary seating in the barn as Jacquerie and Sarah came together not as slave and mistress, but as teacher and pupil.

"We'll start with yes and no... oui and non."

"Oui and non," nodded Sarah. "Oui and non. Simple enough."

"Very good. Next is how to greet someone. Hello, Mister LeGare, how are you? Bonjour, Monsieur LeGare, comment allez-vous?"

"Bonjour, Monsieur, como talley view?"

Jacquerie shook her head. "*Vous...* comment allez-*vous*."

"*Vous*," repeated Sarah. "Comment allez-vous?"

"Tres bien fait, Miss Talton! Very well done!"

Sarah's pronunciation carried with it a slight flavor of Cajun spice, but it was altogether very passable. She beamed like a young schoolgirl, pleased with her progress thus far.

12

There is neither male nor female: for ye are all one in Jesus Christ.

Galatians 3:28

The city of Winston was thriving in 1860, a hub of commerce in North Carolina due in large part to the train tracks that ran along the eastern portion of its border. Even with the threat of war on the horizon, these were prosperous times with a thriving wagonworks and burgeoning textile and tobacco industries.

Though there wasn't the selection she could find in the more sophisticated shops of Winston, Sarah preferred to do as much of her shopping as she could in the adjacent village of Salem. The merchants were all Moravians, deeply religious and earnest folk of Germanic descent. Sarah found the Moravians to be not only honest and fair in their business dealings, but also a people of simple gentility and humility. She had always thought it appropriate that the Moravians had migrated to the area from Bethlehem, Pennsylvania.

Sarah's favorite shop was a general mercantile enterprise known as the Salem Community Store. The quality of the merchandise was perpetually excellent, and the prices consistently reasonable. The neatly arranged shelves carried everything from horseshoes to horehound candy, and if they didn't already have it, they would promise to get it for you. Since the Moravians made most of their own clothing by hand, there was a limited selection of finery for purchase, but just enough to satisfy the wants and needs of the young girls at Salem College, and the parents who came to visit them.

Sarah had come to the Community Store that day to purchase flannel for a new quilt she thought she might make in her spare time, but she was soon distracted by a beautiful set of ivy-green checkered placemats. As her fingers ran across the stiff edges of the fabric, she knew she neither needed them nor could afford them, but wouldn't they dress up that old poplar table in the dining room?

Sarah's attention was soon to change direction when the tiny copper bell affixed to the shopkeeper's door tinkled. She glanced up to see the pleasing and dignified visage of Monsieur LeGare, removing his smoke-gray Low Topper hat as he dipped his head and entered the shop.

Sarah's heart raced as LeGare perused the selection of gloves in the cabinet near the front window. She realized this was her chance to accelerate the chemistry that simmered between them.

"Bonjour, Monsieur LeGare. Comment allez-vous?"

LeGare was clearly taken aback as he turned heel to see who was addressing him. It had been months since he'd heard his native tongue spoken aloud, and this was not where he'd expected to hear it again.

"Très bien, merci," he responded. "Vous parlez français?" he asked in surprise, not only wanting to know if she spoke French, but also wondering why she hadn't revealed that prior to this meeting.

"Oui," she replied.

"C'est utile de savoir une langue étrangère, n'est-ce pas?" asked LeGare as he tried on a pair of gloves. Just the sound of the words flowing from his mouth made her visibly tremble.

"Oui," she answered again.

LeGare proceeded to the counter and handed the shopkeeper the proper amount of currency to pay for the gloves. After a moment of silence that seemed to Sarah to be interminable, the dashing Frenchman spoke again.

"Voulez-vous me rencontrer cet après-midi à l'Auberge King's Gate pour parler affaires? A quatre heures? D'accord?"

"Pardon?" she asked.

He leaned closer and spoke more slowly. "Voulez-vous me rencontrer cet après-midi à l'Auberge King's Gate pour parler affaires? A quatre heures? D'accord?"

"Oui!"

"Très bien!" declared LeGare as he smiled broadly, enticing Sarah to do the same.

"Oui!" she said with more self-assurance. "Très bien!"

"A bientôt," said the Frenchman with a courteous nod of his head as he departed the store.

"A bientôt!" echoed Sarah, giving LeGare an unseen wave.

Still watching LeGare as he disappeared into the crowded street, Sarah spoke to the shopkeeper. "Might I trouble you for a pencil and paper?" she asked.

"What for?"

"I have to figure out what I was saying yes to. Pencil! Paper!"

The shopkeeper rummaged under the counter and immediately produced her desires. Sarah began to scribble furiously, mumbling to herself as she tried to reconstruct LeGare's words. "Voo lay voo ron-con-tray... low-berge... King's Gate... catra oats..."

She finished the shorthand notes and held them up for inspection. Out of the corner of her eye, Sarah noticed a simple dress hanging in the window of the store with colors as bright as a Marigold garden. She bit her bottom lip as she calculated numbers in her head.

Moments later, Sarah charged out of the store and moved swiftly down the street to the surrey, a package under each arm. She called ahead to Cyrus. "Let's go!"

Sarah hopped into the back of the surrey and flung her arms open wide, filled with the anticipation that at long last, something good was going to happen to her.

An hour later, Sarah and Jacquerie were together in the barn. Sarah looked around her to make sure they were alone, then revealed the scribbled slip of paper in her hand. She stammered as she read her cryptic notes aloud. "Voo lay voo muh ron-con-tray set apray meedee ah low-berge King's Gate poor parlay affair? Catra oars. Dacore?"

Jacquerie listened intently, nodding as she deciphered the code.

"Well? What did he say? Does he want to talk about an affair?" asked Sarah.

"He says he wants to meet you at the King's Gate Inn."

"Monsieur LeGare wants to meet me?"

"Yes, ma'am. That's what he said."

"Did he say why?"

"Business."

"Business?"

"Yes, ma'am. He wants to talk about business."

"When?"

"Today."

"Today?"

"Yes, ma'am."

"*When* today?"

"Four o'clock."

"Four o'clock?!"

"That's what he said."

"But it's nearly three o'clock now!"

"Yes, ma'am."

"Why didn't you tell me that first? We have to get going!"

"Yes, ma'am."

"You'd best change your clothes."

"Change?" replied Jacquerie with a look of puzzlement. "These are the only clothes I got, Miss Talton."

"Not anymore."

Sarah reached behind one of the stalls and pulled out a brown paper package tied with string. She handed it ceremoniously to Jacquerie, who wasn't at all sure what to do with it.

"Well then, quit starin' like a cow lookin' at a new gate. Go on, open it up."

Jacquerie cautiously tore away the plain brown paper and pulled out a brightly colored dress. Her eyes lit up with the same wonder of a child opening a present at Christmas, but she still didn't understand why she was the recipient. She looked up at Sarah, who was beaming with delight.

"If you're going to accompany me to see a gentleman, you need to look more presentable."

"Thank you, Miss Talton. Thank you *so* much."

"The pleasure is mine. Just remember, though, you're not to wear that anywhere else."

"Yes, ma'am. I understand."

"Go ahead now, go put it on."

"Now?"

"Of course now! We're leaving right away! Put on the dress and bring the surrey around to the front of the house. I'll wait for you there."

"But the surrey... that's Cyrus's job."

"Not today. Now hurry up!"

Jacquerie nodded her head obediently as Sarah left the barn. Jacquerie wrapped her arms around the new dress, caressing its fabric and drinking in its aroma. Stepping into an empty horse stall, she quickly shed her tattered work clothes and slipped into her new attire. She ran her hands reverently across the fabric, admiring the delicate texture and precise stitching. She'd never been in a dress before. She felt instantly regal, like a princess preparing for a gavotte in the grand palace ballroom. She emerged from the stall, suddenly now both different on the inside and the outside, and she permitted herself a few immodest struts around the barn.

"What you doin' in heah?" roared the booming voice from the end of the barn.

Jacquerie's self indulgent daydream was instantly shattered as Cyrus marched toward her, clearly incensed. "This ain't no place for you!"

Jacquerie trembled slightly as Cyrus loomed next to her, his nostrils flaring.

"Miss Talton asked me to hitch up the surrey."

"You lyin'! Don't lie to me, 'cause I'll—"

"*Jacquerie!*" Sarah called from the yard. "*Let's get moving!*"

Cyrus froze in mid-sentence as the truth made itself known. His gut churned with confusion and anger as he slowly realized his position as surrey driver was being usurped. Hanging her head to break away from the simmering fury in Cyrus's face, Jacquerie slowly lifted the latch on the horse stall and gently led the animal out of the barn to the awaiting surrey. Cyrus's fingers twitched by his side like an anxious gunfighter as Jacquerie disappeared through the door. "I got my eye on you!" he called after her, long after she was out of sight.

A short time later, Sarah's surrey trundled to the front of a venerable country inn. A family of stately magnolias cast their wintry shadow on the wooden sign reading King's Gate Inn.

Jacquerie reined the horse to a stop, as Sarah leaned over from the backseat to confer.

"All right now, let's just keep our wits about us and we can get through this."

Sarah hopped out of the carriage and straightened her bonnet.

"It's not *my* wits I'm worried about," murmured Jacquerie.

"Did you say something?"

"Just talkin' to the horse, ma'am."

Within minutes, Sarah was seated on a stone bench in the rear garden of the manor house, with Jacquerie standing several feet away. She nervously smoothed the wrinkles of her dress, her stroking motion having absolutely no effect other than to fritter away her nervous energy. Her heart was suddenly flushed with adrenaline as the door from the manor house opened and Monsieur LeGare stepped through it into the garden. Sarah leapt to her feet with unrefined eagerness as the Frenchman greeted her with a passionate yet respectful kiss of her hand.

"Bonjour, Mademoiselle Talton."

Jacquerie took several steps sideways to position herself behind LeGare but still in Sarah's line of sight.

"Bonjour, Monsieur LeGare. Comment allez-vous? (*Hello, Mr. LeGare. How are you?*)"

"Très bien, merci. Et vous? (*Very well, thank you. And you?*)"

"Bien. (*Good.*)"

Sarah glanced over to Jacquerie for reassurance. She had made it through the opening pleasantries without a hitch.

Sarah returned the jacket she had borrowed that night on the veranda.

"Votre... uh... jacket."

"Merci, merci."

"Et j'ai un cadeau pour vous. (*And I have a present for you.*)"

He handed her a small rectangular parcel, wrapped in brown paper. "Allez! Ouvrez! (*Go on! Open it!*)"

Delighted, Sarah untied the twine holding the paper in place. She peeled backed the edges of the brown paper to reveal a set of four ivy green checkered placemats. Her cupped hand instinctively covered her mouth as she drew in a deep breath of pure excitement.

"Oh my!" she murmured as she held one of them aloft. "They're *beautiful!* Merci, Monsieur LeGare! Merci beaucoup!"

"De rien. (*You're welcome.*) Voulez-vous vous asseoir? (*Would you like to sit?*)"

"Pardon? I mean, par-*dohn*?"

With his outstretched palm, LeGare politely motioned to the garden bench. "Voulez-vous vous asseoir dans le jardin? (*would you like to sit in the garden?*)"

Sarah furtively looked to Jacquerie for help. Jacquerie pointed to the bench in the corner of the garden, pretending to sit down. Sarah finally understood.

"Ah! Le jardin! Oui! Oui!"

Sarah took a seat on the bench, with LeGare taking his place next to her at a respectful distance. Her nerves were jangled in his presence as she looked to Jacquerie for encouragement.

"Uh... bonjour. Il fait beau, (*It is beautiful,*)" she began as she looked up at the sky to offer her thoughts on the weather.

LeGare gave her a somewhat curious look as he surveyed the cold, windswept day.

Jacquerie shook her head in embarrassment.

"Non," he replied with hesitation. "Il fait très froid. (*It is very cold.*)"

To reinforce that it was indeed cold outside, LeGare draped his jacket around Sarah's shoulders.

"Oui... très froid," she said as she nestled into its warmth.

An uncomfortable silence hovered over the garden as they both searched for something to say.

"Quel beaux jardin, n'est-ce pas?" said LeGare, referring to the beauty of the garden.

Jacquerie motioned to Sarah to nod yes.

"Oui."

Again the uneasy silence enveloped them as LeGare examined the flowers behind him. "J'aime ces fleurs, mais je ne sais pas leurs noms. (*I love these flowers, but I do not know their names.*)"

Jacquerie mimed a shrug of her shoulders.

"Je ne sais pas," offered Sarah. It was an honest answer, because she truly didn't know the names of the flowers in any language.

"Mais est-ce-que vous êtes venu pour parler du jardin, ou des affaires? (*But did you come here to talk about gardens, or business?*)"

Jacquerie held up two fingers. Sarah nodded subtly in recognition, then cleared her throat.

"Je sais que vous êtes ici pour acheter du coton et du tabac, mais est-ce que vous voulez aussi acheter du blé? (*I know that you are here to buy cotton and tobacco, but would you also want to buy wheat?*)"

Monsieur LeGare mulled over the thought, then leaned closer to Sarah and spoke in a hushed tone.

"Est ce que c'est rentable? (*Is that profitable?*)"

Jacquerie was unable to hear the Frenchman, and wasn't sure how to respond. She shook her head vigorously, attempting to indicate to Sarah that she didn't comprehend.

"Non!" Sarah replied confidently.

"Non?"

Behind the Frenchman's back, Jacquerie shrugged her shoulders.

"Je ne sais pas! (*I don't know!*)"

"Je ne peux pas gagner d'argent? (*I cannot make money?*)"

Sarah looked to Jacquerie for guidance, but got only another shake of the head.

"Mais non, Monsieur LeGare. (*But no, Mr. LeGare.*)"

LeGare forced his eyes closed and shook his head, as if he'd just tasted something bitter. "Alors pourquoi est-ce que je voudrais acheter blé? (*Then why would I want to buy wheat?*)"

"Mais oui! (*But of course!*)" replied Sarah. She flashed a quick glance at Jacquerie, hoping to soak in her approval. She received none.

LeGare slowly drew the tip of his index finger from the valley below his lower lip to the edge of his jutting chin, trying to piece together some sense in Sarah's sudden rash of non-sequiturs. His eyes suddenly widened. He spun around to look at Jacquerie, who quickly turned away, pretending to be engrossed in the needles of a nearby Norfolk Island pine. He turned back to Sarah, who held fast to a blithe smile. A wry grin slowly blossomed across LeGare's face as he deciphered the message and its messengers.

Sarah wrapped herself in a cocoon of blankets in the back of the horsedrawn surrey, shaking her head in utter disbelief as Jacquerie steered the horse homeward.

"I can't remember being more humiliated," she said to Jacquerie and any other woodland creature who cared to listen.

"At least you got to talk to him."

"Talk? I didn't talk! I rambled on like a schoolgirl! An *insane* schoolgirl, at that!"

"Couldn't have been *that* bad. He promised to see you again."

Sarah considered the point, and poked her head out of her protective woolen shell. "You're right. He did, didn't he?" She heaved a sigh of self-induced relief. "I shall remember this day for the rest of my life. November 11th, 1860. The day I first conversed with the dashing Edouard LeGare! Only next time, a few more language lessons beforehand!" Sarah erupted in laughter. "Did you see the look on his face? *What are you talking about, woman?*"

For a dozen revolutions of the surrey wheels, Sarah and Jacquerie giggled like young sisters, with no barriers of caste or color.

Sarah capped off her bout of laughter with an audible sigh, then nodded her head in approval of the decision she had just made.

"You provided a great service for me today, Jacquerie. I intend to reward you by purchasing you from Mr. Duval in Louisiana. What do you think about that?"

The joy of the preceding moments instantly evaporated from Jacquerie's face. "Whatever you decide, ma'am. But beggin' your pardon, you don't have the money."

"I can sell a horse... that's a fair trade, don't you think? You're worth as much as a horse, aren't you? If not more, I would venture to say."

Jacquerie didn't respond. The indignity was nearly too much to bear. Sarah leaned forward, sensing she'd offended her. "You know, you speak better than any slave I've ever met. But you seem to say the most when you're not saying anything at all."

Jacquerie raised her chin and remained silent. Sarah slumped back into the rear of the surrey.

A small tempest of red dust kicked up on the road in front of the surrey as Braxton Smithwick headed toward them at a full gallop. With unnecessary drama, he waited until he was nearly on top of them before grabbing hard at the reins and yanking his steed to a furious stop.

"Have you heard the news?" he blurted out.

"News? No, I've been—uh, no. I haven't heard. What is it?"

Braxton pulled a newspaper from his saddlebag like a knight brandishing a cutlass. He held it out for Sarah to see.

"The results are in... Abraham Lincoln is going to be President! The Democrats split between Breckenridge and Douglas and that was all the Republicans needed. Lincoln takes over from Buchanan in March of next year."

Sarah quickly glanced at the typeset. "This is trouble. Lincoln will see to it that slavery is excluded from the new territories, and eventually they'll get to the South."

"Precisely. There's a meeting at Charles Duffy's tonight to talk about how we fight this thing."

"Who's meeting?" asked Sarah.

"All the local landowners. I'll let you know what we decide."

Sarah's eyes flashed. "Am I not to be included? I'm a landowner!"

"I said I'd let you know!"

Braxton snatched back the newspaper and galloped away. Her anger smoldering, Sarah kicked the floor of the surrey.

"Take me home!" she ordered.

Jacquerie coaxed the horse back into motion and the surrey rolled on. Sarah fumed in the backseat as the dry tinder of inequality threatened to combust inside her mind. The social order of the day was patently unfair to women, and she railed in her unspoken thoughts as she stared infinitely deep into the forest. She worked just as hard as the men in the town, in fact, harder than most. She paid equal taxes, paid equal sums at the feedstore, and suffered equally the vagaries of rain, drought, and pestilence on her crops. The only thing separating her from having an active voice in the business and political affairs of the town was gender. How blatantly discriminatory, she thought. How disgustingly inequitable. One's makeup at birth should have no bearing on one's abilities, she argued in her head. It should not diminish one's influence or power. It should present no obstacles to one's future. Yet it did. It always had. Perhaps always would. How unfair, she seethed, to be excluded simply for being a woman. How tyrannical. How infuriating. How insulting. How could one segment of mankind do that to another? How utterly, foolishly, morally wrong.

Inexplicably, as if guided by an unseen power, Sarah slowly removed her gaze from the dulling blur of the passing trees, and with imperfect awareness, now focused her attention on the slave woman in front of her. She studied her, as an artist studies a still life before putting brush to palette. At that moment, a mustard seed of illumination was planted deep in her consciousness.

13

For now we see through a glass darkly;

I Corinthians 13:12

Sibby served a watery-thin stew to Will, Luzanne, and Jacquerie as they sat in a semi-circle on the cabin floor. Over the rim of his bowl, Will's eyes were locked on Jacquerie as he devoured his meal with a crude soupspoon.

"Look to me like ya gettin' pretty friendly wit Miss Talton deez days. What ya spose yo lil' husband would tink 'bout dat?"

Jacquerie looked Will squarely in the eyes.

"My husband is the *only* reason why I'm getting friendly with her, and if my husband were here, he'd take that soupspoon and cut off your tongue for thinkin' anything else. Who knows, I might just do it myself."

Will momentarily stopped eating as Jacquerie stared him down like a school marm intimidates a misbehaving child. He looked to Sibby for support, but received none. He focused his attention on his bowl as he talked.

"In da ole days, a woman wouldn't talk to no man like dat."

Jacquerie snickered with derision. "The *old days* are for people who are either too scared or too ignorant to change. Which are you?"

"Mebbe I jes don't *wants* thangs to change. Mebbe I'm happy right heah."

"Uh huh... which is why you keep runnin' off." Jacquerie finished the last sip of her stew and set her bowl on the floor. She rose to her feet and paced the cabin floor. "Change is inevitable."

"What's dat mean?" said Will.

"It means it's comin' whether you want it to or not. Things are going on out there beyond this old farm that can't be stopped. Men like Abraham Lincoln see a new tomorrow."

"Who dat?" asked Luzanne.

"Abraham Lincoln is goin' to be our next President." Sibby, Luzanne, and Will stared back blankly. "The President is the leader of the country. People have to listen to him... follow him... do as he says."

"Like Moses?" asked Luzanne.

"Yes. Very much like Moses."

Will shook his head. "One man cain't change da whole land."

Jacquerie's eyes flew open. "But you see, it's not just one man! People all over the North want to abolish slavery."

"Where ya hear such thangs?" asked Luzanne. "Dey don't care nuttin' 'bout us."

"Yes they do... I'll prove it to you."

Jacquerie dug her arm deep into her corn shuck mattress and pulled out the crumpled pages of *The Liberator,* stained from having been wrapped around freshly cleaned fish. Their eyes wide, Sibby, Luzanne, and Will recoiled in instinctive fear when they saw the contraband.

"Where ya git dat?" whispered Will.

"Borrowed it." Jacquerie smoothed out a page of newsprint and leaned forward to read the words in the fading light. "Southern Negro slavery by all accounts is intolerable. Humanitarians and reformers—"

"Ya knows how to read?" exclaimed Luzanne as they all backed away.

"Of course I do. Anyone given half a chance can learn to read. Now be quiet and listen... 'Humanitarians and reformers cannot rest until there is immediate and uncompensated emancipation of these oppressed people.' " She looked up to gauge the reaction of her audience. "That's a *white* man writin' those words! And there's tens of thousands more that think just like him!"

The other three slaves sat in stunned silence, as if they'd just witnessed a genuine miracle. Will finally slid a foot closer to Jacquerie, and spoke in the hushed voice of the persecuted. "So... what do all dat mean?"

"It means there's a new wind blowin', and it's comin' from the North."

Without warning, Sibby snatched the pages of *The Liberator* out of Jacquerie's hands and angrily hurled them into the fire. The orange flames jumped to life as they greedily welcomed the unexpected fuel.

"Whatcha think ya doin', chile?" barked Sibby. "Ya tryin' to git us all kilt?"

"I'm tryin' to warn you people that things are goin' to change, and we need to be ready."

Sibby leaned into Jacquerie's face with a boiling anger her children had never before witnessed. "We don't need no changes, ya hear? We got a roof over our heads, warm clothes, and plenty to eat! We don't want no changes!"

Jacquerie didn't flinch; she pressed her face closer to Sibby's. "You've got plenty to eat when they *say* you get plenty to eat. A free man eats when *he* wants to."

"What you know 'bout bein' free?" said Will, rising to his feet to get more involved in the fray.

"I know enough about slavery to know there's somethin' better out there."

"Yeah, ya *think* der is, but der ain't. I spent three months in Ohio, where I was spose to be free, but I weren't treated no better than I am here... worse, most of da time. As long as you a Negro, y'ain't never gonna be free."

"Then why do you keep runnin'?"

"I jes done tole ya... it was a mistake. I ain't runnin' no mo."

"No, but you're always *thinkin'* about it, aren't you?" Will opened his mouth to reply, but his genuine feelings stopped him. He slammed his lips shut and turned away.

"The change is comin'," preached Jacquerie. "I promise you, and we all need to start gettin' ready. Last year in Virginia, a white man named John Brown tried to lead a slave rebellion... he was hanged, and you know why? Because the slaves refused to fight. If that happens around here, I'll be the first to take up arms, and you'd be smart to do the same."

Sibby exploded with anger. "I will *not* have dis kinda talk in heah, ya unnerstan? I had a husband who used ta talk like you, ramblin' on 'bout things like *freedom* and *rights*. One night dey came and dey took him away. He come back in a pine box. So I ask you... how free is he now?"

Jacquerie soaked in Sibby's speech for one measure, then issued her cold response. "Freer than any of us."

Sibby's old eyes narrowed from an unsettling mixture of anger, fear, and painful memories. She had no response other than to tremble.

With no remorse for her brutal honesty, Jacquerie turned to the door and slammed it nearly off its hinges on her way out. Will took one glance at the others, then back at the door.

Sibby shook her head slowly. "Dat woman is dangerous, and if ya know what's good for ya, you'll keep clear of her, ya hear? Ya promised me ya wasn't gonna run no mo, and I don't want nobody comin' in here and temptin' ya to break dat promise."

Will nodded in obedience. "I best go git her, 'fore she git us all in trouble." He quickly slipped outside.

Will saw Jacquerie's silhouette moving quickly toward the barn.

"Hold up!" he called as loudly as he dared.

She glanced over her shoulder, but continued to march away. Will ran to catch up to her until he was walking alongside.

"Come on now, don't git in no trouble. Unless ya goin' to the outhouse, y'ain't supposed to be wanderin' 'round outside."

She turned on her heels and faced him jaw to jaw.

"This is *exactly* what I'm talkin' about! We can't even go for a walk without white folks tellin' us it's all right! How much longer are we gonna stand for that?"

"Shhhhh! Hush up, now! If ya want to talk, we'll talk, but let's go sumwhere's that Cyrus ain't gonna hear us."

She resumed walking as Will followed after her. "I know what you mean by *talk*."

"No, no, no, dat ain't what I mean a'tall. Look, I know we started out on da wrong foot, but all dat's outta my head now. Fact is, you be needin' a friend, and right now, I'm 'bout your only taker."

She stopped again and looked at Will long and hard. "You?"

Will glanced over his shoulders to make sure they were alone. "Listen... der's a lot of us dat feel the same way you do... we jes too scared to do anythin' 'bout it. We need somebody to tell us what's really goin' on out der... someone to give us some hope."

"I thought you promised your Mama you weren't gonna run away again."

"Yeah, probably 'bout da same way you promised Miss Talton *you* ain't gonna run." Will nodded his head at her ankle. "Sho look like dat limp be gittin' a whole lot better, hum?"

Jacquerie couldn't help but crack a devilish little smile. Will took her gently by the arm. "Come on now, back inside 'fore Cyrus make his rounds." She nodded and followed Will back to the cabin.

As they walked back through the door, Sibby refused to acknowledge Jacquerie's presence. What had been said had been said, and no amount of explaining or apologizing could bridge the gulf between them.

In the fireplace, the ashes of *The Liberator* quivered from the chilled air that blew in through the open door.

14

He that trusteth in his riches shall fall:
but the righteous shall flourish as a branch.

Proverbs 11:28

Sarah flinched as the old plowhorse kicked the wooden planks in the stall. She circled the four-legged problem, trying to summon the courage to take control of a tense situation that was growing worse by the moment. With each stamp and snort, however, it was becoming increasingly more evident that between the animal's belligerence and her own reluctance, the halter and lead rope Sarah carried with her had a much greater chance of remaining in her hand than it did ending up on the horse's head.

Jacquerie suddenly appeared in the barn doorway. "You called for me, Miss Talton?"

Momentarily startled, Sarah smoothed back her hair and did her best to pretend she was in control of the situation.

"Yes. Yes, I did. Cyrus told me this morning that you left your cabin after dark last night. I want to know why."

"I went for a walk."

"A walk? With a sprained ankle?"

"Yes, ma'am."

"If you're not getting enough exercise during the day, perhaps you're not working hard enough."

"But I was with *you* yesterday."

"Yes. So you were. Well, just so you know, you're being watched."

"Yes, ma'am."

"You're free to go now."

"Yes, ma'am."

Without warning, the plowhorse kicked violently, and Sarah nearly lost her balance from the concussion of hoof slamming into wood.

"What's got her so riled up?" asked Jacquerie.

Sarah turned around to see that Jacquerie was still there. "I thought I told you to go on."

"She sick?"

"She's fine. She just doesn't want to work. Thinks every time she leaves the barn, she's gettin' hitched up to a plow, so now she doesn't want to leave the barn. Imagine that."

The horse bucked again, narrowly missing Sarah's thigh with her outstretched fetlock. Sarah grabbed the stout pitchfork leaning against the corner of the stall and smacked the horse's hindquarter in frustrated anger.

"Ignorant beast! Won't eat, won't work, won't even let me take her out to graze! Stupid animal!" She struck the horse again.

"Beggin' your pardon, ma'am, but you're goin' about it all wrong."

Sarah slowly turned her head while transferring her anger from a stubborn horse to an unmannerly slave. "Excuse me? Begging *your* pardon, but I believe I know what I'm doing. The key to dealing with ornery horses is to show them who's in control. My father did it this way, my grandfather did it this way, and *his* grandfather did it this way."

"Just 'cause *they* were doin' it wrong too doesn't mean *you* can't change."

Sarah's eyes flashed with swelling anger as she tossed the pitchfork aside and made a beeline for Jacquerie. "You know, sometimes you—" Two steps closer is all she got, as the plowhorse unleashed another volatile strike with its hind leg, this time clipping

Sarah's hip and sending her flying sideways onto a landing pad of straw and manure.

Unhurt for the most part, but embarrassed and disoriented, Sarah scrambled to her feet and took refuge in a corner of the stall out of harm's way. She pressed her back to the wall like a frightened young girl. Jacquerie calmly opened the stall door and stepped inside.

"Would you at least let me show you *my* way?"

Daunted by her sore hip and bruised ego, Sarah silently nodded, accepting the offer for help. Cautiously but confidently, Jacquerie made her way to the head of the horse, dragging her fingers along the mare's dusty flank. She scooped a handful of oats out of the feed bucket on the floor of the stall and held it to the old girl's mouth. The plowhorse turned away, unwilling to eat. Puzzled, Jacquerie smelled the oats in her hand and having passed olfactory inspection, tossed them back into the feed bucket. She spied a grooming brush on the top of the stall wall, anchoring a network of cobwebs. She slid her hand into the strap of the brush and gently caressed the glistening skin below the animal's mane. You could see the tension gradually release in every sinew of the horse's muscular frame as Jacquerie broadened the strokes of the brush.

"Smart as they are, a horse can only think about one thing at a time, and all she could think about before was how uncomfortable you were makin' her. Now we got her thinkin' about somethin' else." She continued to brush, as fine dust rose from the horsehide and filtered into the stagnant air of the barn.

"Why you so afraid of horses?" asked Jacquerie, making more of a statement than seeking information.

"I'm not afraid of horses. Whoever said I'm afraid of horses? I tend to these horses every day. They don't scare me."

"All right then, you're not scared of horses. Just makes you wonder, that's all."

"Wonder about what?"

"Why you always ease out of the surrey next to the wheel, as far away from the horse's hindquarters as you can get. Why you always walk through the barn on the opposite side of the stalls. Why you feel the need to hit the horses whenever they don't cooperate with you. Just makes you wonder."

"Just because I have to whip them from time to time does *not* mean I'm afraid of them. It simply means I'm... I'm... it means that I'm making sure they understand I'm in control."

"I see," Jacquerie nodded. "In control. Hmmm."

After an extended period of silence, in which the only sounds were the scraping of bristles against horseflesh and the swishing of a wispy tail to keep the flies at bay, Sarah finally spoke with uncommon honesty.

"If you must know, when I was seven years old, I was thrown by a horse. A gelding. Meanest creature God ever allowed on this earth. I cried my eyes out, but my father yelled at me to get right back in that saddle."

"And did you?"

"Yes." Sarah's eyes wandered off to a painful place and time from a quarter-century before.

"And what happened?"

"I got thrown again."

"And did you get back on?"

"I tried to."

"But you didn't?"

"I couldn't."

"Why not?"

"He bit me. Wrapped his jaws around my arm and didn't let go until my father laid into his hind end with his riding crop." Sarah slowly shook her head, still in disbelief. "This horse that I had raised, that I had cared for, that I'd fed with my own hands... *bit* me. I think he would have killed me if he'd had the chance. I haven't been on the back of one since. So, yes, I'm afraid of horses. Deathly afraid, to be honest."

Jacquerie nodded in appreciation for Sarah's plight. "Horses are like people. You're gonna find some mean ones now and again, and there's nothin' you can do about that. But most of the time, it's all in how you treat them. Show them love, show them respect, and they'll do the same to you. What's this horse's name?"

"Name? I don't think it has a name."

"No name?"

"Well, no. It's just a horse."

"Every horse ought to have a name."

"Why?"

"What's the most important thing to a human? It's their name. You greet somebody by their name, and it builds a relationship. It builds trust. Brings you closer together. Same thing for a horse."

Sarah rolled her eyes and shook her head. She flicked the back of her hand in the direction of the horse. "Very well, then, give it a name."

"Let's call her... Sweet Pea."

"Sweet Pea? You want to call an ornery old plowhorse Sweet Pea?"

"Seems to suit her."

"Fine. We'll call it Sweet Pea."

Jacquerie motioned to the halter in Sarah's hand. "Go ahead, try it now."

Sarah cautiously slid the halter over the horse's nose as Jacquerie continued to apply the soothing brushstrokes. Within a matter of moments, Sarah had fastened the headstrap behind the horse's ears without so much as a grumble from the animal. As proudly as a child who had just learned to tie her own shoes, Sarah stood up and stroked the meaty flank of the old horse. She exchanged a genuine smile with Jacquerie.

"So where'd you learn so much about horses?" she asked.

"My little Missy in Louisiana loved horses, loved to ride them, so I spent a lot of time in the stables. You keep your eyes and your ears and most of all your *mind* open, you can pick up just about anything."

"Can you ride?"

"Fairly well. We'd go way off in the far corner of the plantation and take turns ridin' and jumpin' the split rails. Somethin' about gettin' ahold of those reins and thunderin' down the pathway... kinda makes you feel—"

"Feel what?"

"Free. Kinda makes you feel free."

Sarah nodded in agreement. "My Daddy used to recite this poem... 'Give a man a horse he can ride, give a man a boat he can sail, and his rank and wealth, his strength and health, on sea nor shore shall fail.' "

"What happened to your father?"

"Don't really know. I suppose it was something with his heart. He'd gone out on a hunting trip. Probably the hottest day we had in August. His horse wandered back to the barn and he was slumped over in the saddle. That was it. I never got to say goodbye."

"And your mother?"

"Died giving birth to Rebecca. I was fourteen at the time, so I had to grow up in a hurry. I had to take care of my sister, plus tend to all my other chores, so I didn't have much time to grieve." Sarah's mind briefly wandered back in time as she nearly allowed herself a moment of grief, but then quickly returned to the present. "What about *your* parents? They still in Louisiana?"

"I never knew my parents. From what I hear, they were sold off when I was a baby."

"So who raised you?"

"Everybody. Nobody. I ate and slept where I could. Didn't know any different."

"I'm sorry."

Jacquerie nodded in thanks as she patted the horse and stared off into space, trying to rein in emotions she hadn't touched in years.

Sarah deftly changed the subject. "Do you have time for a French lesson?"

Jacquerie cocked her head. The question was insulting. Did her mistress not have any realization that a slave had nothing *but* time? Had she not once considered that a slave's life was not one of hopes and dreams and futures, but only of here and now? Existing, subsisting, languishing in a timeless world of endless and infinite hedgerows. The slave needed no clock or calendar because time was irrelevant and meaningless. There was no free time, no spare time, no down time. Sunrise only meant it was time to work, sunset only meant it was time to sleep and prepare for another timeless day in the fields. No Alpha, no Omega, just perpetual durations of hard work in nearly unendurable conditions.

Jacquerie raised the brush as if to throw it angrily on the ground, then smiled ruefully and calmly hung it on a peg on the stall. "Yes, ma'am. I got time."

Seated on their familiar bales of hay, Jacquerie and Sarah collaborated as teacher and student. Narrow shafts of late afternoon sun crept through the thin, vertical gaps in the barn siding, casting shadows akin to a prison cell around the two women. As the French lesson wore on, and the sun's umbrage gradually shifted, Sarah's white skin would temporarily darken with the shadows, while Jacquerie's black skin would become effulgent with the sunlight, until the difference in their skin tones was nearly imperceptible. Within minutes, however, the shadows would shift as the earth continued its rotation, and the disparity in their color became greater than ever. This dance of heat and light continued until the sun expired for the day, and the lesson was over.

Sarah rose to her feet, beaming with pride over her progress. "Merci, Jacquerie," she said with an ever-improving accent. "Merci beaucoup."

"Bien. Very good," replied Jacquerie with some pride of her own over her student's increasing competence. With unrestrained joy, Sarah suddenly stepped forward and embraced Jacquerie. Taken aback by this significant break in protocol, Jacquerie stood rigid, arms by her side. Sarah suddenly realized what she had done, and quickly backed away into the safety of her own space.

The two women stood facing each other in an awkward silence. Sarah drummed her fingers across the top of her thighs. She opened her mouth halfway as though she wanted to say something, perhaps something revealing or insightful, but she couldn't grasp the right words in either language. All she could manage was a nervous tug on her right ear lobe and an exhalation of breath.

"Well then," stammered Sarah. "I believe it's time to get back to our duties."

"Yes, ma'am."

"We'll meet again soon?"

"Yes, ma'am. Whatever you say."

"Very well. Have a good evening."

"Yes, ma'am."

Sarah dipped her head as she forced a smile and ambled out of the barn. She simultaneously felt pleasure from their time together, but twinges of guilt for the dynamic of their relationship as mistress and slave. It was starting to gnaw at her soul, to swirl inside her consciousness in the same way leaves rustle and turn in the breezy precursor of a gathering thunderstorm. She could feel it happening deep inside her, yet she honestly couldn't understand why.

Her spirits were lifted as she looked far across the fields to the four acres down by the creek. The field of mustard greens now had an intricate grid of irrigation canals winding through it, and the first hint of green leaf was breaking heavenward through the cold ground. Her father would be proud, she thought to herself. At least she hoped.

That night in Sibby's cabin, as the others slept, Jacquerie gingerly unfolded the letter she kept in her shoe and read it over and over by the light of the fire. It gave her strength. It gave her comfort. It gave her hope. A single tear rolled down her face as she carefully folded the parchment along its threadbare creases and tucked it safely back into its hiding place in her heel. Rising to her feet, she positioned the heel under the back of her shoe and mashed down with all her weight, sinking the cobbler's nails back into the leather. She shifted her weight from leg to leg, testing her ankle.

15

For where envying and strife is, there is confusion and every evil work.

James 3:16

There was a nervous energy circulating through the parlor of the Talton house, the kind of pleasant anxiety that only comes with the entertaining of special guests. Sarah's disquiet disposition was understandable, for seated in front of her was Monsieur LeGare. His visit to the Talton farm was ostensibly business related, but they both knew better. He knew that his meeting with Sarah was why he took extra time in the dressing mirror earlier that day, and she knew his impending arrival was the reason she'd spent an hour of valuable daylight making sure every cushion and candlestick in the parlor was exactly where it needed to be. The mere thought of having LeGare in the same room made it difficult for Sarah to swallow or catch a deep breath, but now that he was there with her, all the unease and apprehension of the morning had been worth it.

Jacquerie was across the room, pretending to polish a pewter charger, while making sure she was stationed squarely in Sarah's line of sight.

LeGare narrowed his eyes as he gently questioned Sarah on the subject of American politics. "Votre nouveau Président, Monsieur

Lincoln... est-il un politicien sans préjugés? (*Your new President, Mr. Lincoln... is he a politician without prejudices?*)"

Jacquerie nodded as Sarah caught her eye.

"Mais oui, *(But of course,)*" came Sarah's delayed but appropriate response.

The look of mild surprise on LeGare's face was proof the French lessons in the barn were clearly paying off.

"Ça c'est bon, mais je m'inquiète... est ce que Monsieur Lincoln amènera la guerre? (*This is good, but I am worried... will Mr. Lincoln bring war?*)"

Jacquerie casually shrugged her shoulders as a signal to Sarah.

"Peut-être. Je ne sais pas. *(Perhaps. I don't know.)*"

"Vous n'êtes pas comme des autres femmes américaines que j'ai rencontrées. Vous êtes forte... indépendente... mais si jolie. (*You are not like other American women I have met. You are strong... independent... yet so lovely.*)"

Sarah could tell from the tone of the Frenchman's voice that the text of the conversation had shifted. She glanced over at Jacquerie for a translation.

"Ça, c'est bon? (*Is that good?*)" she asked. Jacquerie nodded with great enthusiasm. "Well in that case, merci."

Monsieur LeGare moved closer to Sarah. She inched forward, closing the distance between them. She raised her chin and pursed her lips to wet them, inviting him to kiss her. That dull ache she'd harbored inside for more than twenty years, ever since their abrupt separation in the pond at the Talton farm, was about to be healed. Without saying a word, the Frenchman reached into his coat pocket and produced a gold necklace. It was a delicate chain not much thicker than a single strand of hair, with a heart-shaped pendant dangling at the end. LeGare circled behind Sarah and lifted her flowing hair off the nape of her neck. Gently and deliberately, he reached over her shoulders and pulled the two ends of the necklace around her neck, the golden heart gradually rising along her breastbone. LeGare joined the end of the chain with the clasp, allowing the pendant to hang freely. Eyes closed, Sarah reached up and held the heart between her thumb and index finger, feeling its texture and conjecturing as to its meaning. She felt LeGare's breath now closer to her neck. He leaned forward and placed the softest and most respectful kiss on Sarah's shoulder. Her knees buckled slightly. She turned to face him, treading the line between desire and decorum. For several seconds they simply gazed at each other in disbelief that their open wounds caused by time and space were finally going to be healed. They kissed as if they might never kiss again.

From across the room, now unnoticed, Jacquerie watched the two lovers embrace. It was too much to bear. Her mind was racing to Canada, to the arms of a man who showed her the same kind of affection. Her translation services no longer needed, she brushed aside a tear and swiftly exited the room.

Just a few steps into the kitchen, Jacquerie fell to her knees, clutching her chest in a vain attempt to hold back the pain from her sobbing. Within moments, her mind was back in Louisiana. Her last kiss in the storehouse had been followed by weeks and months of tears. It was not only the heartache of missing her husband, but the sickening feeling of not knowing if he'd survived the journey. When she finally received his letter, it brought her comfort that he was safe. It gave her tangible hope that they would be reunited. But it also filled her with dread. How could she ever find the words to tell John Bodin she'd lost their baby to the closed fists of a vengeful Owen Duval?

On the grounds outside the Talton farmhouse, Monsieur LeGare prepared to mount his horse. He gave Sarah's hand one final kiss.

"Au revoir, Mademoiselle Talton. Au revoir."

"Au revoir? Until we meet again?"

"Oui. Again."

As they parted company, the underlying desires of what they wanted to say to each other swirled between them like a rushing river on the verge of spilling over its banks after a summer storm. Sarah gazed longingly at LeGare as he swung high into the saddle. All she wanted from him was the gift of his time, and the pleasure of his company. LeGare politely doffed his hat, then spun his horse around. The aching knot of missing him grew tighter in Sarah's stomach as LeGare raced away.

She turned and trudged slowly up the three brick steps to the landing and went inside. She closed the door behind her, barely expending enough energy to make it latch. She made her way to the staircase, moving languidly, as if suffering from the sudden onset of influenza. Having ascended but halfway, she turned and sat down, elbows on knees, head in hands. The heart-shaped pendant dangled freely below her chin. It was tortuous to miss somebody. It enveloped the body and soul in nauseating incompleteness. Was it healthy to feel that way about someone? Should one man, especially one she had known for such a brief period of time, be allowed to have that kind of emotional power over her? Sarah had more questions than answers, and more raw feelings than rational thoughts.

Suddenly, she lifted her head from her hands. The blood rushed back into her cheeks where her fingers had been pressing against her skin. Were those hoof beats? Sarah's boot heels clattered down the staircase. Yanking open the front door, she burst outside and negotiated the trio of brick steps in a single bound.

"I just *knew* you'd—" blurted Sarah.

"Now *that's* the kind of reception I've been hoping to see for years!" came the voice from tall in the saddle.

"Braxton," she moaned almost inaudibly. She turned to look down the gravel drive to confirm that LeGare was indeed gone.

"Who were you expecting?" asked Braxton, knowing full well the answer because he had passed the departing Frenchman along the path not two minutes ago.

"Is there something you want?" asked Sarah, collecting herself as best she could.

"I just wanted to know if you'd considered my offer for that section of land on the lower end. I've just noticed you aren't preparing it for spring planting, and thought maybe the time was right to sell. My offer is plenty generous, and it would allow you to clear up some of your untended business affairs in town. So what do you say? Can I draw up some papers?"

"I'm just letting it lay fallow for a season."

"But it's not plowed. You still have to put the harrow to it."

"I realize that, thank you. I just haven't gotten around to it. I've had some trouble with my plowhorse that put me behind, but I'm catching up. I have other matters that require more immediate attention."

"I'm sure you do." Braxton's look grew more serious as he surveyed the field behind the barn. Three inches of lush green plants obscured the red clay below. "You plantin' winter wheat?" he asked.

"I am. Twelve acres."

"Since when did the Talton farm grow winter wheat?"

"Ever since I realized how profitable it was. I've got eight acres of acorn squash in the ground as well, and my mustard greens seem to be taking off. I figure by spring, I'll have enough money to clear up my 'untended' affairs. So the answer is no, I'm not selling."

"Well then." Braxton drummed his fingers on the top of his saddlehorn. "Looks like things are turning around for you. I couldn't be happier." He turned his head and spit.

"Why thank you, Mr. Smithwick," replied Sarah in the same disingenuous vein. "I know you want what's best for me."

Still staring at the field of winter wheat, Braxton reined his horse hard to the right and spun around to leave. He finally looked back at Sarah. His look of contempt was no match for her visage of contentment.

"You have a nice day, then," said Braxton. He spit again, but this time in Sarah's general direction. He spurred his horse and galloped away.

"I already have, Mr. Smithwick," came Sarah's smug rejoinder, long after he was out of earshot. "I already have."

That night, Sarah went into the parlor to seek comfort and escape in the pages of a book. She suddenly noticed her Bible had been returned to its original spot on the shelf, but now a different book was gone from the shelf below. She made a mental note to ask Rebecca about it tomorrow. For now, she would immerse herself in a few chapters of Nathaniel Hawthorne by candlelight, then off to bed.

16

And thou shalt be secure, because there is hope;

Job 11:18

With an arthritic gait typically reserved for octogenarians, Jacquerie limped across the grounds of the Talton farm, scattering a handful of peafowl that were out scavenging a morning meal. With several furtive glances over her shoulder to make sure she wasn't being watched, she vanished from view behind the barn. Pausing briefly to make one last visual check that she was indeed alone, she suddenly broke into a full sprint, racing the length of the barn with no pain in her ankle. She came to a dead stop, drew several rejuvenating breaths, then resumed her trek with a full and convincing limp.

As Jacquerie turned the corner and passed by the double doors on the end of the barn, she heard a thrashing of hooves and horsehair emanating from one of the stalls inside.

"Why are you doing this to me?" she heard Sarah cry out in frustration, exhorting the old plowhorse to obey her wishes.

"Ma'am?" called out Jacquerie as she stepped deeper into the barn and closer to the source of the thrashing. "Ma'am? You in here?"

"Of course I'm in here!" snapped Sarah, her head popping up inside the stall with the disobedient creature.

Jacquerie moved closer to the stall and saw the horse writhing on the ground, a look of fear swirling in the enormous equine eyes staring back at her.

"This is *your* fault!" bellowed Sarah at Jacquerie. "See what happens when you spare the whip? When you give them foolish names like Sweet Pea? They get lazy! She won't even get up to work anymore!"

Jacquerie absorbed none of Sarah's whinings as she yanked open the stall door and charged inside, taking control of a situation she had quickly and accurately grasped.

"We got to get her on her feet!" commanded Jacquerie with no regard as to who was giving orders to whom.

"Excuse me, but that's what I've been *trying* to do for the last half an—" Sarah suddenly abandoned her complaining. It was clear from Jacquerie's tone and temper that the situation was serious, if not critical. With quicksilver speed, Jacquerie grabbed the halter draped on a rusty nail on the side of the stall and strapped it on the horse's head. She tugged firmly on the lead rope and lifted the mare's muddled head, hoping the listless body would follow, but the horse wasn't moving. Neither was Sarah. She stood at a safe distance, paralyzed by her childhood fears.

"Miss Talton, we have *got* to get this horse on her feet *now* or she's gonna die! Get over here and help me!" Sarah took one tentative step closer to the ailing horse but couldn't bring herself to come any closer. Still clinging to the lead rope of the halter, Jacquerie stretched her free hand as far as it would go and latched onto Sarah's wrist. She pulled Sarah toward her, slowly closing the gap between Sarah's trembling hand and the halter rope. As flesh met fiber, Jacquerie wrapped Sarah's fingers around the braided hemp until her bloodless white fingers were tightly clenched. Without any more prodding, Sarah wrapped her other hand around the cord. "Now hold on and lift up her head!" commanded Jacquerie. "Pull her toward you as hard as you can!" Sarah nodded obediently, tightening her grip and pulling the rope taut. She was now standing directly in front of the mare's face. The eyes of both human and horse were wild with panic.

Jacquerie lifted a bridle off the wall and gripped tightly around the leather straps of the reins. She closed her eyes briefly, as if to beg forgiveness, then lifted the reins up over her head and spanked the horse as hard as she could on the animal's flank. The horse groaned and slid forward on the ground to escape the source of the pain. "Pull harder!" Jacquerie yelled. Sarah swallowed hard and dug in her heels. She pulled on the rope until the mare's neck was grossly contorted. Jacquerie raised the leather straps again and flogged the horse's backside. The whipping was as painful to administer as it was to absorb. Above all, it was necessary, and so it continued until finally the mare struggled to her feet. Heaving for breath, Jacquerie unclenched her fingers from the leather straps of the bridle and let them fall to the ground.

"What's wrong with her?" asked Sarah.

Jacquerie knelt down and pressed her ear to the animal's midsection. "Ain't nothin' movin' in there. She got colic. Bad."

"Colic? Like a baby?"

"In a way, 'cept worse. It means her stomach's all blocked up. If it gets to pressin' on her heart, or if she gets her innards twisted up, it'll kill her in no time. I've seen it happen."

"So what do we do?"

"First thing we do is get her to walkin' some. Get things movin' inside again. Come on, Sweet Pea, you gotta get movin', ole girl."

Sarah opened the stall door as Jacquerie led the mare towards the barn door. Together, they induced the old plowhorse to follow them outside into the bright sunshine that was bringing its full force to bear on the morning dew.

"How did she get colic?" inquired Sarah.

"Can't say for sure. It's usually somethin' they ate that didn't sit well. She get out of her pasture recently?"

Sarah thought about it for a moment. "Actually, the last few days, she's nudged over the fence in the lower field. I've found her drinking from the stream down by the edge of the pine forest."

"Any fresh mowed grass in that field?"

"No."

"Any fruit trees?"

"A few old persimmons. Why?"

"Persimmons. That's it. She went after those persimmons. Ate too much, drank too much, and now she got the colic."

Sarah wrinkled her brow in puzzlement. "Why would she do that? Why would she break out of her regular pasture, when there's more grass in there than she could possibly eat? That doesn't make sense."

A wistful smile crossed Jacquerie's face as she reached up and stroked the horse's neck. "The French have a saying for it. They call it *faute de mieux.*"

"Faute de mieux? " repeated Sarah. "What does that mean?"

"It means, 'for want of somethin' better.' Kind of a fancy way of sayin' the grass is greener on the other side."

"I see." Sarah, nodded in understanding. "Faute de mieux. For want of something better."

The mistress, maid, and mare strolled on in silence. Three of God's female creatures, all wanting something better in their lives.

With timidity, Sarah extended her arm and stroked the horse's flank as they continued to walk together. "So what do we do now?"

"We gotta get rid of that blockage."

"How do we do that?"

Jacquerie pursed her lips and scrunched the muscles in her forehead. Her eyes had a devilish twinkle. "You know those India-rubber gloves your sister uses in the garden?"

"Yes."

"You best go get them. I'll see you back in the barn."

With great uncertainty as to what the very near future had in store for her, Sarah nonetheless turned back and headed for the farmhouse to retrieve the gloves.

Fifteen minutes later the long rubber gloves were on Jacquerie's hands, but only one was visible. The other was shoved deep into the plowhorse's hind end, the fingers inside feeling blindly around for the half-digested remains of the offending persimmons.

At the head of the horse, with both hands clamped tightly around the lead rope, Sarah snatched occasional glimpses of the crude veterinary procedure as her own digestive system fought to stay in check. Jacquerie leaned over and saw Sarah stoically standing her ground next to the horse's languid head.

"With all due respect, ma'am, seems like you're gettin' over that 'scared of horses' thing pretty good." Jacquerie retreated back behind the horse's tail and bit her lower lip to keep from laughing out loud.

With a sudden trumpeting of flatulence, the old mare summarily emptied her aching stomach. Jacquerie yanked back her captive arm and with the grace of a fencer avoiding a killing foil, sidestepped the flood of relief now flowing expeditiously out of the mare.

"Ugggghh!" groaned Sarah, turning her head and using her free hand to shield her eyes from the disgusting sight of vast amounts of horse manure now covering the floor of the stall. Her amazement over the sheer volume of manure that was still exiting the horse forced her to turn back and at least witness a portion of the expulsion of excrement. She quickly realized her free hand was better utilized pinching her nose to diminish the abominable smell that immediately followed.

Within moments, the old plowhorse was stamping her feet and nibbling at the wad of hay in the corner. The light had returned to her soulful eyes, and the crisis was over. She whipped her head around in Jacquerie's direction and let it bob repeatedly up and down, almost as if to express her gratitude for an unpleasant job well done.

Too physically and emotionally exhausted to even clean up, Sarah and Jacquerie leaned against two bales of hay, their legs stretched out in front of them. They both stared directly ahead.

Sarah tapped the side of her foot against Jacquerie's boot. "You sure know a lot about horses."

"You're learnin' a lot yourself."

"You seem to know a lot about a *lot* of things."

"Thank you, ma'am."

"How old are you?"

"I don't rightly know, for sure. About twenty-six, twenty-seven maybe. Why you wantin' to know?" It was more than an innocent question. Most slaves weren't asked their age unless they were on the block to be sold to a new master.

"Just curious. You have a wisdom about you that most people don't acquire until they're well on in years. Some folks never reach that point. But you're already there at age twenty-six or twenty-seven."

"And may I ask how old you are?"

"Uh... about the same," replied Sarah. She closed her eyes and pinched the bridge of her nose, then exploded with laughter. Jacquerie joined in, laughing as hard as she dared. Sarah gave her a playful shove on the shoulder as their bodies convulsed with girlish giggling. As their laughter waned, they both allowed a contented smile to spread across their weary faces as they continued to gaze at the woodworm patterns of the planks in the barn.

That evening, just as the sun retired below the horizon, Jacquerie scurried across the gravel path that led from the slave cabins to the main house. Several yards from the front door, she fell back into a rehearsed limp as she ascended the front stoop and knocked on the door. Sarah answered, clearly anticipating the visit.

"You call for me, Miss Talton?"

"Yes, yes! Come in, get out of the cold!"

Jacquerie obeyed, closing the front door behind her as she entered the warmth of the farmhouse.

"This way!" said Sarah, motioning Jacquerie into the parlor. "Sit!"

Jacquerie sat down in the ladderback chair as Sarah pulled up another chair and sat down next to her, a little closer than normal.

"How's that ankle feeling?"

Jacquerie gauged the tone of the question, trying to determine its sincerity. She concluded the inquiry into her health was genuine. "Not too good, ma'am. I think it's still swollen up pretty bad."

Sarah lurched forward. "Let me take a look at it."

" 'Scuse me?"

"Your ankle... I'd like to examine it."

Jacquerie narrowed her eyes and tucked her legs under the chair. "Actually, I'm fine. Ankle's fine."

"Now don't be silly! How can anyone's ankle be badly swollen and fine at the same time?" Sarah scooted her chair closer to Jacquerie. She extended her hand and motioned with her index finger. "Let me see it."

Jacquerie crossed her legs underneath the chair, stalling for time.

"Come now, I haven't got all night." Impatience was seeping into Sarah's tone of voice and Jacquerie realized there would be no substitute for obedience. With great reluctance she extended her leg and raised it off the floor for inspection. Sarah gently grasped Jacquerie's foot and rested it on her knee, cautiously squeezing the bones in her ankle with her thumb and index finger.

"Owww!" cried out Jacquerie.

Sarah momentarily pulled away, but didn't stop. "Don't worry, I'll be careful." She continued to examine the ankle. "Actually, it looks like most of the swelling has gone down. But you say it isn't getting any better?"

"No, ma'am. I think maybe it's slightly broken."

"You know what I think?"

Jacquerie's heart pounded faster with near certainty that Sarah may be onto her.

"I think your problem is with your old shoes." Sarah reached behind her chair and produced a rectangular box. "Which is why I bought you... these!" Sarah whisked off the top of the shoebox, revealing a new pair of women's shoes that had recently been on a shelf at the Salem Community Store. Sarah's face radiated with the joy that comes with finding someone a perfect gift. "Now don't go bragging to everyone about these, then everyone will want some!"

Jacquerie trembled as she shook her head. "But I don't need any new shoes, ma'am. These I got will do me just fine."

"Nonsense! Those old things are worn down worse than cobblestones. These'll make you feel a lot better."

"Please, Miss Talton, I don't *want* any new shoes."

"Oh, stop it! You're as bad as old Sweet Pea! Am I going to have to stroke your neck and feed *you* oats to get new shoes on you? Come on now!"

Without warning, Sarah grabbed the heel of Jacquerie's old boot and started to untie the laces. Jacquerie jerked back her leg. The leg and boot flew out of Sarah's grasp, but the heel did not, exposing the secret cavity inside. The tattered letter fluttered to the ground.

Jacquerie's eyes blazed with wild fear as the letter screamed trouble from the wooden floor of the parlor. She bolted forward to snatch it back, but Sarah beat her to it. The carefree delight of just moments before was now long gone as Sarah carefully unfolded the letter, keeping her eyes riveted on Jacquerie. She stood up, paced back and forth, and read silently. Jacquerie sat frozen in place, tremulant with fear as she awaited the verdict for her sins.

Sarah turned to face her, glowering with anger. "You can *read*? You *know* it's against the law for slaves to read! I hear of masters who have killed slaves for lesser crimes!"

Jacquerie remained rigid with terror. There was a long, chilled pause as both women contemplated their next move.

"How did you get this?" Sarah demanded.

Jacquerie hung her head.

"Tell me!" bellowed Sarah, "or your troubles will get worse than they already are! Where did this come from?"

Jacquerie wrung her sweating hands. She looked heavenward for strength, then drew a deep breath. "There's a man named John Purvis. He's with something called the General Vigilance Committee. He met my husband in Canada and tracked me down in Louisiana. That's the truth."

Sarah nodded silently, accepting the answer as plausible.

"What are you going to do?" whispered Jacquerie.

"I don't know... I need time to think. You've created a serious problem for me. If word gets out that I'm keeping a slave who knows how to read and I did nothing about it—how could you *do* this to me?"

Sarah rubbed her brow in anguish. She stared again at the letter.

"It says *both*."

" 'Scuse me?"

"The letter says 'I know in my heart that one day you will *both* join me. Both. Two people. What's that mean?"

Jacquerie looked away. "A baby. I lost it. He doesn't know."

There was a long pause before Sarah could think of anything to say. "I'm sorry." She folded the letter, which now seemed more precious, and clutched it in her closed hand. She tossed the hollow heel back to her slave.

"Get out. And not a word to anyone about this."

Jacquerie stood up and exited the room, emitting a dissonant *clunk* with each plodding step of her unheeled boot. She turned back briefly to see Sarah standing there holding her letter, the new shoes, and her future.

Sarah sat somberly at the dinner table, stirring her butternut squash with her fork, but unable to bring it to her mouth. Rebecca sat across from her, dabbing the edges of her mouth with a napkin as she studied the troubled look on her sister's face. Rebecca cleared her throat to breach the abnormal silence. "You're unusually quiet this evening. What's wrong?"

Sarah wrinkled her brow and swished her tongue from cheek to cheek, not quite certain how to begin a delicate conversation.

"Do you believe that colored people can read?" said Sarah, still staring at the food on her plate.

"What?"

"Colored people. Do you think, with proper training, they can learn to read?"

"Of *course* they can read! Why would you say such a foolish thing?"

"It's just hard for me to believe, that's all."

"Why is that so hard to believe?"

"It just is." Sarah shook her head. "I'm sorry, but it just never occurred to me that colored people could read, no more than it occurred to me that horses can dance. It just never crossed my mind before. That's all I'm saying."

"Thomas Jefferson's slave, Sally Hemmings, who was also later his mistress I should add, spoke perfect English and was fluent in

French. And in 1831, there was a slave named Omar Iben who ran away from right here in North Carolina, and when he was recaptured he wrote a summary of his life on his cell wall *in Arabic*!"

"Where do you learn all this?"

"I know how to read too." Rebecca ate the final morsel on her plate and excused herself from the table. "Incidentally, in Spain… they have horses that can dance." She kissed Sarah playfully on the temple and carried her dishes away. Sarah put her elbows on the table and touched the tips of her fingers on both hands together, pondering all this new information and trying to extract some sense from it. She meshed her fingers together and dropped them into her lap. She rolled her neck over the top of the chair and stared at the ceiling. She'd never before noticed how the flickering candlelight gleefully danced off the linen-white plaster, pausing and bouncing and pausing again like a hummingbird in a summer meadow. She made a mental note that in the future, she would look at more ceilings.

17

Let your speech be always with grace, seasoned with salt,
that you may know how ye ought to answer every man.

Colossians 4:6

A light frost was melting off the veins of fallen oak leaves as
Monsieur LeGare galloped onto the Talton farm.

With a broom in hand, Rebecca Talton stood on the front porch
of the main house to greet him.

"Monsieur LeGare! What a surprise!"

"Parlez-vous français? (*Do you speak French?*)" asked the
Frenchman as he swung out of the saddle and hitched his horse.

"Uh... I'm not sure what you're saying."

"Mademoiselle Talton? Est-ce qu'elle est ici?(*Miss Talton? Is she
here?*)"

"Sarah?"

"Oui! Sarah!"

Rebecca nodded in exaggerated fashion. She responded with
pantomime and a loud and stilted voice, as if LeGare were deaf,
not French.

"Sarah is not here! She has gone to town! Gone! To the town!"

LeGare pursed his lips in disappointment. "Informez la soeur
ce je vais au Charleston aujourd'hui. Je retournerai en Janvier.

(Tell your sister that I am going to Charleston today. I will return in January.)"

Rebecca squinted her eyes and nodded her head. "Yes. Whatever you say!"

LeGare removed a sealed envelope from his breast pocket and handed it to her.

"Savez-vous lire le français? *(Can you read French?)*"

Rebecca shrugged and cocked her head to one side as she took the letter. "Ummm..."

"Pour Sarah."

"Yes, yes, for Sarah! I understand!"

"Au revoir," said LeGare as he tipped his hat, unhitched his reins, and swiftly swung back into the saddle.

"Oar ray-vwah!" mimicked Rebecca, nodding and waving.

LeGare turned his horse to leave, tapped his boot heels into his horse's flanks, and raced away.

Sarah emerged from the Salem Community Store with a modest collection of provisions. She suddenly stopped, her dispirited mood souring even further as she saw Braxton Smithwick leaning smugly against her surrey. Jacquerie sat motionless at the reins, making herself as invisible as possible.

"Good morning, Sarah!" chirped Braxton, as if the storm cloud of tension hovering over them weren't there.

"Mr. Smithwick," nodded Sarah. She brusquely made her way to the surrey and placed her purchases on the seat.

"My goodness, such a long trip into town for so few provisions. No coffee today, Sarah? No loaves of fine sugar? Don't tell me you spent so much on those shoes you just bought that you can no longer afford some of the finer luxuries in life. Is that the case here?"

A mixture of embarrassment and indignation swept through Sarah. She took a quick glance up at Jacquerie, swallowed hard to summon her courage, then turned abruptly to face Braxton.

"With all due respect, Mr. Smithwick, I believe my business dealings and finances are a private matter, and I'm quite capable of handling them myself. If the time comes that I need some sage advice in these affairs, I will seek the counsel of someone more astute and knowledgeable than myself. Perhaps you know someone who fits that description?"

Braxton's smile didn't wane. "I'd like to make you an offer for that eighteen acres of land in the southeast corner of your farm. I'm lookin' to plant another field of tobacco."

"Not interested."

"It's a very generous offer... one that would allow you to buy all the coffee and sugar you need for quite awhile."

"I believe I have all the provisions I require."

"Well that's a shame. We'll certainly miss all your visits to town, which I've noticed have become more frequent in recent months. How many miles do you suppose you've traveled this fall, just on the off chance you might cross paths with Monsieur LeGare?"

Sarah trembled with anger at the insinuation, mostly because she knew it to be true. "Good day, Mr. Smithwick." Sarah stepped quickly into the surrey.

"Of course, all good things must come to an end," replied Braxton with a glib smile. "I believe the Bible says that?"

"What do you mean by that?" said Sarah.

"Oh, haven't you heard? LeGare is leaving Winston."

Sarah's face turned ashen white.

"What?" she replied in a disbelieving whisper.

"I'm sorry, I thought surely you would have known that." Braxton tossed a look over his shoulder. "Yes, word is he's headin' to South Carolina. Don't know why... perhaps these rumblings of war have him a little frightened."

Braxton took an evil delight in watching Sarah's reaction to his volley of information and speculation. She was doing her level best to retain her composure, but the thought of LeGare's departure was cutting into her soul like jagged glass. She was shaken to the point of nausea.

Sarah's quivering hand lightly tapped Jacquerie on the shoulder. "Home, please."

Jacquerie snapped the reins against the horse's back and the wagon wheels clattered away.

"Have a pleasant day!" shouted Braxton as the two women departed in silence. "And think about my offer!" He tipped his hat, more to himself in congratulations than to the two quiet figures in the surrey.

Sarah stood in the middle of the parlor of the Talton farmhouse, holding LeGare's letter at arm's length as she arbitrated a happy medium between dim candlelight and aging eyesight.

"What does it say?" prodded Rebecca, craning to get a look at the missive.

"I can't read it," said Sarah.

Rebecca held the candle aloft and moved it closer to the fine linen stationery. "Is that better?"

"I can't read it because it's in *French*."

"Oh. Would you like *me* to try?" offered Rebecca.

"You can't read French either!"

"No. But I'd be willing to try!"

Before she could finish her sentence, Sarah was already folding LeGare's letter and pulling on a cloth coat. She reached into a wooden box on the bookshelf, removed something, and slid it into her pocket. As she turned to leave, her eye was suddenly caught by the bookshelf. Every volume was now back in its original place.

"Rebecca, have you been borrowing my books?" asked Sarah as she buttoned her coat.

"No."

"It's perfectly fine if you have."

"I haven't touched them. Why?"

Sarah didn't respond, but simply shook her head and walked briskly to the front door.

"Where are you going?" called Rebecca. The only response was the thudding of the door as Sarah vanished into the night.

Sibby used a gourd ladle to dish out a helping of stew from an iron kettle resting on the coals of the fire in her cabin. Luzanne, Will, and Jacquerie held their bowls in their outstretched arms like famished children in an orphanage.

Will sneered at the meal in his hands. "I sho is sick a venison and squash every night. Sick of it."

"It's mo than most git, ya 'member dat. Weez lucky we got any meat at all, so ya hush up."

"Free men eat what they want," muttered Jacquerie as she tested the stew with small sips.

Sibby tossed the gourd into the kettle and waved a menacing finger at Jacquerie.

"Hush yo mouth! I don't wanna hear no mo talk 'bout dat, ya unnerstan me, chile? No mo! Ya gonna git us all kilt!"

"Don't you get it? The fact that we're afraid to even *talk* about freedom is proof enough—"

A sudden knock at the cabin door snuffed out her sentence. They froze in place with the very same panicked alarm they'd just been discussing. Sibby glared at Jacquerie as she drew several deep breaths.

"Come in!" she called out as calmly as possible. Sarah pushed open the door and leaned her head inside. Luzanne and Will leaned their faces closely to their soup bowls in an attempt to disengage themselves from any interaction. "Why Miss Talton! Somethin' wrong?"

Sarah looked directly at Jacquerie and spoke with the solemnity of someone delivering bad news. "I need to speak with you. Outside. Now."

Jacquerie slowly set aside her meal and rose to her feet. Not a word was spoken as the four slaves each wondered to themselves how much of their conversation Miss Talton may have overheard. The ever-present fear of the "White Master" was thick in the room, weighing them down like wet wool. Sibby, Luzanne, and Will each slowly turned their attention back to their stew, as if the act of even watching Jacquerie shuffle to the front door would make them guilty by association.

Sarah struck a match and held it to the wick of a small kerosene lantern. The light penetrated the vast darkness of the barn as best it could, straining to illuminate even a small portion of the area. Sarah pointed to a bale of hay.

"Sit," she ordered.

Jacquerie obeyed, her eyes still fixed on Sarah. Sarah held out the letter from LeGare.

"Read it."

Jacquerie's eyes widened with suspicion. "But Miss Talton, we both know that's against the law."

Sarah rattled the letter in her hand and pushed it closer to Jacquerie. "Read it. Out loud."

Jacquerie reluctantly accepted the letter and unfolded it, wetting her lips with the tip of her tongue as she examined the message inside. She glanced over both her shoulders to make certain there were no eavesdroppers listening to her commit the deadly sin of reading. Sarah moved closer with the lantern, standing behind her.

"'Mon cher Sarah... my dear Sarah,'" began Jacquerie, slowly warming to the task of translating LeGare's words into English.

> "*My dear Sarah... It is with great sorrow that I travel to Charleston at this time. I very much wanted to remain here with you, but the current political affairs in your country compel me to conclude my business here as quickly as possible. I will think of you often these next few weeks, and eagerly anticipate my return and the opportunity to share your company once again. I miss you already.*
>
> "*With deepest affection, Monsieur Edouard LeGare.*"

Jacquerie gingerly handed the note back to Sarah, who carefully folded it and returned it to her coat pocket as if it were breakable. Sarah moved away from Jacquerie and sat down on a bale of hay, staring at the flickering shadows on the barn wall as she spoke to no one in particular.

"Life is cruel, is it not? From the time of my father's death, I've been responsible for watching over my sister and keeping the family farm in operation. I have never been permitted the luxury of falling in love, and now, the first time I allow it to happen, a language barrier and a nation on the brink of war conspire against me." Sarah shook her head and forced an ironic smile. "You have no idea how that feels." She dragged her middle and index fingers across her eyelids to suppress mounting tears, and only then did she see the tears forming in Jacquerie's eyes. For Sarah, it was another brief epiphany, a sudden realization that white people were not the only ones susceptible to the fragilities of the human heart. For the first time in her life it occurred to her that love sees no color and that pain knows no bounds. She cast gentle eyes toward her slave. "Perhaps you do."

Jacquerie gently nodded, as part of her mind was now somewhere in the North, envisioning a reunion with her husband.

Sarah suddenly leaned forward, her mood brightening as she spoke in a loud whisper. "If you can read, I'm assuming you can write?"

"Yes, ma'am."

"Very good. We will write Monsieur LeGare every day until he returns from Charleston." Sarah scrambled to her feet with renewed purpose. "They say that absence makes the heart grow fonder, but I'm not willing to take that chance."

"So I'm staying?"

"Why wouldn't you?"

"I just thought that with him leaving, you wouldn't need—"

"Of course you're staying." Sarah reached into her coat pocket and produced the crumpled letter from the boot heel. "And you might want this back."

More tears welled up in Jacquerie's eyes as she accepted Sarah's token of gratitude. She gently kissed the note.

"Thank you, Miss Talton. Thank you kindly."

"Time for you to get back. I'll see you tomorrow, first thing."

"Yes, ma'am."

Sarah started to leave the barn, then abruptly turned back. "Oh, one more thing. Don't let me catch you borrowing any more of my books."

" 'Scuse me?" said Jacquerie.

"You know perfectly well what I'm talking about," replied Sarah. She suddenly broke into a wide smile. "I didn't say stop doing it... just don't let me *catch* you."

Jacquerie bit her lower lip and returned a sheepish grin.

"Yes, ma'am."

" 'Night."

Sarah exited the barn, leaving Jacquerie alone. She unfolded the precious letter from her husband and read it for the thousandth time by the waning light of the lantern.

18

Therefore if thine enemy hunger, feed him;
if he thirst, give him drink:

Romans 12:20

Christmastime in 1860 would find itself immersed in irony. The gentle spirit of *peace on earth* was starved for attention amid the growing hatred between North and South. *Goodwill toward men* did not extend past certain borders.

Despite the looming political storm, Rebecca and Sarah intended to mask the black cloud with red and green. They decorated the fireplace mantle with sprigs of holly and ruby velvet ribbon that had been carefully rolled up and preserved each year for a generation of holidays.

"I've been thinking," said Sarah, "that maybe we shouldn't do very much for Christmas this year. Maybe we could *make* our gifts for each other? What would you think about that?"

"I think that means we don't have enough money to buy presents this year. Is that what that means?"

"Braxton Smithwick is coming for dinner tonight. He's going to make us an offer for a portion of the farm."

Rebecca let a roll of ribbon fall to the floor. "No! No no no! There *has* to be another way, Sarah!"

"It's just a few acres, down by the stream... we won't miss it."

"Sarah, he's buying us up parcel by parcel! Soon he'll own the entire farm!"

"I won't let that happen, but right now, I don't have much choice. I'm running out of things to sell, except furniture and slaves."

There was a brief period of silence as the two women continued to adorn the fireplace. Finally, Rebecca spoke her young mind.

"Does it ever bother you that we buy and sell people the same way we sell horses and chickens and wagon wheels?"

Sarah stopped her sprucing of holly sprigs and stared intently at her precocious baby sister. Part of her was shocked over the brazen question that tore at the very foundation of their southern existence, while part of her was proud that Rebecca had the courage to mention the unmentionable. Sarah resumed her work with the holly.

"It's starting to. The world is changing faster than I was taught to keep up, and I'm not doing a very good job of adapting. Frankly, I'm not doing a very good job at anything these days."

Sarah wanted to cry. For that moment, she wanted to put away Christmas decorations, push away politics, and run away from the prison of farm life. She wanted to let down her stalwart defenses against the outside world that demanded so much of her and simply weep to purge her anguish. How good it would feel to set down the yoke of her many responsibilities and anxieties for even ten minutes and simply have a good cry. But she wouldn't allow herself the luxury. Not in front of her sister. Certainly not in front of the portrait of her late father hanging over the fireplace mantle. He detested weakness, and to him, tears were the hallmark of the disempowered. Instead, she forced a resolute smile and fluffed up a red ribbon that needed no assistance.

"We need to finish up. Braxton will be here in a few hours." Sarah wrapped her arms around her sister and stroked the back of her head, like a parent comforting a child. "We'll be fine. I promise." Rebecca nodded her head, wanting to believe it. Sarah pulled away and allowed a genuine smile to wrinkle her face. She shook her index finger at Rebecca like a schoolteacher.

"And you promise to be nice at dinner!"

"I promise to be as nice as I can be!" replied Rebecca.

Dinner was just concluding in the dining room of the Talton farmhouse. Braxton Smithwick still gnawed on the leg of a roasted chicken, the juices dribbling down the corners of his mouth and all over his fingers.

"Wonderful meal! Wonderful!" He licked his fingertips. "I'm constantly amazed at what today's woman can do with a chicken!"

"I imagine you're amazed by a lot of things, Braxton," interjected Rebecca.

Sarah pursed her lips to stifle a smile, but visually implored Rebecca from across the table to *be nice*! Smithwick ignored the slight and continued on.

"I must admit I prefer a good pheasant to chicken, but this was not bad. Not bad at all. Now then, let's talk about why I'm here."

Braxton dug his chicken-greased fingers into his breast pocket and pulled out a sheath of documents. It was a contract to purchase part of the Talton farm. He slid the stiff papers across the table to Sarah.

"When might I expect you to accept my exceedingly generous offer?"

"How about never?" piped in Rebecca.

"Rebecca, please!" Sarah turned her attention to Smithwick. "The fact of the matter is, Mr. Smithwick, that we're still thinking it over. You can understand that, can't you?"

"Indeed I do, but *you* need to understand that my offer won't be on the table forever."

Rebecca jumped in again. "And how soon can we look forward to that?"

"Sarah, can you please control your sister?"

"Rebecca, that's enough!"

"What's wrong, Mr. Smithwick? You afraid of strong women?"

"Rebecca!"

"I'm no more afraid of women than I am of my dog."

"You mean the dog that *bit* you last summer? *That* dog?"

"Rebecca Talton, that's enough! Mr. Smithwick did not come here to pick a fight! The truth is, Mr. Smithwick..."

Rebecca jumped to her feet. "The truth, Mr. Smithwick, is that you will *never* own the Talton farm! I'd rather it burned down!"

Sarah banged her hand against the table, hard enough to rattle the dishes. "Enough! Rebecca! You apologize!"

"The truth requires no apology!"

Braxton leaned closer to Rebecca. "I'll tell you one thing, Missy. No woman in *my* house would talk like that and get away with it!"

"That's because there will never be a woman in your house who is *smart* enough to talk like that! And we're *not* selling any more of this farm!" Rebecca threw her linen napkin in Braxton's general direction and stormed out of the dining room.

"Since when did a schoolgirl start runnin' your affairs?" said Smithwick, appearing amused.

"She doesn't run my affairs. She just likes to speak her mind."

"And you allow her to talk to all of your guests like that?"

"I'm her sister, not her mother. She's got a mind of her own. In most ways, I believe that's a good thing."

"You may not be able to see it, Sarah, but you're changing. You're not the Sarah Talton I used to know."

"Sometimes change is good."

"And sometimes it's not. Sometimes it's dangerous. There's a certain order to things, Sarah, and it's worked for generations. The day women like your sister start tryin' to change everything is the day the South goes up in flames! Your Daddy would tell you the same thing. *And* he'd tell you to sell me this farm. And *that*, Sarah Talton, is the *truth*."

Braxton rose from the table and swigged the last inch of wine from his goblet. "I best be going now." He donned his topcoat and quickly buttoned it from top to bottom. As he passed by the dinner table, he dug his fingers into a pristine rhubarb pie and pulled out a steaming sample, then stuffed it into his mouth. He sucked at his fingers, eyeing Sarah, then picked up the documents and placed them in Sarah's hand. "Take good care of these. They're your future."

Outside the Talton farmhouse, Sarah remained motionless in the whirlwind of dust Braxton left behind. She glanced at the passel of legal documents he'd given her, now fingerprinted with rhubarb stains. It *was* a generous offer, one that would immediately rescue her from the brink of bankruptcy. Sarah then looked up and scanned the dwindling acres of her family farm. She dared to wonder how important it was to her to hold onto it.

Sibby and Luzanne sat by the robust fire in their cabin, fashioning toy dolls out of dried cornhusks and scraps of brightly colored cloth. Will had stretched out on the floor by the fire with his hands tucked under his head, gazing at the ceiling.

Jacquerie stood with her back turned to the others, staring intently out of the window at the main house.

"I 'member when ya wuz makin' dolls for me and Will when we was kids," said Luzanne.

"Hey! I dint never play with no dolls!" yelled Will.

"Oh, yes, ya sho did," chuckled Sibby. "Ain't no chile ever been born dat dint like to play with a good cornhusk doll." Sibby looked over at Jacquerie. "Ya gots any chillin?"

"Not yet," said Jacquerie, never removing her gaze from the window. "But we will. Someday."

Sibby shook her head. "Oh, chile, ya still thinkin' 'bout dat man of yours, ain't ya? I tell ya what, the sooner ya git dat man out yo mind and figure out ya ain't never gonna see him agin, the sooner ya gonna stop mopin' 'round here like the weight of da whole world is on yo shoulders. For all ya know, he ain't even alive, and if he is, he's fo sho taken up wit someone else by now. Dat's jes the way men is."

"Not this man. He's alive and he's waitin' for me. We'll be together again someday. I don't know when or how, but I know we will."

"What make you think dat?" asked Luzanne.

"There's some things in this world you just *know*. You can't explain it, but deep in your soul you know it's true. It's like that feelin' you get when you know someone's lyin' to you, or when you know that someone close to you is in trouble... or when you fall in love. Those are all things you just *know*. It's like God leaned down and whispered it in your ear, and from that point on you believe it with all your heart."

Sibby shook her head again. "It don't do nobody no good to git their hopes up over somethin' that ain't never gonna happen. It eats away at ya. Make ya sad all da time."

Jacquerie shook her head. "You give up hope, you might as well give up everything."

Not another word was offered on the subject of hope. The only sound in the cabin was the raspy sound of cornhusks being given new life as a child's toy.

Candlelight suddenly illuminated a window on the bottom floor of the main house. As if responding to a signal, Jacquerie pulled a thin blanket over her shoulders and exited the cabin without saying a word.

"Crazy woman," said Sibby. Nobody disagreed.

Jacquerie sat at the rolltop desk in the living room of the main house as Sarah poked her head out of the door to make sure they would be undisturbed, and more importantly, undetected. The candlelight in the room flickered as Sarah closed the door, the motion ushering in a fresh zephyr of wind into the dark room.

"Ready?" asked Sarah in a hushed tone.

"Yes, ma'am." Jacquerie dipped a quill pen in ink, poised to take dictation.

Sarah paced nervously, searching for the right words. "Dear Monsieur LeGare..."

Jacquerie quickly scribbled Sarah's words in French onto the parchment, then obediently waited for the next line.

"Dear Monsieur LeGare..." she began again. "You got that?"

"Yes, ma'am."

"Dear Monsieur LeGare... how are you? I trust the weather in Charleston is pleasant. It is quite cold here."

Jacquerie stopped writing and twisted in her chair to face her mistress. "Miss Talton, with all due respect, I understand that this is *your* letter, but I doubt he wants to hear about the weather."

"Yes. Yes, you're probably right about that. So what *should* I be saying?"

"Just speak from your heart. Tell him how much you miss him.

Tell him how wonderful you think he is. How important he is to you."

"But I'm not good at saying those things."

"It's easy! Just think of all the things you'd say if you were whispering into his ear."

"Oh my, I don't believe that's in my nature."

"Well then, I suppose we can just talk about the weather."

Jacquerie turned her back on Sarah in a subtle display of displeasure. Sarah paced for several more seconds, then suddenly stopped as an idea struck her. "I know! *You* do it!"

" 'Scuse me?"

"You know the right things to say! Just put them down on paper, then I'll sign it."

"Well... I suppose that would work."

"Of course it will! We can do this!"

Jacquerie mulled it over for a moment, then pressed the tip of her pen to the paper. The words sprang from her heart, were translated into French, and then flowed freely into the letter. As she wrote, she read aloud the sentiments that Sarah would be sending to the Frenchman.

> "*My dearest Monsieur LeGare... not a day goes by, not a minute, not a single moment, that my thoughts are not filled with you. How I miss your gentle touch, the sound of your voice... the way you look at me in quiet moments where words are not enough to express our feelings.*"

As Jacquerie continued to write the letter, her mind was filled with hazy visions of her husband, John Bodin. Handsome and sturdy, he came alive in her thoughts. The memories racing through her mind flashed from one to another as she retraced their courtship. Sensing that first hint of chemistry as she slipped him two molasses cookies after a long day of hard labor. The silent nights of soothing his hideous wounds from a day of lashing. Two young lovers stealing a fervent kiss behind a giant oak tree on the edge of a cotton field. The unforgiving ache after one final, desperate kiss goodbye as he pulled up the lapels of his coat and ran into the forest, headed northward. Tears of both fond and bitter recollections mingled in Jacquerie's eyes as she continued to write.

> *"Circumstances beyond our control have pulled us apart, but I trust in God that the affection we share for each other will bring us back together. I read your letter every day and pray for the time when the words between us are once again spoken. I know in my heart of hearts that we belong together. Yours truly..."*

So enraptured was she with her own fantastic visions that Jacquerie nearly signed the letter with her own name. As she dipped the quill in the black ink one last time and placed it in Sarah's hand for the signature, she felt like a young woman who had just given birth to something rare and wonderful, but was now handing the child over to the adoptive mother. Sarah took the pen, dipped it gently into the inkwell, and carefully signed her name.

> *"Miss... Sarah... Talton."*

Unable to read the French words, Sarah's face nonetheless lit up with delight as she held the letter up to the candlelight to help speed the drying of the ink.

"Amazing. Simply amazing. You speak and write as well as any white woman. How did you learn to do all this?"

"Why do you want to know?"

"Don't be so cautious... *I'm* certainly not going to tell anyone. I'm just curious, that's all."

Jacquerie drew a deep breath. "When I worked for Mr. Duval, my job was to take care of his daughter. Every morning, her private teacher came to her room for her school lessons. I just sat in the corner and pretended like I was sewin' on somethin', but I was listenin' the whole time, soaking up every word. Then at night, I'd stuff the little girl's schoolbooks under my dress, read them by the fire, and put 'em back the next mornin' before she woke up."

"You risked your life just to learn how to read and write?"

"What kind of life is it if you can't?"

Sarah shook her head in amazement and respect. "I've never met anybody quite like you."

Jacquerie nodded in agreement. "I guess I could say the same thing about you."

The two women stood silently, unsure what to do or say next. "Well then," said Sarah, ending one awkward moment while creating another one. "I guess you should be getting back."

"Yes, ma'am."

Returning to her role as slave, Jacquerie picked up her thin blanket from the back of a chair, wrapped it around her shoulders, and quietly left the room.

As she exited the front door of the main house and trudged back to her cabin, Jacquerie caught a distant glimpse of Cyrus standing next to the storehouse. He stood motionless, his hulking frame blotting out a sizable portion of the faint moonlight behind him. He watched her every step as she found her way back to the cabin.

19

For we are saved by hope.

Romans 8:24

*T*he well-appointed townhouse had a panoramic view of the Charleston Harbor, but Edouard LeGare ignored the seaside scenery as he sat hunched over a Hepplewhite desk, engrossed in numerical values for the cost and exportation of cotton and tobacco. He didn't notice the servant who entered the room until the young man was almost next him, holding a letter in his outstretched hand. LeGare rubbed his weary eyes as he took the letter and examined the postmark. He instantly realized it was from Sarah, and with a sudden surge of adrenalized eagerness, tore it open and consumed every word. Holding the note in one hand as he continued to read and reread, LeGare spontaneously wrapped his free arm around the quiet servant, unable to contain his effervescent joy.

Despite a brisk early December wind, the streets of downtown Winston were teeming with life, full of pedestrians shopping for Christmas and laying in supplies ahead of an uncertain winter.

Sarah pulled back the woolen scarf wrapped over her head as she ducked into the post office and quickly shut the door behind her.

"Miss Talton, you're quickly becomin' my most frequent visitor," said the postmaster.

"Anything today?" she inquired.

"No. Nothing today."

Sarah's shoulders slumped, and the warm glow that comes with the anticipation of something good vanished from her face. She turned to leave.

"Except for this," said the postmaster with an impish twinkle in his eyes. He reached underneath the counter and produced an envelope bearing a red wax seal. Sarah broke into a broad smile as she snatched the envelope from his hand and examined the postmark. Charleston, South Carolina was all she needed to see.

"Thank you! Thank you *so* much!" she exclaimed as she burst out the door, not even taking the time to pull her scarf back over her head.

"And Merry Christmas to you!" called the postmaster after her.

Barely three steps outside the post office, Sarah stood in the middle of the crowded sidewalk like a rock in a rushing river. She fumbled with eagerness as she carefully cracked the wax seal and opened the letter. Within seconds of unfolding the parchment, her smile evaporated.

"Ugghh! French!"

Sarah gathered up the bottoms of her dress and ran to the carriage where Jacquerie awaited, reins in hand.

A quarter mile outside of town, the carriage stopped along the edge of the woods. Sarah climbed into the front next to Jacquerie, brimming with excitement as they unfolded the stiff pages of the letter.

"Quickly, read it! What's it say?" begged Sarah, sliding closer to Jacquerie.

Jacquerie cleared her throat and began to read aloud.

> *"My dear Sarah... the words in your letter sustain me through these long December nights. How I look forward to returning to North Carolina to see you again."*

Sarah closed her eyes and leaned back against the bench seat of the carriage, savoring the Frenchman's words like a vintage Bordeaux.

"Oh my." She exhaled. "Don't stop."

Jacquerie looked slightly askance at the ardent reaction of her mistress, then continued.

> *"Even though we are many miles apart, your letter made me feel closer to you than ever before. Such wit! Such charm! I have never seen such emotion put forth in the written word. You are a woman of extraordinary ability in all you undertake, including matters of the heart."*

Jacquerie paused for a moment, puffing up with pride. Her head still tilted back in a position of contentment, Sarah cocked one eye open and grinned.

"Read!"

"Where was I?" continued Jacquerie. "Wit, charm, extraordinary ability... oh, here we are...

> *"My business meetings are going well. I have made excellent contacts that will serve me well upon my return to France. But I must confess, at this moment, my thoughts are not of business... they are only of you, and when I shall see you again. My weary heart tells me it must be soon. With deepest regards, Monsieur Edouard LeGare."*

Sarah leaned forward and wrapped her arms around her own shoulders, twisting back and forth with a strange mixture of anxiety and glee.

"He cares for me! The object of my affection truly cares for me!"

Jacquerie glanced over the letter. "He said he's going back to France. When?"

Sarah's mood instantly changed to a more somber tone.

"I'm not certain. Spring, perhaps. Sooner if war breaks out."

"Then what happens?"

"I don't know. I've been entertaining thoughts of... of..."

"Of what?"

"Of asking him to stay here. Of convincing him to marry me."

"You're thinkin' about marrying a man you've only seen a dozen times?"

"I've thought of nothing else from the *first* time I saw him."

"But beggin' your pardon, ma'am... a woman doesn't ask a man to marry her. It's just not—"

"Not what? Not proper? Not normal? Not *socially acceptable*? I've never been accused of being any of those things before, so why should that stop me? I'm tired of the rest of the world telling me what to do just because I happened to have been born a woman."

"Would you consider going with him to France?"

"I couldn't do that. I couldn't leave here. This is the only life I know."

"But is this the life you want?"

Sarah took several moments to reflect before answering.

"Do you mean *faute de mieux*? For want of something better?"

"Somethin' like that."

"Right now, what I want, and what the world will allow me to have, are two very different things. Maybe one day that will change... but not right now."

They sat in silence as the horse nibbled on the scarce clumps of green grass along the side of the road. Sarah stood up, took LeGare's letter from Jacquerie's hand, and moved into the backseat of the carriage.

"We best be getting home."

"Yes, ma'am."

Jacquerie brought the leather straps of the reins gently onto the back of the horse. He obeyed her command and once again trotted down the dirt road.

Sarah leaned forward and rested her chin on her clasped hands. "By the way, I gave this horse a name. I'm calling him Onyx. Thought you should know."

Sarah leaned back, never seeing the soft smile covering Jacquerie's face.

20

Ye hypocrites, well did Isaiah prophesy of you, saying, This people draweth nigh unto me with their mouth and honoreth me with their lips; but their heart is far from me. But in vain they do worship me.

Matthew 15:7-9

*A*Christmas wreath fashioned from boxwood stems and holly sprigs filled each window of the Friendship Presbyterian Church. A light snow fell outside, the pristine white flakes mingling with brown needles being dislodged from their moorings in the pine boughs and hurtling toward earth like tiny daggers.

The sanctuary inside was filled to capacity, the two dozen rows of rigid oaken pews radiating with the warmth of body heat and a stout woodstove. Sarah and Rebecca were among those in the congregation, seated in their customary spot on the left-middle of the church next to the center aisle.

The minister, cloaked in black, ascended to the pulpit and gazed out over his flock. Once assured that he had their rapt attention, he pushed his spectacles further up the bridge of his angular nose and turned his focus to the enormous Bible splayed before him on the lectern. He clasped his hands together, gathered his thoughts, and cocked his head to one side.

"During this season of Advent," he began in an uninspiring monotone, "in this season of eager anticipation of great things to come, and in some ways, trepidation over the unknown, we are reminded of the words found in the book of Judges... 'God is raising up one side against the other for the scourge of their sins.'"

Though her eyes remained focused on the preacher, Sarah's mind was quickly disengaged from his droning message. Her thoughts were of Christmas days past, sitting in the same rigid pew with her stolid parents. She recalled how hard it had been to sit still during the sermon even as a young teenager, but how she had always dutifully behaved in an effort to avoid the frightening admonitions of her father in the form of icy stares. Rebecca, on the other hand, never worried about such things. Even then she was always the one with the fidgeting hands and the restless legs that swung freely off the edge of the bench seat. A firm grasp of the knee by her father would interrupt her only for a moment, then it was back to cavorting in her corner of the pew. How little had changed, thought Sarah. The sermons were still arid and vapid, and Rebecca still never seemed comfortable in the pew. On occasions like this, Sarah dared to question herself as to why she came to church at all. It did nothing to fill her soul or satisfy her hunger for deeper knowledge. She had always derived much more spiritual enlightenment simply by reading her own Bible by candle flame. Though she would never admit it, perhaps not even to herself, the only reason she attended church as an adult was because it was expected of her. The people of the town certainly expected it, and she knew she would be ostracized if she didn't attend virtually every Sunday. Anything less was socially unacceptable. And Sarah believed that God expected it as well. If nothing else, Sarah felt that attending formal worship showed that she was trying to walk in His path. Nonetheless, it was confusing to her to sit there week after week and hear the minister's words of *love thy neighbor* and *turn the other cheek*, only to depart the meeting and immediately hear the men of the church discuss their hatred of the North and the need for war and bloodshed. She wondered if anyone else sitting in the sanctuary felt the same way. Probably not, and if they were smart, they wouldn't admit it.

After more than a half hour of rambling, the preacher mercifully closed his remarks. By the grace of God, thought Sarah. At least one of her prayers had been answered that morning.

Though sorely in need of tuning, and someone more accomplished at the keyboard, the old upright piano behind the pulpit nonetheless did its best to fill the sanctuary with a joyful noise. Sarah and Rebecca rose to their feet and shared a hymnal, joining the congregation in singing James Montgomery's hymn, "Hail to the Lord's Anointed."

Sarah had always believed that music was the best part of any worship service, and although not blessed with a nightingale's voice, she nonetheless took great joy in singing.

"Hail to the Lord's Anointed, great David's greater Son!" she began in unison with the others. But as she stood tall, hymnal resting on one open hand, Sarah could now see outside the church window. There was Jacquerie, sitting in the surrey, huddled under a blanket to fight off the biting wind and swirling snow. Her lips were moving as she appeared to be praying.

Sarah surveyed the others in the congregation. Braxton Smithwick, the elders and deacons, the town fathers and their well-heeled wives, all proudly raising their voices to God.

"Hail, in the time appointed, his reign on earth begun," sang the assemblage with growing evangelical enthusiasm.

Through the garland hanging in the church window, Sarah's eyes connected with Jacquerie's, as the slave woman sat motionless in the winter chill, unwelcome inside.

"He comes to break oppression, to set the captive free," chanted the congregation in unison.

Sarah turned away and stared straight at the large wooden cross hanging behind the pulpit. She felt like Saul on the way to Damascus. The words of the hymn now seemed to burn her lips as they passed through. *"To take away transgression, and rule in equity."* Sarah's voice trailed off as the nauseating sensation of hypocrisy stole through her body. Heavenly love on the inside of the church walls, earthly contempt on the outside. The ungodly paradox had simply never occurred to Sarah before that moment in time, and now that she could see it, she wondered how she could have ever been so blind. She couldn't bring herself to sing another word.

The ride home from church was a quiet one. Sarah was physically unable to look at Jacquerie.

"Are you all right?" asked Rebecca.

"No," was the only reply. They rode on in silence.

Sarah sat across from Rebecca at dinner, still mute. She stirred her mashed sweet potatoes with her fork but had no desire to bring any food past her buttoned lips.

"You haven't spoken two words since church," said Rebecca. "What is it?"

Sarah frowned and shook her head, still mingling her food on the plate. "I don't know what it is, exactly. It's just this feeling of being terribly unsettled."

"Unsettled about what?"

"About everything. Everything I know to be true, everything I've been taught to believe, everything I see and feel and hear everyday. The Bible says to 'do unto others,' but is that truly what we do? Suddenly it seems to be... inconsistent."

"I'll be right back," said Rebecca, springing from the table and bolting upstairs. Seconds later she was back with a section of newsprint in her hands.

"You used the word inconsistent? Listen to what Frederick Douglass says about inconsistency.

> "We have men stealers for ministers, women beaters for missionaries, and cradle plunderers for church members. The same man who wields the blood-clotted cowskin whip during the week, fills the pulpit on Sunday, and claims to be a minister of the meek and lowly Jesus. The slave auctioneer's bell and the church bell chime in with each other, and the bitter cries of the heartbroken slave are drowned in the religious shouts of his pious Master."

Rebecca slid the newspaper over to Sarah, who stared at the words without really reading them. She appeared distraught as the debate raged on inside her head.

"But what does he propose? That we just wave our hands and set all of the Negroes free? What would happen to our farms? How would we survive?" Sarah banged her open palm on the table, rattling the dishes and utensils. "Nobody seems to be able to explain *that* to me!" She flung the newspaper into the air as she shoved her chair back under the table and stormed from the room.

The revelations of the day still weighed heavily on Sarah's mind long after the coming of night. She paced nervously alongside the fireplace in the parlor, unable to ease the turbulence that swirled inside her. Fresh air, she thought. Perhaps that would provide the panacea to her mounting troubles. She slipped on her wool coat and gloves and ventured into the solitude of the quiet night.

The snow showers from earlier that morning had moved on, leaving a light dusting of pristine white on the ground and tree limbs that reflected the starlight. Sarah breathed deeply of the rejuvenating air that comes to North Carolina on clear December nights. It soothed her and cleared her mind, like washing her face in a bold mountain stream.

As her lungs drew deeply again, she suddenly heard a faint sound being carried along the arctic wind. It seemed to be voices, perhaps even song, emanating from the far reaches of the Talton plantation. She took several steps in various directions as she tried to detect the source. The sound was coming from the south, and she started to walk in that general direction. It grew louder, then suddenly disappeared altogether. Sarah stopped and waited. Eventually the sound rose again from the dead of night and Sarah continued to follow the low tones, stumbling through thorns of the wild raspberry bushes in her path.

As Sarah crested a small hill, she could see the faint glow of a pine torch in a hollow just inside the tree line of the woods. She moved closer to the light. The wind shifted slightly and now the sounds coming from the brush arbor grew stronger. There was hand clapping, foot tapping, and a dull, droning hum. She moved closer still, taking up position behind an immovable granite rock not fifty yards from the gathering.

A dozen slaves, including Jacquerie, were in the throes of worship. One voice would call out for mercy, the other eleven would respond with incantations to their Lord.

The religious fervor of the praying ground grew more intense. Polyrhythmic clapping and stepping. Call and response, call and response. Unrestrained dancing in an African style, appearing wilder in the windblown shadows of the pine torch.

At one point, Jacquerie suddenly stopped dancing and abruptly swiveled her head directly in Sarah's direction, like a deer sensing danger. She seemed to look right through the veil of darkness and fix her gaze directly at her mistress, still hiding behind the fieldstone. She slowly turned back toward the gathering in the brush arbor and resumed her worship.

Waves of adrenaline raced through Sarah's body as she eavesdropped, and a unique clarity filled her mind as she sat transfixed on the wild scene in front of her. She contrasted the effusive, unharnessed devotion to the Holy Spirit she was currently witnessing to her own experience in organized worship earlier that day. The gathering in the brush arbor seemed so much more genuine, more fundamentally spiritual, so much closer to God and Christ than anything in her religious experience. An irrational urge to race down the hill and join in the worship swept through Sarah's subconscious. It was fear more than reason that stopped her from acting on her primal impulses.

Without warning, an owl flew directly over Sarah's head, its powerful wings moving the air above her as it silently swooped past. It startled Sarah so badly she could only offer one response, and that was to run. She fled from her hiding place and raced back through the wild brambles to the safety and sanctuary of the farmhouse.

Slamming the door behind her, she charged up the stairs and threw herself into her bed, heaving with exhaustion and drenched in malarial-like sweat.

21

The fear of the Lord is the beginning of wisdom: a good understanding
have all they that do his commandments: his praise endureth for ever.

Psalm 111

he next morning, Sarah stood outside the well at the
pumphouse and washed her face with fresh spring water.
Jacquerie approached from behind with two empty water buckets
in tow.

"Mornin', Miss Talton."

"Good morning, Jacquerie."

"If you don't mind me sayin' so, you look mighty tired this
morning. You sleep all right?"

"No. Not much sleep."

Sarah started to speak again, but stopped, grasping for words.

"Is there somethin' troublin' you, ma'am?"

Sarah bit her bottom lip. "May I ask you something?"

"Yes, ma'am."

"When you pray... do you pray to a white God, or a black God?"

Jacquerie opened her eyes just a little wider, the smooth lines in
her forehead forming wrinkles of perplexity.

"Just God, ma'am."

"I see," Sarah nodded. "It's just that I have a difficult time imagining a black God. You know, all the paintings of Him, things like that. I've just always seen Him as white. But I suppose it doesn't really matter, does it?"

"Maybe it all depends on where you see God. I see God in flowers, in sunsets, in rainbows. I see God in rainwater, morning dew, and fresh air. He can be every color, or He can be no color at all. So much in life is simply how you choose to see it."

"Yes, yes, I suppose that's true. And when you pray, you pray out loud, am I correct? In fact, rather loudly at times?"

"Yes, ma'am, I do. Why do you ask?"

"Because I tend to pray silently when I pray... a whisper at most."

"That's all right. God can hear whispers."

"Yes. Of course." Sarah laughed nervously as she sorted things out in her flustered mind. "Of course He can! I mean, why wouldn't He? If He knows every hair on our head, then surely He could hear a whisper, don't you think?"

"Yes, ma'am, I believe you're right about that."

"Well then... you apparently came to fetch some water... I'm standing in your way... so why don't I move aside, and you can do what you came here to do."

"Yes, ma'am."

Despite what she'd just said, Sarah didn't move. Jacquerie stared back, patiently waiting. It eventually dawned on Sarah that she was still blocking access to the pumphouse.

"I'm sorry, I haven't moved, have I?"

"No, ma'am."

Sarah nodded her head and slowly stepped away from the pumphouse. She took three backwards, then gathered up her skirt and suddenly bolted toward the main house. Just steps from the front door, she turned on her heels and called back to Jacquerie.

"Can you have the surrey ready in an hour? We're going into town!"

"Yes, ma'am!" replied Jacquerie, shaking her head in mild amusement over the bizarre behavior of her mistress.

Moments later, Sarah was at her desk in the parlor, engrossed in her Bible. She was rapidly flipping the pages, dragging her index finger down and across the lines of scripture, and inserting strands of yarn between the pages to bookmark selected passages. The electricity of newfound spiritualism ran through her as the printed words suddenly carried new meaning. They were verses to which she had listened all her life, but never really heard. Each new thread she cut seemed to bolster her growing enthusiasm.

It was shortly before noon when Sarah took a seat in the front pew of her church alongside her minister.

"Now then, my child, what's troubling you so much that you rushed over here to see me?"

Sarah clasped her hands together and placed them firmly in her lap. She arched her back and cleared her throat.

"I need you to help me understand something. Does it not seem strange to you that we celebrate the Prince of Peace, while at the same time we ask God to condone our wars, and even seek his help in winning them?"

The preacher smiled wryly, clearly amused by the line of questioning.

"My dear woman, war has always been a part of Biblical history... David and Goliath, the Maccabees, the Battle of Jericho... the sound of trumpets then, the sound of bugles now... war and religion are not mutually exclusive." He paused, looked briefly toward the heavens, then leaned closer to Sarah. "What's important in these conflicts, is that God is on your side."

"What about slavery?" asked Sarah.

"What about it?"

"With all due respect, Reverend, if you follow the tenets of the Bible, doesn't it seem morally inappropriate to enslave your brother?"

The preacher wet his lips and smiled. "There again, slavery is as much a part of the Bible as the miracles. The Bible teaches 'Slaves, obey your earthly masters with respect and fear.' "

"True," said Sarah, sifting through her handwritten notes. "But doesn't the Bible also say 'And masters, treat your slaves in the same way. Do not threaten them for you know that He who is both your Master and theirs is in heaven and there is no favoritism with Him.' Doesn't it say that?"

The preacher sat upright against the pew, crossed his arms, and drummed the fingers of his right hand across his bicep. "Let me try to explain this in words you can understand. Slavery is everywhere in the Bible, and nowhere, *nowhere,* does it say it's wrong! The Israelites, slaves themselves, also owned slaves when they settled in the Holy Land! God in fact *commanded* them to enslave their captive enemies! Jesus never spoke about it, and if you care to read the book of Philemon you'll see where Paul sends a slave back to his master and never denounces it! The Bible was *written* by slave owners!" The preacher stood up and began to pace. He spoke again with the same voice he used in the pulpit. "I'm not so naive as to say there aren't abusers of the system, but as good Christians, we take care of the slave, from the cradle to the grave! We feed them! We clothe them! Ours is the compassionate system! Young lady, instead of questioning its authority, you really ought to be applying the teachings of scripture to convert your slaves to Christianity. Slavery is in truth a providential gift from God, to rescue these people from their pagan beliefs! For the first time in their lives they have the opportunity to learn about the Christian messages of docility and love and patience and forbearance, and in the end it will make them far easier to control."

"But how can the man who wields the blood-clotted cowskin whip during the week fill the pulpit on Sunday?" Sarah said this more as a statement than a question.

The Reverend shook his head and uttered a *tuh* sound with the top of his tongue. "And where did you hear that? Clearly that's not original thought."

"It's from Frederick Douglass."

"Oh. Him."

"Do you want to know what else he says?"

"Not particularly." He sat down heavily and crossed his arms.

"He says that slavery mocks the laws of God and man by unjustly subjecting one man... or woman... to the will of another. He says that so long as it is allowed to persist, no man's freedom would be secure."

"That's nothing more than the rubbish of northern agitators. It's simply their opinion, not the word of God."

"But it seems to me that it *is* the word of God." Sarah quickly turned the pages of her Bible to another strand of yarn. "Here it is, Matthew twenty-two, verse thirty-seven... "Isn't the supreme commandment of the New Testament that we are to love our neighbors as ourselves?' "

"What that passage means—"

"Or here, Matthew twenty-five, verse forty, 'What you do to the least of my brethren, you do unto me.' "

"Miss Talton, I must say that I appreciate this stimulating discourse surrounding the scriptures, and your enthusiasm in presenting them. I encourage women to occasionally speak their minds." The minister leaned forward and placed his hands on top of Sarah's. "But the fact of the matter is, these are not subjects on which pretty young women such as yourself need to spend time pondering. The church has carefully considered all the factors, both ecclesiastical and political, and you need to trust our judgment. These matters are highly complex, and if you don't mind me saying so, they are simply beyond your realm of comprehension."

Sarah sprang to her feet and slammed her Bible shut. Her jaw was set and her head shook back and forth as she searched for exactly the right words. Just as the molten indignity inside her was about to erupt, the doors of the vestibule flew open and Braxton Smithwick barged into the sanctuary.

"Come quickly!" he yelled out, his frantic voice reverberating through the hollow room. "It's war!"

Minutes later, the telegraph in the mercantile store chattered with the rhythmic *clicking* and *clacking* of an urgent message speeding down the line.

A group of men leaned forward in unison, paying rapt attention as the telegraph operator decoded the message.

"What's it say?" asked one of the men, cutting through the silence.

The telegraph operator cleared his throat and began. "December

20th... South Carolina secession convention adjourns... delegates vote—" He paused and hung his head. "May God help us all."

Sarah stood alone in the corner of the store, taking it all in and gradually realizing what had been left unsaid.

The surrey rolled up in front of the Talton homestead on a night that seemed darker than usual. Sarah gathered up her skirt, jumped to the ground, and headed straight for the front door.

"Meet me in the barn in five minutes," she called back to Jacquerie.

"Yes, ma'am."

Inside the Talton house, Rebecca was standing on a footstool primping the Christmas tree when Sarah entered in her winter coat. The ashen look on her face spoke volumes as she sank into the cushion of a wingchair and stared straight ahead.

"I have bad news. Terrible news, in fact."

The holiday cheer on Rebecca's face melted away as she stepped off the stool and moved closer to her sister.

"What is it? Is someone hurt?"

"No. Not yet, anyway. South Carolina has voted to pull out of the Union."

"What does that mean?"

Sarah exhaled loudly. "I'm not entirely sure. Maybe nothing, maybe the start of something awful."

"War?" asked Rebecca.

Sarah slowly nodded, still gazing straight ahead. "Promise me this... that you'll keep the news from the slaves. They don't need to know."

"I promise. Is there anything else I can do?"

"Pray. Pray like never before."

Sarah rose from the chair and hugged her sister, her eyes still staring blankly ahead. She pulled away and fumbled with the top button of her coat as she exited the room.

"Where are you going?"

"Out to the barn. I'll come in before supper."

"Sarah? Perhaps it's none of my business, but you seem to be spending a great deal of time in the barn these days. Can I ask why?"

Sarah buttoned up her coat and left the room.

The dim light of a kerosene lantern peeked through the slats of the barn, dying a quick death in the ink of nightfall that enveloped the Talton farm.

Inside the barn, a wide wooden plank was stretched across two bales of hay. Jacquerie squatted on her knees, using the board as a makeshift writing desk as Sarah nervously paced in front of her, dictating.

"And include in there something about getting out of Charleston and returning to North Carolina where it's safe. And make sure you tell him how much I miss him. You got that?"

"Yes, ma'am," replied Jacquerie, carefully penning Sarah's thoughts onto the parchment.

Sarah continued to pace, talking to nobody in particular. "Live and let live! What's wrong with that? Why do some people feel the need to always be in control? Agitators, that's what they are! Agitators! And the next thing you know we're at each other's throats!"

"Miss Talton?"

"What?" she snapped.

"Well, beggin' your pardon, ma'am, but you seem mighty agitated yourself about somethin'. Is everything all right?"

Sarah suddenly realized she'd been ranting. She collected herself, taking a deep breath as she grabbed an old horse blanket that had been tossed anto a bale of hay. She *snapped* the tattered old wool to shake out the dust, then handed the loose end to Jacquerie. In minuet fashion, they came together, then moved away with each new fold.

"I'm sorry. I'm not myself tonight. It's just that I miss him *so* much! I didn't realize how you could physically ache from missing somebody! It's this gnawing in your stomach that won't go away. You can't sleep through the night, you don't feel like eating... you're just consumed by the thought of being with that person again. I just want to see him so badly, to just look at him, to hold him, to feel his touch... but because of circumstances so far beyond my control..."

"I understand, Miss Talton," Jacquerie whispered. "I understand."

Sarah tossed the newly folded blanket back onto the bale of hay. With the back of her index fingers, she pushed hard against the dark flesh under her weary eyes, refusing to allow tears to escape.

22

A time to weep, and a time to laugh;
a time to mourn, and a time to dance.

Ecclesiastes 3:4

Sarah breezed into the post office, brimming over with anticipation that was about to be richly rewarded. The postmaster was already holding aloft a letter with a familiar red wax seal.

"Merry Christmas!" chimed Sarah.

"And to you, Miss Talton! I figured I'd see you today."

"A week between letters is starting to feel like months! I believe if *I* were President, the first thing I'd do is improve the postal service!"

"I'm afraid Mr. Lincoln's going to have a lot more than just slow mail to worry about. The news I hear today is that Mississippi is making plans right now to secede, and Florida and Alabama aren't far behind. We might be smelling gunpowder in the air before the first spring flowers."

"It's Christmas," said Sarah, clutching the letter to her chest. "We'll worry about those other matters at another time. I'll see you soon."

Sarah moved quickly out of the post office, repelling all attempts to dampen her mood. She held the letter high in her outstretched arm, waving it triumphantly to Jacquerie as she scurried back to the waiting surrey.

"Let's hurry!" she exhorted as she climbed aboard. Jacquerie snapped the reins in tandem and rolled quickly toward home.

Safely back in the confines of the Talton barn, Jacquerie translated the letter aloud as Sarah stood behind her, peering over her shoulder at the handsome French cursive on the paper.

> *"My dear Sarah, I shall be back in Winston on the thirty-first day of December. I have been invited to a cotillion at the home of Mr. Clitherall to bring in the New Year, and I would respectfully request the pleasure of your company. Until then, I will see you in my thoughts and dreams.*
>
> *"Yours truly, Monsieur... Edouard... LeGare."*

Sarah nearly melted as the Frenchman's name rolled off of Jacquerie's tongue.

"Oh my. The man certainly has a way with words." Suddenly, mild panic set in. "Wait a minute! Did he say cotillion? As in *dancing?*"

"That's what it says."

"But I don't dance! I *can't* dance!"

"What do you mean, you can't?"

"I mean I can't! I don't know how!"

"You've *never* danced?"

"No!"

Jacquerie shook her head in disbelief. "I don't think I've ever met anybody who's never danced!"

"Who works on a farm and has time to dance? Between planting tobacco and pulling in beans, it doesn't leave a lot of time for waltzing, now does it?"

"Then you got about half a week to learn. Unless you don't *want* to be in the arms of Monsieur... Edouard... LeGare."

The eyebrows on Jacquerie's face bent upwards as she cocked her head slightly to one side and shot Sarah an impish, beckoning grin. Sarah covered part of her mouth with the side of her palm and broke into a wide smile as she audibly snickered.

"So what am I going to do?" she said, clearly amenable to the prospects of expanding her social horizons.

Jacquerie took a step closer and extended her arms.

"Come here," she commanded her mistress. "Take my hands."

After a fraction of reluctance, Sarah cautiously raised her arms and joined her hands with Jacquerie's.

"A waltz has the rhythm of a heartbeat. Just listen to your heart. Dancin' is nothin' more than takin' what you're feelin' inside and lettin' your body express it. Like this... follow me."

Jacquerie began moving slowly, rhythmically swaying to an unheard beat, as Sarah awkwardly followed her lead. "Relax... let yourself go. Just *feel* it."

Sarah responded gradually, becoming slightly more at ease and adept with each gentle step. Their smiles grew broader as they shared the same rhythm. Inhibitions dwindling, confidence growing, as the pair moved in small circles across the floor of the barn.

"Good! Very good!"

"Look at me! I'm dancing! I'm *dancing!*"

A fresh shaft of sunlight streamed through the slats of the old barn as the dance lesson continued unabated. For the first time, they were not master and slave... they were not black and white... they were simply two women finding common ground through the most basic of human pleasures, and for that unique moment in time, the rest of the tumultuous world didn't matter.

Sarah was stoking the evening fire in the parlor when Jacquerie appeared at the door, shivering from the chilled air that moved in after sunset.

"You wanted to see me, ma'am?"

Sarah spun around, letting her amplified smile provide more illumination for the room than the burning logs.

"Come in, come in!" said Sarah, waving Jacquerie into the room. "Stand by the fire, get warm."

Sarah paused momentarily to glance in both directions out the front window as she scurried to the door. She quietly shut it, and turned the key to lock it.

"Is somethin' wrong?"

"Oh, heaven's no! It's Christmas!"

"I don't understand."

Sarah held up a rigid index finger as if to say 'just wait,' then dashed over to her desk. From the bottom drawer, hidden underneath a raft of old papers, she removed a small white box tied in a scarlet bow. Holding the box in both hands like a ringbearer's pillow, she ceremoniously carried it across the room and offered it to Jacquerie.

"Take it."

Paralyzed by circumspection, Jacquerie didn't move. "Go on, take it," urged Sarah. "I got it for you. It's a Christmas present."

Jacquerie cautiously extended her arms and allowed Sarah to place the box in her open palms. "Open it."

Only slightly warming to the task, Jacquerie's willowy fingers slowly but deftly removed the bow from around the box. With a nod of encouragement from Sarah, she gently lifted the lid. Her eyes grew wide and her head pulled back.

"Oh my," she whispered, bringing her trembling hand to her lips.

"Do you like it?"

Jacquerie could only nod her head. Inside the box were two dozen sheets of creamy-white stationery with matching envelopes, and a wood-cased Munroe lead pencil. Jacquerie's fingers caressed the fine linen paper as if it were gold and myrrh.

"Remember the man you told me about with the General Vigilance Committee, the man who met your husband in Canada?"

"Yes, ma'am. John Purvis."

"Well tell me, if he can get a letter from your husband to you, can he also get a letter from you to your husband?"

"I would think so."

"Then you go write all the letters you want. I'll see to it that they get to Mr. Purvis."

"But Miss Talton, you could get in a lot of trouble doing that."

"Nobody has to know. Just don't let anyone catch you writing, especially Cyrus. You can leave this box in the kitchen and write where no one will see you."

Jacquerie suddenly hung her head. "I have nothing to give you."

"That's quite all right. You've already given me more gifts than I can count."

23

Ye have heard that it hath been said, Thou shalt love thy neighbor,
and hate thine enemy. But I say unto you, Love your enemies,
bless them that curse you, do good for them that hate you,
and pray for them which despitefully use you, and persecute you.

Matthew 5:43-44

*W*ith rapier speed and precision, the kitchen knife sliced through the gill of a large catfish that was moments away from the hot skillet. Jacquerie wielded the blade with power and control, making quick work of the catch of the day as she separated flesh from bone.

"Where's the lady of the house?" boomed a loud voice. Startled by the sudden intrusion, Jacquerie looked up from the carving table to see Braxton Smithwick in front of her, hat in hand.

"Don't rightly know, suh. I ain't seen her in a spell. Sorry, suh." Jacquerie resumed her work with the knife, but now much more deliberately.

"That's a very trusting mistress to leave a slave alone in her house and with a sharp knife. Or perhaps a foolish one."

Jacquerie said nothing as she continued to prepare the fish.

Braxton moved two steps closer, leaning over the table until she could feel his breath. He clamped his lower lip in his front teeth and narrowed his eyes, focusing on the nape of the slave woman's neck. "Then again, I get the feeling you're not just any ordinary slave. There's something about you... something, I don't know, out of the ordinary." Braxton slowly raised his hand and touched Jacquerie just behind her ear. He drew his index finger down her jawline. "I just can't seem to put my finger on it."

Jacquerie gripped the knife tighter than she needed to, aggressively drawing the blade through the slimy flesh of the catfish hard into the scarred wood of the carving table. "Well, suh, you is right 'bout one thang. This heah *is* a sharp knife. Very sharp indeed."

"What's going on here?" blurted out Sarah, suddenly standing in the doorway to the kitchen.

Braxton quickly pulled away. He grabbed the brim of his hat in both hands and approached.

"Sarah! My dear Sarah! So good to see you! How have you been?"

"Why are you here?" she asked.

"Just a social visit. Just trying to be a good neighbor."

"I thought good fences made good neighbors, not unannounced visits."

"Well, I admit, there's another reason I dropped by."

"Yes, it would appear there was." She exchanged a quick glance with Jacquerie.

"There's a cotillion at the home of Charles Clitherall on the eve of the New Year. I would be most honored if you would permit me to escort you to that event."

"I'm sorry, but I already have plans for that evening."

"Plans? Sarah, you can't miss this! This is truly the social event of the year!"

"I didn't say I wasn't going. I'm just not going with *you*."

The dawn of realization washed over Braxton's face. "I see. Very good. Perhaps I will see you there."

"Perhaps you will. Good day, Mr. Smithwick."

"Yes. Well then, I best be going. By the way, that's a fine slave woman you have there. She would be a welcome addition to any farm around here, I do believe." He nodded to both women and tugged his hat onto his head as he quickly brushed past Sarah and made a humiliating exit.

Keeping an eye on the door to make certain Braxton was gone, Sarah moved slowly to the carving table and began cleaning off the scraps of the catfish carcasses. "You all right?" she asked. Jacquerie bravely nodded. "I hate that man," offered Sarah. Jacquerie nodded again, squeezing the knife in her hand.

"Hate's a strong word, Miss Talton."

"Yes it is. But at times, a very appropriate one."

Sarah opened the cupboard and reached for the tin canister of red pepper. As she shook it in her hand, it seemed half as heavy as usual. She tapped her index finger against her chin, trying to recall the last time she'd had occasion to use it.

New Year's Eve found Sarah in front of her dressing mirror, with Rebecca judiciously spritzing her with perfume. She had been transformed, from farmwoman to fairy princess. Her hair was pulled on top of her head in graceful ringlets, and powder and makeup accentuated her natural beauty. Her flowing gown showed off a trim figure usually well hidden under work clothes. Rebecca stood back and admired her subject. "I'd say one look at you, and this Mister LeGare fellow will forget all about France!"

Sarah didn't share the same confidence as her sister as she looked in the mirror. "I don't know about all this... maybe it's too much."

"Sarah, for once in your life forget that you're a farmer! Tonight, you're a woman. A beautiful, desirable *woman!*"

Sarah sighed and took another long look at herself, pursing her lips and cocking her head for a different view. Deep down, she actually liked what she saw, even though it didn't really look like her. She drew a deep breath and allowed herself one contented smile. She wrapped her arm around Rebecca's neck and pulled her sister's head next to hers. "Thank you."

"You're welcome. And tell LeGare that *he's* welcome too!"

A loud knock at the front door interrupted the moment.

"That's him!" squealed Sarah, hopping up from the dressing chair and nervously making unneccessary adjustments to her dress and hair. She gathered up the bottom of her gown and bounded down the stairs to the front hall. One final primp, a calming breath, and she confidently pulled open the door to receive her suitor.

"Bon soir, Monsie—" She stopped mid sentence, her knees nearly buckling. Standing before her was Braxton Smithwick. She blinked uncontrollably and searched for something to say.

"Mr. Smithwick... it's...what a surprise."

Braxton examined Sarah from head to toe and back again. "I could say the same."

"Is there some reason you're here?"

"Yes, in fact there is." From his breast pocket, Braxton removed a letter with LeGare's distinctive wax seal and placed it in Sarah's hand. "This came for you. I was in the vicinity, thought I'd drop it off."

"Thank you," said Sarah.

"And something I forgot to mention on my last visit here. I wanted to remind you that my offer for your farm still stands." Braxton again ogled Sarah. "And I must say, the offer is looking better all the time."

"I'll keep that in mind. Thank you again. I must be going now."

Sarah attempted to close the front door, but Braxton stepped across the threshold and blocked it with his muddy boot. He edged closer to Sarah, breathing in her perfume.

"The pleasure was all mine, Sarah. And I'll look forward to seeing you again at Mr. Clitherall's tonight. It's undoubtedly the finest affair this town has ever seen, and I'm so glad you'll be in attendance. It would be an *awful* shame to miss it, don't you agree?"

"Agreed. Goodnight, Mr. Smithwick."

Sarah pushed hard on the door and abruptly closed it in Braxton's face.

With her eyes closed, Sarah leaned against the inside of the front door, clutching the letter from Monsieur LeGare. She held it to her nose and extracted as much aroma from the parchment as she could, then exhaled loudly as she allowed her mind a few moments to run free. Finally she cracked the wax seal and revealed the handwritten note, penned in French. Sarah bolted outside and raced across the yard to the slave cabins, banging on the door.

"Jacquerie! I need you! Jacquerie!"

Moments later, the two women had found some privacy in the barn. Sarah was pacing with anticipation as Jacquerie held the letter close to a candle flame and began to translate.

"My dear Sarah..."

"Oh!" gushed Sarah. "I just *love* it when he says that! Go on!"

Jacquerie began again, but immediately the tone of her voice dampened.

> *"My dear Sarah... by the time you receive this letter, I will have departed on my return voyage to France."*

Sarah froze in sudden horror and snatched the letter from Jacquerie's hand.

"Departed?" she whispered. "*Departed?* It doesn't say that! You made a mistake! Read it again!"

Jacquerie looked into Sarah's eyes, knowing it was no mistake. "That's what it says, ma'am. Departed."

"But that can't be! He was supposed to come here first!" Sarah started to pace, unable to immediately process the bad news unfolding in front of her. "Departed? Gone? Just like that? Did he say why?"

Jacquerie slowly brought the letter back to the candle and resumed reading.

> *"I regret deeply that I was unable to be with you on the eve of the New Year. My father has taken gravely ill and I have no choice but to return home and be at his bedside in his final days. I should be back in Paris within the month, and will look forward to corresponding with you from there. Such unfortunate timing for us, but I pray you will understand my obligations to family.*
>
> *"The voyage home will be long and difficult, made even harder knowing that each breath of wind in the sails is taking me further away from you. I long for the day when this pen I now hold will be replaced by your hand. With deepest affections..."*

Jacquerie's voice trailed off. "Monsieur... Edouard... LeGare."

Sarah's chin quivered as Jacquerie gingerly handed her the letter. The parchment fluttered in Sarah's trembling hand as she leaned against the splintered wall of the barn.

"Wouldn't you know it? The first time I allow myself to care for someone? One day I'm dreaming about going to cotillions, about marriage, about children, and then with no warning... gone. I'll never see him again."

"You don't know that."

"Oh, but I do. We both do." The makeup that had moments before highlighted a face that held so much joy and promise now covered deep lines of despair.

The days and weeks that followed would take Sarah through a numbing monotony, as though grieving a death. With a never-ending ache in the pit of her stomach, she completed her chores in a state of near catatonia, unable to concentrate on the simplest of tasks.

At night, she would struggle to find the right words as she dictated love letters to Jacquerie.

> *"I worry that the void I feel in my heart will never go away. It's an emptiness, an unsettling, a longing that I can't fully describe. It's as if part of your soul is constantly separated from the rest of your being, and you are incessantly searching for it in everything you see and everything you do. It's like being in a prison with no bars, but no means of escape. And while this feeling ebbs and flows, the emptiness never completely goes away. It captures my thoughts every waking moment, and invades my dreams even while I sleep. I have come to the daunting realization that my only path to wholeness is through you. How painful it is to have tasted love so sweet, only to have it taken away before I've had my fill. It is only when I close my eyes that you don't seem so far away. My thoughts are only of you and future days when we are together again.*
>
> *"Until then, Sarah."*

Dutifully translating Sarah's words into French, Jacquerie swept aside her own tears as hazy images of John Bodin crept through her mind.

Each visit to the post office brought only disappointment. On the surrey ride home, Sarah mused aloud as she stared into the winter wood.

"It's the worst of all situations. To be madly in love with someone you can't see or touch. Time and distance are very cruel partners." Jacquerie nodded in silent agreement as she steered the horse along the well-worn path.

24

Oh Lord my God, in thee do I put my trust:
save me from all them that persecute me, and deliver me:

Psalm 7:1

*T*he carving table inside the Talton kitchen was again laden with fresh fish as Jacquerie swiftly gutted them and arranged the fillets in neat order for the night's meal. She scraped both sides of the bloody blade on the edge of the table, then tossed it into the steaming water of a ceramic basin for cleaning. As she wiped her hands on her apron, she noticed that the remaining droplets of blood on the fish knife turned the water in the basin into a light rose color. The knife at the bottom shimmered through the pale pink, while the surface of the water captured Jacquerie's murky reflection. She suddenly thrust her hand into the water and snatched the knife. She held it aloft for three heartbeats, admiring the glinting steel, then swiftly tucked it into her waistband and made a hasty exit.

Cloaked by dim firelight in their cabin, Will, Sibby, and Luzanne gathered around Jacquerie as she read aloud from a stolen newspaper.

"'On February 4th, the Confederate States of America was officially formed in Montgomery, Alabama. Jefferson Davis has been elected as provisional President. President Davis has instructed his provisional legislature to seize all federal forts and arsenals within the borders of South Carolina, Alabama, Mississippi, Florida, Georgia, Louisiana, and Texas.' "

"What all dat mean?" asked Sibby.

"It mean der's gonna be a war," replied Will with growing animation. "And we'z gonna be right in da middle of it!"

"But what do dat mean to us?" asked Luzanne.

"It means changes," said Jacquerie. "Perhaps big changes."

"Supposin' I don't want no changes?" said Sibby. "Mebbe I likes thangs jes the way they is right now."

Jacquerie stared at Sibby for a moment. "There are many who feel as you do, Sibby. They don't want change. They like things just the way they are. But there are many more who don't. That's why there's gonna be a war."

A shadow suddenly passed by the window. With rehearsed orchestration, a floorboard went up and the forbidden newspaper was dropped into the cavity below. The plank fell back into place just as the front door of the cabin swung open and the ominous figure of Cyrus barged inside.

Without missing a beat, Jacquerie ignored the intrusion. "Know that the Lord is God!" she exclaimed to the others now seemingly gathered in prayer. "It is He that made us, and we are His."

"Amen!" rejoined the others in unison.

"We are His people, and the sheep of His pasture—"

"Amen! Hallelujah!"

"Enter His gates with thanksgiving—"

Cyrus surveyed the situation with instinctive suspicion, but said nothing. Apparently satisfied, he stepped backwards out of the cabin and pulled the door shut.

The group collectively paused, sensing the storm had passed.

Jacquerie broke the silence. "Blessed are the meek, for they shall inherit the earth!"

"Amen! Hallelujah!"

Jacquerie lifted up the floorboard and retrieved the newspaper. She read in a hushed tone as the others moved closer.

"President Lincoln has called for seventy-five thousand volunteer troops to put down the southern insurrection."

"Whazzat?" asked Luzanne.

"It means rebellion... revolt. A new way of doin' things."

With no warning, the door was flung open and Cyrus burst inside. Everyone froze in place. Cyrus pointed to Jacquerie, still holding the forbidden newspaper.

"You!" he bellowed. "You comin' wif me!"

Cyrus grabbed Jacquerie violently by the hair on the back of her head and dragged her to the door. He turned back to the others, snorting in anger. "I'll deal with y'all later!" The three slaves sat in abject fear under the venomous eyes of the overseer. With a firm grip on her nape, Cyrus yanked Jacquerie outside and dragged her through the night air to the front door of the big house. Her efforts to squirm away were no match for his burly arms and adrenalized anger. As they approached the front door, he gave her a sharp slap across her face, drawing blood in the corner of her mouth.

His meaty fist pounded on the door as he held Jacquerie in tow. No answer. He pounded again, prepared to knock it down if need be.

Moments later the door finally opened, revealing Sarah with a candle. The flickering light illuminated the sudden alarm washing over her face.

"Let go of her!"

"But Miss Talton—"

"I said let go of her! At once!"

Cyrus slowly released his grip on Jacquerie's hair.

"What in the world is going on here?"

"I caught dis slave readin', Miss Talton. Readin' from a newspaper, one I 'spect she stole."

Sarah shot a glance at Jacquerie that said "how *could* you?" Cyrus puffed up his chest in triumph. "What ya 'spose we ought to do 'bout dat? I could whip her now, or I could waits til mornin' and whip her den, in front of da others. Or I could wake da others up and whip her now in front of dem right dis minute. Or I could do both. Whip her now, then whip her agin in the mornin'. Teach dem others a real good lesson. So what ya wantin' me to do, Miss Talton?"

Sarah stared squarely at Jacquerie, even though she spoke to Cyrus. "You'll do nothing," she commanded.

Cyrus cocked his head, as if he'd misheard. "Beg ya pardon, ma'am? Did ya say 'nothin'?"

"I did."

"But Miss Talton... readin'? That ain't—"

Sarah shifted her steely gaze to Cyrus, and leaned a fraction closer. "It is not a crime to read on the Talton farm. I do it every day, and don't have to pay for the privilege with the flesh of my back. So there will be no punishment. Is that clear?"

"But Miss Talton—"

"Is that clear?" she said louder, enunciating each word with purpose.

Cyrus shifted his considerable weight back and forth. "Yes, ma'am."

"Good. Now then, I suggest you return to your quarters."

Cyrus didn't immediately budge, still trying to process the bizarre turn of events.

"Is there a problem?" queried Sarah, her confidence growing.

"No, ma'am. No problem t'all. 'Nite, ma'am."

Cyrus fired one more angry look at Jacquerie that hinted of future retribution before lumbering away.

Jacquerie rubbed the reddened patch on the back of her neck as Sarah reached out and dabbed the traces of blood trickling down the corner of her mouth.

"You're not much on authority, are you?" asked Sarah.

"There's only one authority in *my* life," replied Jacquerie with a gentle shaking of her head. "The one I pray to every night."

"And what do you pray for?"

"Strength. Strength to stay alive one more day. Strength to face all the evil and hatred in this world. Strength to keep believin' that a better day is going to come."

"Do you really believe things will ever be different?"

"I do. I believe that some day people will look back in shame."

"And what happens if that day never comes?"

"Every day comes eventually. It's up to us how fast we want it to get here."

Sarah nodded in agreement.

"May I go now?" asked Jacquerie.

"Of course."

Sarah stood silently in the doorway, pondering Jacquerie's words, as the slave limped away into the darkness.

As Jacquerie approached the slave cabin, Will stepped suddenly from the shadows.

"Hey!" he called out in a loud whisper.

Startled, Jacquerie instinctively raised her fist to strike back, until she realized who it was.

"What are you doin'? You scared me to death!"

"You all right?"

"I'm fine."

"Ya gonna git a whuppin'?"

"No."

"No?"

"No. But *you* will if you don't get back inside."

"I needs to talk to ya."

"Can it wait until mornin'?"

"No. What I gots to say can't wait no mo."

"What is it then?"

"I'm gonna run. Head north. And I'll be needin' yo help."

Will had Jacquerie's complete attention. "Go on."

"You'z da only one 'round heah got a chance to git in da storehouse. I needs some food... 'bout three days supply, I reckon. And I needs somethin' to protect myself... knife, gun, somethin', and some red peppah to throw off da dogs."

"How will you know where to go?"

"I'll jes keep a goin' north. Same as you did."

"But it's not that easy. You'll need help along the way."

"Then mebbe you should come wit me."

Jacquerie mulled it over for a second, then shook her head. "I'll see what I can do. No promises."

As the pair quietly slipped back toward the cabin, the haunting screech of an owl pierced the frostbitten night. Will froze in fear.

"What's wrong?" whispered Jacquerie.

"Ya hear dat?"

"That owl? Yes. Why?"

"The old folk believe dat when ya hear an owl screech, it mean somebody gonna die."

"Well I don't believe any of that."

"Dey also say dat iffn a man want a girl to fall in love with him, he need to catch him a bullfrog, boil it, den scratch dat woman with da bone."

"Well I *certainly* don't believe that."

"So what *do* ya believe?"

"I just believe in God."

"Dat's it?"

"That's it."

"How ya know der is a God?"

"I just accept it on faith."

"Faith? Whazzat?"

"Believin' it to be so, even though you can't see it, smell it, touch it, or prove it. You just come to accept it in your heart, and while you may question it sometimes, you never let it go."

"Like da winter chill? I can't see it, but I can sho feels it. Like dat?"

"A little, but not exactly. It's more like love. You love somebody, a baby, a sister, a man, you just *know* it. You can't explain it, but it's how you feel. You just know down deep in your heart that you love them and always will. That's what faith is. Loving God, now and forever."

"That sho is a lot to think about."

"Which is why I think about it all the time. Now get back inside."

They slipped back into the cabin and quietly closed the door.

25

*I*t was now April of 1861, and as she had done nearly every day since LeGare's sudden departure, Sarah made her way through the bustling streets of Winston and into the post office.

"Nothing?" she called out to the postmaster, answering her own question in advance.

"Nothing," he replied. Sarah nodded her head in resignation and spun slowly around, heading back outside.

"Nothing," he repeated. "Except for this."

Sarah turned heel to see the postmaster with a twinkle in his eye, holding a letter with a distinctive wax seal. Her eyes widened with childlike glee as she rushed to the counter and snatched it from his fingers.

"Thank you! Thank you!" she squealed as she held the letter in her hands. She kissed him hard on the cheek then bolted out the door.

Jacquerie was holding the reins of the surrey as Sarah scurried down the street, waving the letter over her head.

"Hold onto this!" she called out as she handed up the letter to

Jacquerie. I have to run into Hollister's for some supplies... I'll be right back!"

A small group of men was gathered in Hollister's dry goods store, Braxton Smithwick among them. They leaned over barrels of foodstuffs as they listened attentively to the man standing in the middle of their circle, holding a newspaper aloft. The banner headline read:

"CONFEDERATE FORCES CAPTURE FORT SUMTER."

The man behind the newspaper read aloud.

> " 'Major Robert Anderson surrendered Fort Sumter
> on the afternoon of April 13th after 34 hours of
> bombardment by Confederate Forces. The attack
> was in retaliation for President Lincoln's decision
> to resupply the federal garrison stationed in
> Charleston Harbor, despite an edict by Confederacy
> President Jefferson Davis that the installation not
> be reinforced.' "

"We warned them!" snorted Braxton. "Lincoln has pushed us too far! If war is what he wants, then Jeff Davis'll give it to him!" The others roared their approval at Braxton's bravado. A tiny bell affixed to the door of the dry goods store *tinkled* as Sarah entered. She paused momentarily and assessed the situation, like a stagehand who had inadvertently barged into a live theatre performance.

"Why, Sarah Talton!" chirped Braxton. "If there's a prettier woman in all of North Carolina, I've yet to meet her."

"There's probably a good reason for that," mumbled Sarah, drawing a few muffled chortles from the other men gathered in the store. She turned her back on the gathering and preceded to the store shelves, carefully selecting her provisions.

Braxton took a step toward her. "You're wise to be stocking up. It appears as though we're going to war!"

"War?"

"That's right!" crowed one of the men. "Them Yanks won't know what hit 'em!'"

"But the South can't *win* a war!" blurted Sarah.

The room fell instantly silent upon hearing Sarah's statement of heresy.

Braxton cast a bemused look at Sarah. "Well now, I certainly wouldn't expect a *woman* to understand such matters. It's not like we're talking about stitching together a quilt, or putting up peach preserves for the winter. But I'm curious, why would you say such a thing?"

"Don't you understand the reality of this? The North has over twenty million people, compared to our nine million, a third of which are Negro slaves! For every one skilled worker in the South, the North has an entire manufacturing plant! They have ninety-five percent of the firearms and railroads, and most of the money too! Do you not realize that going to war is pure folly? It's suicide!"

The case Sarah outlined had a sobering effect on everyone in the room except Braxton. He stepped forward with the swagger of a field marshal and rallied his troops. "It is true, my dear woman, that they may have considerable numbers, but everyone knows the best soldiers at West Point are all from the South, and the Yankees can't come close to matching us in spirit. They may have more gunpowder, but we have more gumption!" The proud boast prompted another round of audible agreement from the gallery.

As Braxton accepted the celebratory cheers of the other men in the store, Sarah calmly gathered herself and forced her voice to rise above the din.

"And tell me, Mr. Smithwick, on the subject of gumption... will *you* actually be going off and putting on a uniform?"

"Excuse me?"

"I'm just curious... with all your eagerness to get us all involved in a war, I haven't heard you mention a single word about you yourself taking up arms. Where exactly will you be when the bugle blows?"

Every muscle along Braxton's cheekbone tightened. He looked

around the room for support from his minions, but found only blank faces. Withering under the pressure, Braxton broke off eye contact. "I, uh... well, unfortunately, due to some ongoing business affairs, and some prior medical complications, I will be unable to *actively* take up the fight." He turned to the others for support, only to see them looking away. "However, that is not to say that I won't be doing all I can back here at home to support our boys in the field... with monetary contributions and, of course, ample moral support."

"Moral support. I see. Well I'm sure they'll find all that quite comforting when the bullets are flying and the blood is flowing." Sarah pushed her way past Braxton and put her provisions on the counter.

"That'll be four dollars and a half," said the storeowner as he scurried behind the cash drawer.

"Put it on my slate," said Braxton in a vain effort to regain control of the situation.

"No need," replied Sarah without hesitation as she dug into her handbag and pulled out a robust sum of cash. "I've got the money."

"Where did you get that?" asked Braxton in disbelief.

"Mustard greens. Sold four acres of them. You ought to see them... as bright and leafy as any greens you ever laid eyes on. Got full market price, and then some."

"Since when did the Talton farm ever grow a decent mustard green?"

"Ever since I opened my ears. It's amazing what you can learn when you just listen. And wait until you see my winter wheat and acorn squash!" Sarah's eyes twinkled as she paid her tab.

"I see," said Braxton. "Well, that's wonderful. Happy for you."

"I knew you would be," replied Sarah breezily as she scooped up her parcel of goods. "Good day, gentlemen." Head raised high and eyes forward, she strode defiantly through the gauntlet of men and exited the store.

Minutes later, Jacquerie guided the surrey to a cutout in the woods along the route home. With girlish eagerness, Sarah scrambled into the front seat and tore open the wax seal.

"What's it say? Is it good news?"

Jacquerie began reading the letter.

"Miss Talton—"

"Wait… Miss Talton?" interrupted Sarah. "What happened to *my dear Sarah?*"

Jacquerie continued.

> *"In the past several months that I have been back in France, I have had the opportunity to reflect a great deal on what is taking place in America. It troubles me deeply to consider the violations of basic human rights and dignities there."*

Jacquerie glanced up at Sarah to see how the message was being received. The creases in her forehead revealed Sarah's growing concern.

> *"I have recently read the book Uncle Tom's Cabin by your American writer Harriet Beecher Stowe. I cannot fully put into words the anger and indignation I feel when I read of the way your slaves are treated."*

"It's fiction!" argued Sarah directly at the written page. "Doesn't anybody understand that? Slaves are *not* treated like that! Doesn't he realize that our slaves have better working conditions than the so-called 'free' factory workers in the North?"

Jacquerie paused for the debate to end, then resumed.

> *"This book prompted me to also read the writings and teachings of Frederick Douglass, William Lloyd Garrison, and Sojourner Truth. Their articles leave me with the undeniable conclusion that slavery in all forms is… is…"*

Jacquerie pointed to a specific word in the letter and showed it to Sarah. "I'm not sure what this word is."

The tip of her index finger pointed to the word *despicable*, which translated identically into English.

"Despicable," murmured Sarah.

"What does that mean?"

"It means deserving to be despised... contemptible."

"Oh. Despicable. Hmmm."

Sarah tilted her back toward Jacquerie, indicating her suspicion that her slave knew precisely what the word meant all along and had tricked her into saying it aloud with her own tongue.

"Keep reading."

> *"What is your opinion on these matters? I am sure that someone as gentle and kind as you must feel the same way, and I trust you are doing all that is within your power to change a most troubling situation."*

Sarah turned her head away and stared into the forest as the letter continued.

> *"It is also my deep concern that trade with your country will be impossible in view of the increasing threat of war. I must also tell you that my father is not well. His health has declined to the point that I have been forced to assume all the responsibilities of the family business. Is this what will bring me happiness? I can't say. The future is uncertain, but I feel as though I have little choice in the matter. There are many people in his employ depending on me to succeed, and to fail is to certainly lose whatever future I may have as well. It is therefore with a most heavy heart—"*

Jacquerie suddenly stopped. Tears of awful realization welled up in her eyes as she surveyed the words of the final paragraph, words that would impact both their futures.

"Keep going," said Sarah stoically.

> *"—it is therefore with a most heavy heart that I must end*

our relationship. I'm sure that you will understand that with so many insurmountable obstacles in our way, I cannot fall deeper in love with a woman an ocean away. My thoughts and prayers will be with you always. Deepest regards—

"*Monsieur Edouard LeGare.*"

Jacquerie slowly lifted her head to inspect Sarah's reaction. Sarah sat motionless, her eyes buried deep in the forest. There was an interminable silence as both women pondered their immediate futures.

It was Sarah who finally spoke. "Do you dream?" she asked Jacquerie, her gaze still fixed in the distance.

"Do I dream?"

"Yes. Do you have dreams?"

"Of course. We all have dreams."

"And what do you dream about?"

Jacquerie thought for a moment, quietly sniffing and dabbing her teary eyes with her sleeve. "Sometimes I dream about him."

"Your husband?"

"Yes. But mostly, I'd say I dream about miracles."

"Miracles?"

"Yes."

"You believe in miracles?"

"The Bible tells us to believe in them."

"Yes it does, doesn't it. So what kind of miracles do you dream about?"

"Changes."

"Changes?"

"That's right. Miraculous changes."

"Changes in what?"

"Everything. Everything we think, everything we do, everything we are."

"Such as?"

Jacquerie drew in a deep breath and fixed her eyes straight ahead, peering infinitely into space. Not so much to another place, but to another time, distant and future.

"I dream of a day when people will be measured through the touch of their hands, and not the color of them. I dream of a day when our differences will be seen as our strength, and not our dividin' line. I dream of the day when *all* children can learn to read and write without fear." She raised her chin a few inches higher. "And I dream of the day when the world will listen to what a black woman has to say."

Sarah nodded and spoke softly. "Maybe some of us already are."

They turned to face each other, each trembling with emotion.

"I know it's hard to believe," said Sarah, lifting her eyes and staring at the changing clouds, "but someday this *will* all be different for both of us. I know that in my heart. I don't know when, and I don't know how, but I know it will... someday."

A gentle whisper of wind swirled across the two women as they sat in somber silence underneath the canopy of Carolina pines.

26

Blessed are they that mourn: for they shall be comforted.
Blessed are the meek, for they shall inherit the earth.

Matthew 5:4-5

Late that night, Sarah sat alone in front of a dwindling fire, running her fingers across the parchment of Monsieur LeGare's numerous letters. Rebecca entered in her nightclothes.

"Are you all right?"

"I will be."

"It's over?"

"Over. No more soft kisses of my hand. No more dreams of marriage and summer days riding to the river in a carriage with our children."

One by one, Sarah tossed LeGare's letters into the fireplace and watched the flames eat them alive. The red sealing wax dripped onto the logs like tiny droplets of blood.

"And no more letters. No more beautiful... French... letters."

Sarah watched the rising fire with a faraway look... a gaze that carried her across the Atlantic.

"This is not what I want," said Sarah, as much to herself as to Rebecca.

"What do you mean? What's not what you want?"

"Everything. This is not what I want. I don't want to be in a war. I don't want to be a farmer. I don't want to have to worry about too much sun, or not enough rain. I don't want to feed horses, or pitch hay, or pluck chickens. And much of the time, I don't even want to be a woman."

"You don't want to be a woman? Why would you say a thing like that?"

"Because it's too difficult. No matter what you accomplish, no matter what you're capable of doing, no matter how intelligent you are, you're never *really* treated quite the same as a man. There's a meeting in town at this very moment of all the local landowners, talking about what we're going to do about this war, and I wasn't invited. Why not? Because I'm a woman, plain and simple. And a woman who will never get married, at that."

"Sarah, you don't need a man to survive in this world. Men are like the wind... sometimes they push open a door for you, and sometimes they cool you off, but most of the time, they're just annoying."

Sarah laughed out loud. "Part of me believes that. The other part says I don't want to die an old maid."

"There are worse things in the world than being an old maid."

"Not in the South, there's not."

"Sarah, listen to me. You are older than me. You are wiser. But if there's anything I've learned at that expensive school you send me to, it's this... don't let the result of your birth dictate the results of your life."

Sarah stood up and embraced her sister as the paper in the fireplace quickly turned to ash. "Perhaps I'm not the wiser one after all."

The gentle silence was abruptly breached by the violent clanging of the alarm bell outside. The two sisters instinctively jumped up and rushed outside into the yard. Cyrus, standing in his bare feet, was yanking full force on the knotty rope of the signal bell, bringing the entire plantation out into the night.

"What's wrong?" yelled Sarah above the din.

"It's Will! He ran off!"

"How do you know?"

"Right after I goes ta sleep, he come into my cabin and stole my shoes, den he done took off. I couldn't chase him, 'cause now I ain't got no shoes! I'm sorry, Miss Talton! I'm sorry!" yelled Cyrus as Sarah raced over to him. "I shoulda knowed better!"

"Stop it! Stop it right now!" Sarah nearly tackled Cyrus to make him stop tolling the bell. She took a deep breath, battling to remain calm.

"All dis talkin' round heah, 'bout freedom dis, freedom dat... I shoulda kep a devil's eye on him all the time! It's my fault, Miss Talton! I'm sorry!"

"It's not your fault. It's not anyone's fault."

"You want I should hitch up and go afta him?"

"No. You'll do nothing."

Sarah took a moment to collect her thoughts, then ran across the yard to Jacquerie's cabin, her hot breath crystallizing in the arctic air. She pushed open the door.

"Miss Talton? What's wrong?" Sibby scrambled out of her bed and onto her feet.

"You know exactly what's wrong."

"I sho don't, ma'am. What is it?"

Sarah marched over to Will's bed and flipped over the empty pile of blankets. Sibby and Luzanne looked at each other in horror, clearly unaware that Will wasn't there.

"Where's Jacquerie?" barked Sarah.

"I dunno, ma'am," replied Sibby with trembling fear. "I thought she was right heah."

"Where is she?" screamed Sarah, stepping menacingly closer to the old slave woman.

"I dunno! I swear it!"

"Don't lie to me!" thundered Sarah, instinctively raising her hand to strike, but then consciously pulling it back.

"I'm right here."

Sarah spun around to see Jacquerie framed by the doorway. "Was this your idea?" said Sarah, heaving with anger.

"No, ma'am."

"Do you not realize he'll be killed? Not just captured... killed!

Those slave patrols are being told to shoot to kill! They're starting to see that the flood of Negroes to the North is stirring up more agitators, and they can't have that! Don't you understand? They'd rather make an example out of a runaway than bring him back alive! Do you *want* him to get killed?"

The two women stood face to face in a defiant stalemate, but the anger washing over them was not at each other, but rather at a world beyond their control that had brought them both to this crossroads. Sarah shook her head, placed her open palms over her furrowed brow, and pulled them outwardly toward her flushed cheeks.

"Get inside," she said to Jacquerie in a more controlled tone. "Close the door."

Jacquerie obeyed as Sarah sat down on Will's empty bed, desperately trying to organize her thoughts. "How far can he get?"

"I honestly don't know."

"Did you help him with provisions? Food? Warm clothing? And tell me the truth. This is no time for secrets."

"Three days supply. That's all he could carry and still make good time."

"What about a map? Does he even have any idea where he's trying to go?"

"No, ma'am. He's just gonna follow the rivers."

Sarah exhaled loudly as she shook her head and closed her eyes.

"Whatcha goin' do?" asked Sibby, quaking with fear.

Sarah sat quietly for a moment, unsure what to say or do next. "I don't really know. Not much I can do at this point. Just pray, I suppose. I would suggest we all do that."

Sarah slowly rose from the bed and silently made her way to the cabin door, brushing past Jacquerie as she exited.

She walked across the yard, heading directly to the front door of the main house. "Go to bed, Cyrus. We'll worry about this in the morning." She vanished inside, leaving her overseer standing by the muted bell in stunned silence.

The bloodthirsty tick hounds yelped like anguished old souls as they ran serpentine through the thorny underbrush of the pine forest. A cluster of bounty hunters with guns and torches chased behind, steam pouring from their flaring nostrils.

Braxton Smithwick dug his heels deep into the flanks of his horse as he led the charge.

"Kill him on sight!" he commanded to the others.

"But that's Miss Talton's boy!" replied one of the hunters. "Don't she need him in her fields?"

"I said *kill* him! He's nothin' but trouble, and right now, we don't need any trouble."

Fueled by fear, Will stumbled blindly through the thicket, now within earshot of the river that might give him a fighting chance to escape the keen noses of the dogs. Suddenly he could see the water, the ripples reflecting the pale moonlight as they surged downstream. With a surge of fresh energy, Will burst from the tree line and headed for the riverbank. A full sprint now. Almost there. A single gunshot rang out, echoing for miles around. Will dropped to his knees, gripped with pain from a fire-hot bullet embedded in the back of his thigh. He pulled himself to his feet, staggered a few more yards, then collapsed.

Will remained prostrate on the frosted earth, clutching and squeezing handfuls of the sandy loam along the riverbank to ease his suffering.

The slave hunter ran up to the motionless figure on the ground. He kicked his muddy boot into Will's abdomen, then got down on one knee to inspect his quarry. He grinned with pride, as if he had just killed nothing more than a ruffed grouse.

"Hey!" he called back to the others. "Y'all come over heah! I done killed me a—"

Without a fraction of a warning, Will thrust himself upward and slammed a river rock into the pigskin-pink forehead of the slave hunter, sending him reeling violently backwards and onto the ground, writhing in pain. Will staggered to his feet and sat on the patroller's midsection, straddling his waist. He wrapped his ashy, black hands around the hunter's neck and tightened his grip. The hunter's lungs fought for breath as his bulging eyes begged for mercy. There would be none, as Will's fingers pressed harder into his throat. The patroller's legs kicked with involuntary spasm as the final bits of oxygen coursed his body. Moments later, he lay still on the frozen ground, the miserable life choked out of him.

Will finally released his grip on the man's throat and rolled off of him. With a fresh surge of energy, he pushed himself to his feet and resumed his flight. Another gunshot cracked through the night. Will's heaving lungs reached out for one final breath. He fell dead to the ground, free at last.

In her useless bed, Jacquerie fought for sleep. Her eyes flew open momentarily when far off in the distance, the strident call of a screech owl echoed across the fields.

Before the sunrise, Sarah was awakened again as the uneasy thunder of a dozen hoofbeats invaded the Talton farm like the devil's timpani. She threw off her coverlet and raced to the window, nearly collapsing from the sight.

Moments later, with only her woolen coat covering her nightclothes, Sarah stood in the yard. She faced a land armada of men on horseback, including Braxton Smithwick. Front and center to their cavalcade was a buckboard wagon with a bulging canvas tarp.

"Mornin', Sarah. I heard your warning bell last night... I rode this way, didn't see smoke, so I figured you had a runaway. Lucky for you my men were able to pick up the scent right away."

The doors to the slave cabins were all creaking open as the bleary-eyed field hands gradually gathered in the yard, Sibby and Luzanne among them.

"Where's Will?" whispered Sarah, already knowing the answer.

Braxton motioned to the lifeless heap under the canvas on the back of the buckboard.

"With all due respect, Miss Talton, you have got to do a better job of keepin' up with your personal property. I hate that you lost your best field hand... I imagine that's gonna make it harder to take up that winter wheat and acorn squash. But look at it this way... one less mouth to feed."

"No! No! Please God, *no!*" screamed Sibby as she ran toward the buckboard. Braxton swiftly dismounted and grabbed her before she could get there.

"Let her go, Braxton!" snapped Sarah with unwavering firmness.

"Excuse me?"

"I said... let her go."

Flashing a grin of derisive amusement, he finally relented. Sibby staggered to the buckboard, pulled back the canvas covering, and draped her body over her dead son. She sobbed with the anguish only a mother knows as Sarah ran over to comfort her.

"My, my. You seem to be gettin' quite a soft spot for your coloreds, Miss Talton," said Braxton. He turned to the collection of men on horseback. "You see that, gentlemen? A prime example of what happens when Yankee liberalism invades our southern way of life... white folk hugging coloreds, like they were human beings or some such. And that, my friends, is why we need to fight for our land and our liberty."

Sibby suddenly pulled away from the buckboard. Enraged, she turned to Jacquerie and pointed an accusing finger in her face.

"You! You did dis! Everythin' was jus' fine 'til you showed up, stirrin' up people's insides! You da one dat put dem thoughts in his head, and now ya done put him in da ground! You and yo speeches 'bout freedom and a better life! Now he ain't got no life a'tall!"

"You should be proud of what he tried to do!" argued Jacquerie. "He went down fighting, because he wanted something better for all of us!"

Sibby coupled her palms together as if in prayer. "When ya gonna understan', chile? There *ain't* nothin' better! When you a Negro, the world is the way it is, and no amount of dyin' gonna change dat!"

Sibby broke down in tears, and Jacquerie realized this was not the time to make a stand. She hung her head in remorse and out of respect for a mother who had just lost her son. Luzanne stepped in to pull Sibby away and lead her heartbroken mother back to her quarters.

Sarah stepped closer to Braxton and stared him down with eyes as cold and hard as Sheffield steel. "You'll be leaving now."

Knowing her words were more of a direct order than a suggestion, Braxton turned back to the posse of slave hunters, gesturing to Will's body.

"Get him off of there before he bleeds all over the wagon."

The men shuffled toward the buckboard, but Sarah stepped quickly in front of them. With a half nod of her head, she motioned to Jacquerie to join her. Summoning all of their collective strength, the two women lifted Will off the wagon and laid him ceremoniously on the cold ground.

Sarah aimed her incendiary eyes at Braxton. "Get off my farm."

"Yes, ma'am. Happy to oblige. Y'all enjoy the rest of the day." Braxton pulled his thumb and index finger across the brim of his hat and climbed back into the saddle. With a swift nod of his head, he cued the other men to saddle up and go. They cantered away, leaving behind a cloud of dust and a storm of rising anger.

Cyrus marched over to Will's corpse and angrily snatched his stolen boots off the dead man's feet.

27

I am weary with my groaning; all the night I make my bed to swim;
I water my couch with my tears.

Psalm 6:6

*A*soothing Negro spiritual echoed across the Talton farm as the last shovels of dirt were tossed onto the simple grave of Will Quarterman.

Steal away to Jesus!
Steal away, steal away home!
I ain't got long to stay here.
My Lord, he calls me, he calls me by the thunder!
The trumpet sounds within my soul.
I ain't got long to stay here.
Tombstones are bursting! Poor sinners stand a trembling.
The trumpet sounds within my soul.
I ain't got long to stay here.
My Lord, he calls me by the lightning!
The trumpet sounds within my soul.
I ain't got long to stay here.

Propped up by Luzanne, Sibby stood weeping. Even decades

of heartbreak and misery had not prepared her to outlive her only son.

Jacquerie stood a respectful distance away, feeling not only anger toward the men who had put Will in the ground, but also a certain amount of responsibility for putting him in that position.

Sarah laid three fresh jonquils on the newly turned soil, then closed her eyes in prayer. "Beloved, let us love one another, for love is of God, and he who loves is born of God, and knows God. Amen."

"Amen!" responded the gathering in unison.

The others slowly departed, leaving Jacquerie and Sarah alone by the gravesite to watch the sun disappear over the horizon.

Sarah pursed her lips and narrowed her eyes as her mind churned to find the right words to broach a difficult subject for both of them. "When you first came to me, you told me that if I sent you back to Louisiana, they would kill you. Was that the truth, or just something you said to save yourself?"

"The truth is worse than that."

"What do you mean? How could it be worse?"

"You have no idea what it's like other places. Or maybe you do and you just choose not to think about it."

"I only know how slaves are treated on my farm. I realize, more so in recent days, that even here it's harsh sometimes, but I just don't know any other way to keep order. You understand that, don't you?"

Jacquerie offered no reply as she stared back at Sarah with a chilling austerity.

"Then tell me," said Sarah. "Tell me what it's like other places. Tell me the truth. Tell me everything I need to know."

"There aren't enough days in our lifetime to tell you everything."

"But I want to know. I *need* to know."

"Very well. I will tell you the story of Moses Lane, an older slave who showed me much kindness when I was growin' up. He worked as hard as any man I've ever seen. Never complained, never caused any trouble. For years, he just worked to the bone, and then some. But one day Moses came up short in the amount of work he was supposed to accomplish that mornin'. For that, and that alone, the master blindfolded Moses with his own shirt so he couldn't anticipate the whip, and proceeded to flog him mercilessly. He shredded the skin on his back. Blood was everywhere. I can still hear the screams. And it wasn't over. The master tied him up between two posts, his arms and legs outstretched so he couldn't move, and poured pork brine into his gapin' wounds to increase the pain. Moses stayed out there all day in the boilin' sun as the mosquitoes ate him alive, and the yellow flies would lay their eggs in his bloody sores. Finally, they untied him. The women took a weed we called Oak of Jerusalem and boiled it down, then used it as a salve to soothe his wounds. It usually worked, but not this time. Moses Lane drew his last breath that night, and all because he came up a bushel short one day. And *that's* everything you need to know."

"I had no idea," whispered Sarah, hanging her head with physical and emotional nausea. "Please tell me that didn't happen every day."

"It happens every single day, on plantations and farms in every county of every state where people own other people. And even if it weren't *every* day... even if it only happened *once*, don't you think that's still a world that needs to be changed?"

Sarah silently nodded as she fought back tears and massaged her temples, as if trying to banish the unconscionable and repulsive images from her mind. "I'm sorry, Jacquerie. I'm so sorry."

They stood in silence as the evening star gradually appeared in the darkening sky.

That night in her cabin, Jacquerie curled up in her blankets on the floor and clutched her husband's letter.

Inside the main house, Sarah stood in the parlor and leafed through her Bible, desperately searching the testaments for a verse that might provide comfort in her time of spiritual need, but she was too angry to focus, too bitter to hear good news. As she slammed the pages shut, her eyes fixed on her father's portrait hanging over the fireplace. It suddenly struck her that her current situation was as much his fault as anyone's. He'd brought Sarah into a southern world that was rife with irreconcilable hatred, loathing, and enmity, then he'd left her alone to wade through the odious muck of modern mankind. Her seething anger growing, she hurled her precious Bible at her father's portrait, tearing the fabric of the oil-bearing canvas. Nothing made sense anymore.

28

Blessed are those which are persecuted for righteousness sake:
for theirs is the kingdom of heaven.

Matthew 5:10

I'm not sure this is a good idea," said Sarah with growing trepidation as she followed Rebecca along the cobblestone streets of Salem. "We could get into a lot of trouble for this."

"Trouble from whom, the men in town? That's precisely *why* we're going to this meeting! To empower us to do all of the things the men are afraid of us doing!"

"Where did you learn to talk like that?"

"College. Now come on, we're late!"

Sarah wasn't completely convinced, but nonetheless trudged forward in her sister's footsteps.

Minutes later they found themselves in the private home of Irene Murnane, the widow of a respected wheelwright, and a woman with a storied history of civil disobedience. Irene had years ago cemented her reputation as a maverick when she committed the unpardonable sin of wearing her late husband's work trousers while out horseback riding. "They're more comfortable" was her simple and logical reply to the inquisition that followed. In response to the great pantaloon scandal of 1852, the matriarchs of local society and their well-heeled minions had descended upon Irene's cottage en masse and attempted to engage her in an intervention, to explain the gravity of her misdeed, and to once and for all quell her penchant for living life on her own recalcitrant terms. When Irene answered the knocking at her door from the angry mob of fur-trimmed torchbearers, she was not wearing men's trousers. In fact, she was wearing nothing at all. While all mouths were open, only one was speaking, and the conversation consisted of only one sentence, uttered proudly by Irene. "Now then, ladies, let me ask you... which do you prefer?" After that bold display of eccentricity, the ladies of the town had given up on any hopes of reformation, simply washing their hands of Irene Murnane by labeling her as "incorrigible." It was a cross she bore proudly.

Despite the air of estrogenic bravado that permeated the room, the curtains were drawn tightly shut and the only light was provided by candles, giving the gathering place the look and feel of a Roman catacomb.

There were twelve women seated around the room, most of them younger than Sarah. She couldn't recall having ever seen any of them before, but got the sense that some of them knew who she was.

Irene moved to the front of the darkened room and with clasped hands, greeted the assembled guests.

"My dear friends, it is with great joy that I introduce our speaker today. She is the author of *An Appeal to the Christian Women of the South*, and works tirelessly as an anti-slavery campaigner. She has traveled all the way from New Jersey to be with us today, so please give the warmest of welcomes to Angelina Grimke."

To a modest, almost reluctant smattering of applause, the famous abolitionist rose from her seat with authoritative purpose and faced the gathering. Her stern countenance was imperial and august, with deeply set brown eyes buried underneath dark, arched eyebrows. An austere hairstyle was covered by a tight-fitting linen bonnet tied in a bow beneath her jutting chin. But while commanding, Angelina Grimke was not forbidding. She exuded a certain calmness and confidence that radiated throughout the room and captivated her audience.

"I want to thank you for allowing me to address you today, and I more than appreciate the personal risks I know many of you are taking just to be here. My sister and I face arrest if we ever return to our home in South Carolina, and only for the high crime of speaking the truth. The very fact that we are forced to meet in secrecy is empirical proof of the degradation and bondage to which the faculties of our minds have been prevented from expanding to their full growth, and in some cases, wholly crushed. But we are here because we *must* be. We must think for ourselves, and we must act accordingly. The men of the South have created this horrible system of oppression and cruelty, and therefore, it is up to the women of the South to overthrow it."

She spoke without notes, and though her words were rehearsed from hundreds of lectures given on behalf of the Anti-Slavery Society, she delivered them with evangelical fervor as though they were passing her lips for the first time. It was clear to her audience that the sentiment behind her remarks was deeply ingrained in her soul.

As Grimke got deeper into her speech, the restlessness within the room grew. Some of the women were inspired by her thoughts, others frightened, while most, including Sarah, were feeling something in between.

"Go home tonight, read your Bible. It contains the words of Jesus, which nobody in this struggle disputes. Judge for yourselves whether he sanctioned such a system of oppression and crime. Then, if your conscience reaches the same conclusion as mine, that this is sinful behavior, a crime against God and man, then be not afraid to speak freely of it to your friends, your relatives, and yes, even your husbands. Let your sentiments be known. Some of you gathered here are slaveholders yourselves. If you truly believe that slavery is sinful, you must set them free. If nothing else, you must provide them with the knowledge and opportunity to ride the Underground Railroad."

Sarah glanced over at Rebecca and furrowed her brow as if to say *"what's she talking about?"* but Rebecca was completely enthralled with the speaker.

"Slavery must be attacked with the whole power of truth and the sword of the spirit!" continued Grimke, her voice growing louder and her gestures grander and more animated. "If women don't use our moral power to get rid of slavery peacefully, it's going to get swept away in an ocean of blood! You must take it up on Christian ground, and fight against it with Christian weapons! Be the vessels that carry the truth and the light that bursts from the pages of the Holy Book! You *can* do this! Moreover, you *must* do this!"

Thunderous applause erupted from the women as they rose to their feet and pushed forward to be closer to Grimke like new converts at a religious revival.

Sarah stood alone at her seat, soaking it in. She simply hadn't realized that there were women like this, women of independent thought and action. How sheltered and naive she'd been, she thought, because up to this point, Rebecca was the most liberated woman she'd ever known. But now, a new world of possibilities lay at her feet. It was like trudging through a dark forest for days on end only to emerge and discover a lush, emerald green meadow on the edge of the tree line. A secret space where you could lie down and be rejuvenated and your spirit filled and stoked, like a blacksmith fanning a fiery hot furnace. Rebecca was right. It *was* empowering. If only one were willing to leave the safety of the forest and explore the awaiting meadow.

Minutes later Sarah and Rebecca were seated on a bench underneath the sprawling sycamore trees in the center square of Salem.

"So what did you think?" asked Rebecca with brimming enthusiasm.

Sarah shook her head. "In theory, what she says makes perfect sense. But..."

"But?"

"But the reality is, if I set my slaves free, I'll lose my farm! *Our* farm! Then what? Without that farm, I don't have anything else. I don't have food, I don't have shelter, I don't have money to send you to school. Am I to mortgage my entire future on the basis of one speech? I don't know."

"Sarah, you have to ask yourself, when you arrive at the gates of heaven, do you want to have to explain that?"

"I don't know, I don't know!" Sarah leaned over and buried her anguished head in her hands. Rebecca stroked her sister's weary back, vainly trying to console her. Sarah lifted her head and gazed out across the square.

"What's the Underground Railroad?" she asked.

Rebecca's face registered alarm as she glanced around to make sure nobody was eavesdropping.

"It's an elaborate system of safehouses where runaway slaves can find refuge and safe passage to the North. A great many Quakers are involved, but it's run by a woman named Harriet Tubman."

"A woman?" asked Sarah.

"That's right. A woman."

"Hmmm," murmured the older sister. "Tell me more."

29

No man can serve two masters: for either he will hate the one, and love the other; or else he will hold to the one, and despise the other.

Matthew 6:24

*W*ith white, foamy saliva pouring from its mouth, Braxton's horse charged onto the grounds of the Talton farm. Braxton swiftly dismounted and fixed the reins on the hitching post as if he already owned the place.

Cyrus emerged from the barn and approached the visitor.

"Afternoon, Massa Smithwick. Somethin' I can do fo ya?"

"I just dropped by to see how things were going. I understand you had a bumper crop of mustard greens."

"Yessuh. Best ever."

"Well that certainly is good news." Braxton removed a slender cigar from his breast pocket. "Very good news indeed."

He bit off a piece of the tip and spit it onto the dust. With his eyes shut and eyebrows raised, he dragged the sheath of tobacco slowly in front of his nose to soak in its aroma. He pulled a sulphur-tipped match from his watch pocket, raked it across his belt buckle to ignite it, and held it to the cigar now clenched firmly between his teeth. The rich, gray smoke enveloped his head as he twirled the cigar between his fingers to ensure that all the leaves were burning evenly.

Cyrus watched the display with great fascination, licking his lips like a child coveting a candy stick.

"The lady of the house... is she in?" asked Braxton between puffs.

"No, suh. She and Miss Rebecca go into town."

"Into town. I see. How did they get there?"

"Jacquerie drove 'em, suh."

"Oh, Jacquerie. She's the new one, right?"

"Yessuh."

"Driving that surrey... wasn't that *your* job before she showed up?"

Cyrus nodded. "Yessuh, it sho was."

"And how does that feel, having a woman take over your responsibilities like that? I mean, there she is, sitting at the reins of a surrey, and you're back here mucking stalls. That doesn't seem fair to me."

Cyrus hung his head and pawed at the ground. "Well, suh, it ain't up to me."

Braxton intentionally blew a mouthful of cigar smoke in the direction of Cyrus. "You like cigars, Cyrus?"

"I don't rightly know, Mr. Smithwick. Ain't never had a real one."

Braxton held the cigar high between his thumb and index finger and admired it. "This one here is from the Caribbean. You ever hear of the Caribbean, Cyrus?"

"No, suh."

"It's in the ocean. Tropical islands. Hundreds of them. And filled with beautiful black women, hand-rolling fine cigars all day long. You can just picture it, can't you, Cyrus?"

Cyrus allowed himself the hint of a smile as he imagined the picture Braxton painted. "Yessuh, I sho can."

Braxton narrowed his eyes and looked out across the fields of the Talton farm. "Tell you what, Cyrus. You seem like a reasonable man. I have a proposition for you. Perhaps one that could be mutually beneficial." Braxton turned his eyes to Cyrus. "This Jacquerie woman... find out where she's from. Who owns her. In exchange, I'll get you two and a half dozen of these fine cigars, hand-rolled by those beautiful Caribbean women I was talking about. Now how's that sound?"

"Soundin' good, Mr. Smithwick. I can do dat."

"Very good. I'll ride back by in a day or two and see what you've found out."

Braxton started for his horse when Cyrus ran up alongside him.

"There's somethin' else ya should know 'bout dat girl."

"And what would that be?"

"She know how ta read. I caught her last week. And Missus didn't do nothin' 'bout it."

Braxton fought hard to mask his delight upon hearing such delicious gossip. "Really," he said. "Well, well, well. That *is* good to know." Braxton took one last puff from the cigar, then pitched it on the ground and crushed the glowing embers under his bootheel. He snatched the reins off the hitching post, swung into the saddle, and raced away.

Before the dust of the horse's departure had even cleared, Cyrus bent over and picked up the remnants of Braxton's discarded cigar. He flicked away the remaining ash, smoothed the brown leaves with his fingertips, and tucked it into his pocket.

Sarah stood on a knoll in the field just past the barn. It was her favorite time of day, that special hour when the sun melted into the horizon and left the western sky ablaze in a palette of oranges, magentas, and lavenders. While most of the world fell into one of two categories, day people or night people, Sarah was most assuredly an evening person. She was caught somewhere in between the better defined segments of time, in moments that never lingered very long. The quiet minutes and subdued light between sunset and nightfall provided a respite from the burdens of the realities of life, a pause in the spinning of the globe when she felt the greatest sense of personal peace, and the closest to God.

She pivoted slowly in place as she stood in the long grass flowing around her ankles, surveying the land in all directions, but it was not the look of a farmwoman contemplating the spring planting, or deciding which fences needed mending. Sarah instead had the air about her of a traveler on holiday, preparing to board a train to return home, but wanting to soak in one final magnificent look at a paradise she might not visit again.

"As we have therefore opportunity," she whispered aloud, "let us do good unto all men, especially unto them who are of the household of faith." She repeated the verse from Galatians she'd memorized years ago. "As we have therefore opportunity, let us do good unto all men, especially unto them who are of the household of faith."

As the final vestiges of sunlight surrendered to twilight, she walked across the lonely field back to the house.

As she approached the front door, something on the ground caught her attention. It was the ash of cigar, gray and brittle like a hornet's nest. Sarah stared at the ash and contemplated its source. She reached a swift conclusion.

Moments later, inside the parlor of the main house, Sarah yanked her precious copy of Washington Irving's *Sketchbook* off the bookshelf. Holding open the front and back covers, she turned it upside down and shook it violently, forcing the few remaining pieces of currency hidden in between the pages to tumble out and flutter to the floor.

30

And thou shalt do that which is right and good in the sight of the Lord:

Deuteronomy 6:18

The Talton surrey rolled to a gentle stop in front of the post office. From the driver's seat, Jacquerie turned around to see Sarah in the back, intently poring over her Bible, occasionally closing her eyes and mouthing the words on the page.

"What are you readin'?"

"The book of James. It says 'what doth it profit, my brethren, though a man say he hath faith, and have not works? Faith, if it hath not works, is dead.' "

"And what does that mean?"

"You know *exactly* what it means. I wouldn't doubt if you've memorized that passage."

"Well then, what does it mean to *you* ?"

"It means I've got to do something."

Sarah closed her Bible and returned it to her handbag. She scrambled out of the surrey, her jaw firmly set with a look of dogged determination. "I'll be back in a few minutes."

Drawing a deep breath, Sarah marched boldly toward the post office. Just as she arrived at the front door, it swung open to reveal Braxton on his way out.

"Why, Miss Talton," he exclaimed with unusual gentility. "How's your day going? I mean, so far?"

Sarah took a step back and pressed her hand to her breastbone. "Why I'm perfectly fine, thank you. Perhaps soon to be even better."

"Well that's wonderful to hear!" Braxton slowly removed a cigar from his coat pocket and leisurely pulled it under his nostrils, never taking his eyes off of Sarah. "Just wonderful! I'm having a very good day myself! You take care now. I'm sure I'll be seeing you." Braxton tipped the brim of his hat and stepped lively onto the street.

Sarah heaved in another rejuvenating breath and pushed open the door to the post office.

Inside were dozens of men from town, ringing the perimeter of the room in their dark suits and John Bull and Empire hats. They were all men she had seen before. From Braxton's reception for LeGare, from the Community Store, from church. As the den of lions cast their collective gaze, it had all the trappings of an inquisition.

"Good afternoon, gentlemen," said Sarah as brightly as possible. She stepped toward the mail drop but her path was blocked by four dour men who showed no signs of being moved. "Is there a problem here, gentlemen?"

"Perhaps *you* can tell us." It was the voice of her preacher. He stepped forward inside the circle of men.

"I'm not sure what you mean." Sarah cast her eyes downward at the dusty planks on the floor.

"We understand that you have a slave in your keep who can read, *and* that you're allowing her to do so. How do you answer those charges, Miss Talton?"

The shrinking room was filled with a suffocating silence as her eyes darted around the tableau of angry men. Sarah realized the gravity of her situation as she carefully considered the next words that would pass her lips. Six months ago, she would have chosen the path of least resistance, the one paved with apology, humility, and retreat. Six months ago, she felt she had no choices. But that was then. Now, she knew with overwhelming clarity which fork in the road she would travel, despite not knowing the final destination of her new journey. She turned on her heel and faced the preacher.

"A slave... reading... is that a crime?"

"Indeed it is!" the preacher said.

"And tell me, sir, is it also a sin?"

The preacher opened his mouth to quickly respond, but then paused. He cocked his head and pondered the question for a moment before issuing a thoughtful reply.

"It could be considered as such. The Bible says—"

"You're telling me that scripture says it's a sin for a human being to read?" She swiftly pulled her Bible from her handbag and held it a foot from the preacher's face. "You're telling me that contained somewhere within these pages is the decree, 'Thou shalt not read'? Is that what you would have us believe, Reverend?"

The other men in the room took a step backwards.

"I didn't say that!

"What then *are* you saying?"

"I'm saying that it's the law! Divine law! I didn't write it! Those are God's words!"

"Maybe you didn't write them, but you and men like you twisted those words to suit your own unholy purposes."

"Listen to me, you be careful—"

"Could it be that by allowing slaves to read, especially the Bible, that they just might begin to understand the contradictions between what we preach and what we practice? Have we made it a crime to read because we're afraid our black brethren will be awakened to their oppression and this vast moral chasm we've created? Is that not *truly* the reason?"

"Young lady, you have no earthly idea what you're talking about! There are much larger issues at stake here, and unrest among the Negroes threatens us just as much as northern agitators do! You speak of oppression... what about *our* oppression? The Psalmists tell us that the Lord also will be a refuge for the oppressed, a refuge in times of trouble! *We* are fighting against oppression, against an unwanted government that doesn't understand our way of life! We are fighting for *freedom,* and that, Miss Talton, is a noble cause! *We* are the people of moral righteousness, and that is why *we* have God on our side!"

The muted circle of men applauded the preacher's stirring words. With hubris, he stood with his hands on his hips.

Sarah pursed her lips and slowly nodded her head as she began to walk a circle around the preacher. "So what you're saying, if I understand you, is that because you are aligned with God, you are therefore superior, and your beliefs should prevail, and anyone who disagrees with your position is inherently wrong, and therefore inferior. Is that a fair summation?"

"I could not have said it better myself."

"Yes, I'm quite sure of that." Sarah paused, drew three contemplative breaths, then slowly raised her head and riveted her eyes on the southern sons standing defiantly around her.

"Did it ever occur to you, gentlemen, that *God* doesn't want to be aligned with *you*?" Nobody moved as Sarah moved slowly around the circle of men. "Of course you don't want change! You have all the power, all the money, all the birthrights! It's no wonder you're willing to fight to the death to hold onto it! It's no wonder you don't want any slave, or any *woman* for that matter, to realize their potential because that threatens *your* position of privilege! But death is all that will come of this. Death to you, death to your farms, death to your way of life. And do you know why? Because the one thing you cannot kill is the human spirit. And not only are you unable to kill it, you in fact make it stronger with each attempt, like hardened steel that emerges from the inferno of a blast furnace. Mark my words, gentlemen... this will be a tragic chapter in our nation's history, and history will look back on you with shame."

There was an interminable quiet among the men. Despite quaking hands, she stood rigidly within the circle, silently praying to God to shoulder her swelling fears. Finally, an unseen voice spoke from the back of the room.

"So what do you propose? That we just set them all free?"

"Precisely. Starting with my own." Sarah shoved her way through the circle of men and marched toward the postal counter. "If you'll excuse me, I have some business to conduct." She addressed the postmaster directly. "I need to get into contact with a Mr. Duval in

Crowley, Louisiana. He owns the slave woman who's been staying on my farm."

The postmaster hung his head. "Not anymore, he doesn't."

"What do you mean?" said Sarah.

"Braxton Smithwick just received a telegram from Mr. Duval. As of about ten minutes ago, he's now her rightful owner."

Sarah blanched and her knees buckled underneath her skirt.

She pushed past the throng of men and bolted out the door. Ashen and weak, her teary eyes confirmed what she'd quickly suspected. Jacquerie was not in the surrey. To her great surprise, however, Cyrus was there, standing at the head of the horse and holding the bridle.

"What are *you* doing here?" she called out breathlessly. "Where's Jacquerie?"

"I'm here ta drive ya home, ma'am."

"How did you get here?"

Cyrus looked away and didn't reply.

"Braxton! He brought you here, didn't he? Don't you get it? Don't you see what they're doing? They're just *using* you!"

Cyrus looked squarely at Sarah. "Dey ain't da ones who own me, ma'am. You do."

Sarah blinked hard. The truth in his words stung.

"Get in the surrey!" she ordered, scrambling into the back.

Cyrus grabbed the reins and slid back into his old familiar seat up front. "Home?"

"No."

"No?"

"Take me to Bellerive."

"Mr. Smithwick's?"

"That's right."

"Miss Talton, I don't want no trouble."

"Are you disobeying me?"

"No, ma'am."

"Then do as I say! Go!"

Cyrus whipped the brown leather across the ridge of the horse's back and the surrey lurched into motion.

31

Thou preparest a table before me in the presence of mine enemies;
thou anointest my head with oil; my cup runneth over.
Surely goodness and mercy shall follow me all the days of my life:
and I will dwell in the house of the Lord for ever.

Psalm 23: 5-6

"Can you not go faster?" Sarah called from the rear of the surrey as they rumbled across the pocks and potholes of the country lane that would lead them to the Smithwick Plantation.

"Doin' da best I can. Road ain't so good, ma'am."

Sarah leaned back in exasperation. She could only imagine the fate that awaited Jacquerie at Bellerive; a ruthless whipping, a savage beating, or worse. She leaned forward again and yelled above the din of the clacking wagon wheels.

"You have *got* to go faster!"

Cyrus cracked his whip across the flank of the horse. "*Hyaahh!* " he bellowed. The horse immediately obeyed his command and accelerated his already lively pace. The surrey sped down the washboard road, the tall pines flying by like pickets on a fence. Without warning the horse stumbled over a pothole in the road. There was an audible *crack* and the horse reared up on his hind legs and let out a ghastly, unearthly scream. The surrey pitched violently from side to side with a gnashing of wood and iron as it tried to disengage from its coupling with the injured animal, tossing Sarah into the floorboard and Cyrus out of the surrey altogether.

The horse stood in place with his nostrils flaring and his right foreleg held aloft. Sarah scrambled out of the surrey and Cyrus picked himself up off the ground.

"Are you hurt?" she asked Cyrus.

"No, ma'am," he replied, dusting himself off and testing his limbs. "I seems ta be jes fine."

Sarah took a cautious step towards the anguished horse. His shattered cannon bone dangled listlessly below his knee like a pendulum on a stopped clock. "Easy there, Onyx," she called out in a soothing voice as she stepped closer. "Don't worry, everything's going to be—"

The horse suddenly snorted and thrashed aggressively, sending Sarah reeling backwards in fear.

She turned and looked down the road. "How much further to Bellerive?" she asked Cyrus.

"Don't rightly know. Three, four mile I 'spose."

Sarah snatched her handbag from the rear of the surrey and immediately started walking at a brisk pace. "You go back to town and find someone who can take care of this horse. And tell them they'll need to bring a gun."

"Mebbe I should go with ya?"

"No. I don't need another man slowing me down."

Sarah broke into a run, kicking up dust as she hastened down the lonely road toward Bellerive.

A long hour later, as Sarah approached the boundary fence of the Smithwick plantation, she heard the haunting ringing of the warning bell. Though already tired and parched from her exhausting trek on foot, Sarah collected up the bottom of her skirt and ran as quickly as her weary legs would take her.

Within minutes she arrived on the grounds of Bellerive and into a beehive of activity. Black leather saddles were being cinched onto horse's bellies, baying dogs were being clipped to leashes, and kerosene torches and lanterns were being readied.

Sarah moved unnoticed through the frenzy of activity and into the open door of the plantation house. In the dining room she found Braxton and two bounty hunters poring over a hand-drawn map that was rolled out on the table.

"Most likely, she'll head for the river, try to throw off the scent of my dawgs," said the older of the bounty hunters, a man Sarah had seen before.

"Braxton, what's going on?"

He whirled around in surprise. "What are you doing here?"

"What's wrong? Why is the bell ringing?"

"Because that no good slave woman you're so fond of thinks she can run away. I hadn't even had time to give her a proper whippin' before she took off. But she won't get far, and when I get my hands on her—" Braxton narrowed his eyes in resolution as he slapped his open palms on the table.

A young man appeared at the door behind Sarah. "Mr. Smithwick?" They need you outside for a moment. They're wantin' to know how to divide up the groups."

Braxton nodded to the two others to follow him outside. He paused momentarily as he brushed past Sarah, leaning menacingly close to her face. "Hopefully you'll still be here when we get back so you can see how a slave *ought* to be disciplined." He flicked his index finger across the bottom of Sarah's chin as he marched away, causing her to recoil in repulsion.

Sarah had no clear idea as to what to do next, but for some reason, the unfurled map on the dining table beckoned her. Glancing over her shoulder to make certain no one was watching, she darted over to the table and studied the rudimentary lines on the chart. Rivers, mountains, primary roads, railroad tracks and townships were clearly marked, but not much more. However, it was better than nothing, and Sarah was certain that nothing was all Jacquerie had to guide her at the moment.

Sarah dashed to the country Sheraton secretary in the corner of the room and grabbed Braxton's steel pen point and inkwell from one of the poplar pigeonholes. She scurried back to the dining table, where a stark white napkin would be her canvas for fashioning a crude copy of the map. After a brief moment of study in proportion and juxtaposition, Sarah attempted to duplicate the lines of the map onto the linen, but soon discovered her method was fatally flawed. Despite her best efforts to smooth and tighten the napkin, the fine tip of the pen rucked the fabric into ripples, making it impossible to draw even a straight line. In a near panic that the men would return and discover her, Sarah rubbed her temples with her fingertips in hopes of inducing a better idea. When she saw the fireplace, it came to her. She raced over to the hearth and pulled a sizable chunk of charred wood from underneath the grate, then scraped it along the stonework to round off one end. Back to the table she flew, again studying the map, then translating the information to the adjacent fabric. The heavy black ash of the charcoal rode smoothly across the threads of the white linen, leaving behind distinct gray lines. Sarah worked frantically to transfer as much cartographical knowledge onto the napkin as she dared, then quickly folded the linen and furtively stuffed it into her handbag.

Sarah slipped quietly out of the servant's quarters in the back of the Bellerive house just as a young boy was sent inside to retrieve the map from the dining room.

As the bounty hunters gathered on the lawn in front of the house to devise a strategy for tracking down the runaway, Sarah stole across the field to the end of the barn.

In the last stall stood a piebald mare, with a patchwork coat of black and white hair. She appeared to be agitated, either from the flurry of recent activity or from seeing a stranger in her midst. As Sarah inched closer, the fractious horse pawed the floor in warning.

"Easy, girl," whispered Sarah. "Nobody's gonna hurt you. Easy now." Her soothing intonations seemed to calm the mare, allowing Sarah to approach slightly closer. Despite trembling with haunting childhood memories, Sarah summoned the courage to lift the latch on the stall and push open the door.

The piebald moved skittishly backwards, distrusting of the intruder, pinning back her ears and pondering her next move.

"Easy now," repeated Sarah, extending her quaking arm toward the mare's enormous head. Perspiring from fear, Sarah shuffled her feet along the straw-covered floor and edged closer to the high-strung beast. For a moment, neither one moved, each peering through the other's widened eyes to get a sense of their intentions.

Sarah suddenly broke the spell as outside, the yelps of hungry dogs and angry men grew louder as leather boots slammed into iron stirrups.

Sarah turned back to the mare and spoke calmly and clearly. "I'm sorry, I don't know your name, but you *have* to help me. It's very important, and there isn't much time. I really need your help, and I need it now." The mare's ears flicked forward and the muscles along the ridgeline of her back relaxed. The horse stepped closer and slowly lowered her head, allowing Sarah to stroke the soft hide between her eyes.

Still with a measure of uncertainty, Sarah eased the bridle off a peg in the stall and gingerly slipped the bit between the mare's long teeth. She fought it for a moment, stamping the ground and sending Sarah reeling backwards, but calmed down just as quickly and appeared resigned to her duty. With no time to waste strapping on a saddle, the mount stood ready, but it was the rider who now balked. It had been three decades since Sarah had last dared to sit on the back of a horse, longer still since she'd ridden bareback, and she simply didn't know if she could do it. It was like asking someone who had nearly drowned to wade across a roaring river.

"You've *got* to do this, Sarah! You *have* to!" she commanded the scared little girl inside her. Close to panic, she scaled the wall slats of the stall and climbed just high enough to be level with the horse's back. Holding onto the bridle, she bounced twice on the ball of her left foot, preparing to swing her right leg over the mare's midsection, but then suddenly stopped. She couldn't do it. Begging for strength, she bounced again, but still couldn't bring herself to climb aboard. The bloodthirsty bark of the hunter's hounds seemed to grow stronger as Sarah wrestled with her demons inside the stall. Inhaling one last energizing breath, Sarah bounced again, then pulled her free leg up and over the spotted hindquarters of the horse and into the flank on the other side. Trembling like a willow leaf in a summer storm, she leaned forward and wrapped both arms around the mare's neck and simply held on to calm herself. Her fears slowly melted away and she found herself ready to ride. She coaxed the mare through the open door of the stall and outside into the twilight.

Using the barn to shield her escape from the gathering of men in the yard, Sarah stealthily guided the horse toward the tree line, then gradually pressed her knees into the mare's ribcage and eased into a gentle gallop as she fled the grounds of Bellerive.

32

Masters, give unto your servants that which is just and equal;
knowing that ye also have a Master in heaven.

Colossians 4:1

With only a few lonesome shafts of the diminishing sun sneaking through the tall pines to light the way, Sarah paused in a clearing to refer to the crude map she'd sketched on the linen napkin. She listened to the wind, then cupped her hands and aimed her voice to the northwest.

"Jacquerie!" she cried out. The woods offered up no response, except for the cackling of a few birds and the rushing water of the adjacent Yadkin River. "Jacquerie!" she called again, louder. Still nothing. She stuffed the napkin back into her handbag and pushed on.

As the sun dropped lower in the western sky, Sarah would repeat the process again and again, riding as hard as she dared along the bank of the river, pausing, and calling out. She knew Jacquerie would head to the river, she knew she would generally head north, and she knew that with less than an hour's head start, she had to be in the general vicinity. But the woods seemed to grow larger, darker, and more forbidding the longer her vain pursuit continued.

The faint yelping of dogs brushed past Sarah's ears as the sound carried on a blast of cold wind. By now she'd forgotten all about her fear of the horse now sharing in her mission, but her dread over the approaching posse of bounty hunters was growing. They were catching up to her, and it was only a matter of time before they would overtake the runaway.

"Jacquerie!" she hollered, straining her voice. "It's me! Sarah Talton!" Despite her best efforts to hold on to hope, it was becoming clear that her search would be futile. It was the final chapter of a tragic tale, and she knew it. Sarah leaned forward onto the nape of the horse and rested her exhausted head on the mare's grayish mane. Sarah wept. For the first time in years, she gave her tears permission to flow. The droplets rolled down her clenched cheekbones in surrender, mingled briefly with the perspiring shoulders of the horse, then leapt the final few feet to their death in the muddy Carolina ground. The tears came slowly at first, then released into a torrent, like violent water finally bursting through a stubborn dam. Sarah buried her addled head deeper into the mare's coarse hair and convulsed with shameless sobs. She was more than crestfallen, more than defeated. She was collapsing inside, slowly dying from the weight of personal failure. She had tried to live a good life, tried to live up to the expectations of society and the scriptures, but often they hadn't lived up to hers. In her time of greatest need, she felt as though she walked alone. Her tears poured out relentlessly in a cathartic river of anger, disappointment, and sorrow.

As Sarah cried, the horse gently shifted her weight, bearing only a few inches to her left, but just enough to change her rider's direct line of sight to the soil below. Sarah's wallowing eyes suddenly widened. She raised her head as if a thousand miracles were washing over her. There, clearly imprinted in the mud below her right foot, was a heel print from a boot. Not just any heel print, but one Sarah had seen before. She craned her neck to get a closer look. It was obviously fresh, perhaps pressed into the ground just minutes before. Three feet in front of it was another print, then another, marking a distinct line of travel.

Reborn with new hope and energy, Sarah kicked her heels into the flanks of the stalwart piebald and together they charged through the low boughs of the pines and scrub oaks.

"Jacquerie!" she screamed as loudly as she dared. "Jacquerie!"

Up ahead, a shadow darted out of the thicket. It was her. Her chest heaving with exhaustion, Jacquerie waited in the open as Sarah broke toward her.

"What are you doing out here?" said Jacquerie as she gasped for fresh breath. "They'll *kill* you!"

"Only if they see us together, which is why we need to hurry."

Sarah swung her right leg across the horse and dropped to the ground. She whisked the reins around a sapling and pulled her handbag from around her shoulders.

"How'd you know how to find me?"

"Rebecca told me about the Underground Railroad. I knew you had to follow the river. I just hoped I was right, and sometimes prayers are answered."

Sarah pulled the napkin from her bag and held it against the hindquarter of the piebald.

"What's that?" asked Jacquerie, stepping closer for a better look in the dying sunset.

"It's a map. Not a good one, mind you, but good enough to get you where you need to be." Sarah wiped her tear-stained eyes with the back of her hand to clear her vision.

"This thick line at the bottom, that's the Yadkin River, so we're standing approximately here. You need to follow this line for about four miles to a place called Shallow Ford. It should be marked, and even if it's not, you'll know you're there because that's the only place you can get across the river with a horse. You have to get there as fast as you can, because that's where the patrol knows to cross too."

Jacquerie nodded, intently taking it all in.

"Now then," continued Sarah, her voice speeding up in direct proportion to the urgency of the situation, "once you're across, keep following it west, into the setting sun. When the sun goes down, look for the Big Dipper. That'll tell you which way is north. Do you know the Big Dipper?"

Jacquerie nodded that she did. "We call it the Drinkin' Gourd."

"Good. You have to follow the Yadkin about fifteen more miles...

then, when it starts to wind south, you'll see another river, branching off to the right. *Don't* follow that one! That's the Fisher River, and you want the Mitchell." Sarah tapped her finger along the charcoal lines of the map. "The Mitchell is the *second* river, up further, just past this big bend. Don't miss it or you'll find yourself in the mountains of the Blue Ridge and you'll never find your way out. So it's the *second* river you come to. Got it?"

Jacquerie nodded again. "Second river. Got it."

"Now then, follow the Mitchell River due north, it'll fork... take the right hand fork... that's the north fork... and within a few miles it'll lead you to a little town. There should be a church right in the middle. That's where you'll find Quakers."

"I know about the Quakers."

"You knock on that church door and tell them a friend of a friend sent you. They'll know what you're talking about and they'll take you in, keep you safe, then send you on your way. Is all of that clear?"

"Yes, ma'am."

Sarah folded the napkin and handed it to Jacquerie. "Now then, sit down on that stump and put your feet up."

"Why?"

"Just trust me! And hurry!"

Jacquerie eased her weary body onto a mossy stump as Sarah scrambled down the sandy bank of the river, dipped the end of her skirt into the rushing water, then raced back to Jacquerie. She lifted Jacquerie's legs off the ground and proceeded to scrub her boots with the wet fabric of her skirt.

"What are you doin'?"

"Let me guess. You stole some pepper from my kitchen and poured it over your shoes, thinking it would throw off the dogs. Am I right?"

"Yes, ma'am."

"They train their dogs to track pepper."

There was a momentary pause as Sarah diligently cleaned the boots.

"You don't have to do this, Miss Talton."

"Yes I do. The dogs will be on you in no time."

"No, I mean help me escape. You don't have to do this."

"Well, that's where you're wrong. I have no choice."

"Why do you say that?"

"Because *I* have been wrong."

"About what?"

"About everything. Absolutely everything."

She set Jacquerie's cleansed feet back on the earth and continued. "It wasn't too long ago that everyone thought the world was flat. Imagine their fear, their uncertainty, when they found out how incredibly mistaken they were." She paused as she carefully formulated her next thought. "Do you know how difficult, how frightening it is, to wake up one day and suddenly realize that the foundation of your very being is built on the sand? To discover that everything you've been taught... everything you've known your entire life... your customs, your traditions, every last detail... has all been *wrong?* And then after you finally come to accept that, then you have to wonder how it ever *got* that way. And *then* you have to wonder if you can ever change it."

"Miss Talton, the world is the way it is, and it's not your fault."

"Oh, but it is! It *is* my fault, along with everyone like me who saw the world just as it was and couldn't imagine it being any other way. But then I met you, and for the first time I understand it *can* be different! I don't know when, and I don't know how, I just know that it can. And with me, making that difference starts here and now."

Jacquerie and Sarah stood face to face, motionless in the quiet wood, both fighting raw emotion. They suddenly came together in a spontaneous embrace, searching for solace in an uncertain world. Their bodies clung tightly in the pastoral serenity of the forest, as if trying to transfer the inherent goodness in each of their weary souls. The flowing tears on their cheekbones reflected the final brilliant rays of the vanishing sun.

Their embrace was interrupted by the distant cry of hounds giving tongue to the scent of their quarry. Alert and alarmed, Sarah sprang into action. She yanked off her own wool coat and pulled Jacquerie's tattered jacket off her shoulders.

"Take this!"

"But—"

"This is not a time to argue! I'm begging you, as a friend, to just listen!" Jacquerie nodded, agreeing to follow Sarah's instructions.

As Jacquerie pulled her arms through Sarah's coat and fastened the buttons, Sarah removed her Bible from her handbag and slipped various denominations of paper currency in between the pages. She handed the book to Jacquerie.

"For strength," she said. "Strength to keep believing that a better day is going to come."

Jacquerie accepted the gift without question. With Sarah's help, she scrambled onto the back of the mare and looked down at her former mistress.

"I'll never forget you," whispered Jacquerie, choking back tears.

"Nor I you." Sarah pushed against the hindquarter of the horse. "Now go." Go in search of something better. Faute de mieux, my dear Jacquerie. Faute de mieux."

Jacquerie nodded and allowed herself a faint smile through her tears. "Faute de mieux."

Jacquerie pressed her hands against the neck of the horse, turned her westward, and swiftly rode away.

Through the remaining fragments of apricot light from the setting sun, Sarah could see Jacquerie ascend a ridge, linger for one shining moment, and then disappear. Sarah waved goodbye, long after horse and rider had vanished from view.

Hearing the hounds again, Sarah ran through the thicket, dragging Jacquerie's coat behind her, ignoring the ragged thorns of the wild blackberry bushes tearing at her face.

Within minutes, Braxton Smithwick and a portion of his slave hunting party had ridden up to where Sarah was sitting on a fallen oak.

"What are *you* doing out here?" asked Braxton, as he jumped down from his saddle.

"Same as you. I'm looking for Jacquerie."

"This is no place for a woman. Look at those scratches on your face! I'll get one of my men to take you back to Bellerive. I shouldn't be out here much longer."

"I can help you find her."

"No, you need to get on home and have someone attend to those cuts."

"I can call her in. She trusts me."

Braxton raised one eyebrow and pondered the theory, gently nodding his head to give it credence, but then took a hard look at Sarah. "But why would you do that for me?"

"I'm not doing it for you."

"Why do you care about her? She belongs to me now."

"I realize that. I just don't want you to hurt her, that's all."

"And what's in it for me?"

"If you can bring Jacquerie back, unhurt, I will sell you my farm."

Braxton's eyes widened. "I want to make sure I understand your proposition. I bring her back alive and I get your farm?"

"Unhurt, and my farm, at a fair price. You have my word."

"Agreed."

"Do you have a map?" she asked Braxton.

"Indeed I do." Braxton whisked the rolled parchment from his saddlebag and unfurled it on the stump in front of them.

Sarah carefully studied the map as if she were seeing it for the first time. She pointed to the bold line at the bottom. "Is this the Yadkin River?"

"That's right."

"The only way they know which direction to run is by following the rivers."

"That's true." Braxton moved closer to Sarah.

"Well, I used to spend a lot of time in these parts when I was a little girl... my father loved to hunt up here, so I have a pretty good idea where she's headed. Bring that torch closer."

As the posse gathered around her and the torchlight bounced off the parchment, Sarah drew her fingers across the meandering lines that denoted rivers.

"This first river here, that's the Fisher. It heads due north, straight at the North Star. That's surely the one she'll follow."

"Everybody got that?" asked Braxton of the group. They all nodded, eager to resume the hunt. He turned back to Sarah. "Your farm? You swear?"

She nodded. "If you bring her back unhurt. As God is my witness."

"All right, men, let's go!" ordered Braxton as if he were the field general of a great battle. He helped Sarah swing into the saddle of his horse, then climbed on behind her. She clenched her teeth to keep from smiling.

With Braxton at the helm, the posse of slave hunters galloped off in search of a distant river. The thunder of their hoofbeats and yelping hounds disappeared into the darkened wood.

33

I thank my God upon every remembrance of you.

Philippians 1:3

*T*he year was 1866. The war was over, and so was much of the southern way of life.

Like so many of the antebellum plantations across the state, Bellerive was in ashes. Braxton Smithwick had fled before his own slaves could lynch him. He was last seen heading west toward the Blue Ridge Mountains.

The Talton farm was one of the only houses in the surrounding counties that wasn't torched by the advancing Union Army or rebellious slaves. Though it had fallen into disrepair, Sarah was still able to sell it and use the proceeds to open a small bookshop on Main Street in Salem. Rebecca had finished her studies and was working as a schoolteacher, while helping out Sarah from time to time in the shop. They lived together in the former residence of Irene Murnane, who had died peacefully in her sleep just days after Lee surrendered his sword at Appomattox.

On this particular springtime day, Sarah sat alone in the store, gently sliding back and forth in a rocking chair as she immersed herself in a delightful collection of Nathaniel Hawthorne short stories.

Rebecca breezed in the front door with a handful of letters, one of which bore a distinctive red wax seal.

"This came for you from the post office. Doesn't say who it's from. I have to go prepare tomorrow's lesson, so I'll see you tonight for supper." She gave her older sister a quick peck on the cheek and exited as quickly as she'd entered.

Sarah turned the letter over several times in her hands, examining all sides. There was no return address. She slid her long fingernail under the fold of the envelope and gently tore it open. She opened the tri-folded note and focused on the handwritten words.

> *Dear Miss Talton, if you are reading this letter, it means I have found my freedom. It is sweeter than I ever imagined. I will be forever grateful for all the kindness you showed me. I regret that I may never see you again, but I see your goodness in everything. I'm living in Canada, and working for a bookbinder. He treats me very well. My husband John and I had a child. A daughter. We named her Sarah. I will end this letter with four simple words... hope, grace, love, and faith. Hope is all I had when I ran away in search of a better life. Grace is what God showed me when he brought me to you. Love is what you showed me during our days together. And faith is what keeps me believing in the miracles made possible by hope, grace, and love. Godspeed to you and Miss Rebecca. I love you both.*
>
> > *Your friend,*
> >
> > *Jacquerie Bodin*

After a dozen readings, Sarah folded the letter with great care and continued to trace her fingers along the creases. As the runners of her rocking chair rhythmically creaked across the wooden floor of her shop, she closed her eyes and dreamed of miracles. Her face blossomed into a contented smile.

In 1874, a young entrepreneur named Richard Joshua Reynolds rode into the city of Winston. He would occasionally stop in a small bookshop in Salem and purchase leatherbound volumes of poetry for his wife, and a Farmer's Almanac for himself, as he built a tobacco company that would eventually make him one of the wealthiest men in the world. Years later, part of the enormous Reynolds family fortune would be used to purchase a large tract of land near the North Fork of the Mitchell River in Surry County, North Carolina. It was pristine countryside that had embraced the muddy bootheels of a thousand runaway slaves seeking refuge in secret spaces.

They would name it Devotion.

Cameron Kent is the Emmy Award-winning news anchor at WXII-TV in Winston-Salem, North Carolina. He's the author of two previous books, *Make Me Disappear* and *When the Ravens Die*. His film credits include movies shown on NBC, HBO, Lifetime, and at the American Film Institute. Cameron and his family attend Highland Presbyterian Church in Winston-Salem, and are actively involved in Habitat for Humanity.

Cover Artist **Benita VanWinkle** is currently a freelance instructor of photography, altered art, bookbinding, and other creative courses at Surry Community College, High Point University, and other institutions throughout the NC Triad region. She also volunteers at many nonprofits, including Forsyth Habitat for Humanity, the Children's Home of Winston-Salem, The Sawtooth School for Visual Art, and Riverwood Therapeutic Riding Center. She was Program Director at The Sawtooth School for Visual Art in Winston-Salem before leaving to pursue freelance teaching and her personal artistic passions. She moved to the Winston-Salem area from Atlanta, GA, where she was the college admissions director and photography instructor at The Creative Circus, a premier portfolio school.

Benita is a member of the Associated Artists of Winston-Salem where she regularly participates in gallery exhibitions, and has earned awards of excellence in numerous exhibitions throughout the Southeast. Benita is an active member of Brookstown United Methodist Church, chairing multiple art/community festivals and volunteering with the youth.

She graduated with her MFA from Southern Illinois University in Carbondale, IL, where she also served on the Board of Advisors for the Cinema and Photography department. She graduated from the University of Central Florida, Daytona Beach Community College (now Daytona College) and St. Petersburg Junior College (now St. Petersburg College). To see more of Benita's work, visit www.BusyBStudio.com. Benita wishes to thank MaeLena and Teresa Apperson for their kind patience while modeling for this bookcover.

Acknowledgments

My sincere thanks to Meg Scott Phipps and Jim Gilchriest for their willingness to proofread and offer invaluable feedback.

To Steve McCutchan, David Hughes, and Curtis Patterson for sharing their vast knowledge of the scriptures and hymns.

To Philippe Sevin for polishing my high school French.

To Tara Stebbins for her equine expertise and for providing a thoughtful sounding board for new ideas.

To my longtime friend Jimmie Walker, without whose friendship and support I would not be a writer.

To my parents, for raising me in a home where differences in color and culture were celebrated.

To Kevin Watson at Press53 for believing in this story, and for his broad vision and attention to detail in making this project infinitely better, and the process a pleasure.

And to Susan, the love of my life, for reading and re-reading, and for her daily encouragement to pursue all of my dreams.

C.K.

Further Reading

Within the Plantation Household: Black and White Women of the Old South (Gender and American Culture), by Elizabeth Fox-Genovese (The University of North Carolina Press, 7th edition, 1988)

North Carolina Slave Narratives: The Lives of Moses Roper, Lunsford Lane, Moses Grandy, and Thomas H. Jones (John Hope Franklin Series in African American History and Cult), by William L. Andrews (editor/author), Tampathia Evans (author), and Andrea Williams (editor) (The University of North Carolina Press, 2007)

"Angelina Grimke"—The National Archives (http://www.nationalarchives.gov.uk/a2a/records.aspx?cat=133-reas&cid=2-4-2#2-4-2)